# The Adventures
## of
# Bobby Normal

## A.S.Chambers

ISBN: 978-1-915679-29-1

# Dedication

A huge thank you to everyone who kindly backed my
Kickstarter campaign for this book. Special mentions go to
Charlie
Rebecca Armstrong
Simon Brindley
Ron Chick
Nadine Shinfield
Debs the SteamGoth
Bec Pearce
Francesco Tehrani
Paul
Miss Frog
Lee Hardy


Also, special thanks to the members of my Patreon Book
Club for their valued support:
Kevin Denwood,
Jacob Matts,
Paul Lewis,
Gemma Innes.


For more details about my Book Club and how you can
receive signed copies of my books when they are
published, please visit my website:
www.aschambers.co.uk.

Also by A.S.Chambers

Sam Spallucci Series.
The Casebook of Sam Spallucci - 2012
Sam Spallucci: Ghosts From The Past - 2014
Sam Spallucci: Shadows of Lancaster – 2016
Sam Spallucci: The Case of The Belligerent Bard - 2016
Sam Spallucci: Dark Justice – 2018
Sam Spallucci: Troubled Souls - 2020
Sam Spallucci: Bloodline - Prologues & Epilogue – 2021
Sam Spallucci: Bloodline – 2021
Sam Spallucci: Fury of the Fallen – 2022
Sam Spallucci: The Case of The Pillaging Pirates - 2023
Sam Spallucci: Lux Æterna – Due 2024

Short Story Anthologies.
Oh Taste And See – 2014
All Things Dark And Dangerous – 2015
Let All Mortal Flesh – 2016
Mourning Has Broken – 2018
Hide Not Thou Thy Face – 2020
If Ye Loathe Me - 2022
Out of the Depths - 2023
Hear My Scare - Due 2025

Ebook short stories.
High Moon - 2013
Girls Just Wanna Have Fun – 2013
Needs Must - 2019

Novellas.
Songbird – 2019
Bobby Normal and The Eternal Talisman - 2021
Bobby Normal and the Virtuous Man - 2021
Bobby Normal and the Children of Cain - 2022
Bobby Normal and the Fallen - 2023
Bobby Normal and The Black Dragon - 2024
Child of Light - Due 2024
Child of Fire - Due 2025

Omnibuses.
Children of Cain - 2019
Macabre Collection: Volume One - 2022
Macabre Collection: Volume Two - 2023
Sam Spallucci Omnibus: Volume One - 2022
Sam Spallucci Omnibus: Volume Two - 2024

# Contents

# Bobby Normal
## and the
# Eternal Talisman

# Chapter One

People called this place the Divergent Lands. It was a world where there was poor sanitation, little food and monsters lurked around every corner. You could see your loved ones drive their wagon to market in the morning, only to have the same cart carry their cold, stiff corpse home the following evening.

To Bobby it was home.

Sure, it was far from perfect. There were everyday problems to encounter: be quick with your fingers; be careful who you annoy; know when to scarper and always remember to tolerate your kid sister.

Right now, the fourth of these was causing Bobby the most trouble.

"But I don't want to get up!" whined the pile of filthy rags in the corner of the abandoned hut that the two children currently called their home.

"You know we have to get going. Teller saw us last night. He'll know we're here and he'll be after us. You really want that?"

The jumble of rags uttered a far from pleasant noise. "I'm asleep," they said, then proceeded to snore loudly.

Bobby grabbed the dirty bedding and snatched it back. His kid sister glowered up at him, her chestnut brown eyes shining up from her grimy face.

"Not fair."

"Come on Katy," Bobby pleaded desperately. "You know what happened the last time he caught us."

The little eight-year-old gave one more huff and surrendered, albeit ungraciously, rolling her eyes as she sat up. She wriggled out of her mess of a bed before running her fingers through the straggles of knots that made up her hair. "I'm hungry."

"Well we'd better do something about that," Bobby grinned.

It was market day, which meant that there was plenty of food to fill a hungry teenage boy and his young sister. Not that they intended to *trade* for any. It wasn't as if they had anything of value with which they could barter. They were just worthless street urchins.

They had been since the day that their father had died.

Katy was too young to remember either of their parents and Bobby possessed just the vaguest memories of their mother, but not a day went past that Bobby had to hide a tear as he recalled the strength of their love. One day, when Katy had just been a little babe in arms, his dad had taken them to market to get some provisions. He had been a woodworker, so there was always a demand for his creations: stools, tables, other items of furniture. This meant that, when they were young, they had never felt the twisted bite of hunger in their bellies. On that day, when he was exchanging a fine willow basket for some vegetables, his dad had turned to Bobby and said, "You know, it wasn't always like this. Back hundreds of years ago, people used to have to pay for things." He had smiled at Bobby's confused face. "They had shiny pieces of metal that they exchanged for goods. People called them coins. No use for them these days. Not since *they* came."

Bobby remembered that conversation as if it were yesterday.

He had good reason to.

It was at that moment that he had seen his first construct.

It had been taller than the average man, broader across the chest. It walked on two legs and a pair of arms swayed rhythmically by its side. But that was where any similarities ended. This was no creature of flesh and blood. Its skin, if that's what it was, was the colour and sheen of mud from the nearby river. It rippled and undulated as the beast strode unhindered through the marketplace. People stood in silence as it passed. Mothers shielded their children from its gaze.

Not that it had any eyes, nor a neck.

The construct's chest seemed to rise up into what it possessed for a head, rounding off at the top. Across the middle of the face was a jagged slit that opened and shut, causing its skin to part and its deformed tongue to slither as its breathing rasped noisily.

It was the obscenest thing that Bobby had ever lain eyes upon, yet he had stood and stared up at the giant whilst others had cowered in fear.

"Bobby," his father had whispered. "Look away, lad."

But he had not. He had seen the monster and it could never be unseen.

The creature had paused in front of him and his father. It had turned and bent low, its face level with his. There had been startled cries from the other villagers and he had felt his father's fingers like a vice on his shoulder.

But Bobby did not flinch. He just stood and stared up at the monstrosity.

Then a curious sound gurgled from the belly of the beast, as if rocks were being rolled around inside an old wooden barrel. And Bobby realised that the construct was laughing at him. The noise ebbed away as the monster drew itself up. It turned and continued its solitary march out of town.

As one, the whole market resumed its breath. Bobby felt himself swept up into his father's arms and embraced in a hug that could have crushed an oak tree.

In the here and now, he smoothed a stray tear into the side of his face. "What do we want to eat today?" he asked his sister.

"Apples!" she shouted with glee.

Bobby grinned. It was always apples. "Well, you know what you have to do then."

"Oh my! What is it little one?" The elderly man stooped to inspect the small girl that was sat sobbing in the middle of the muddy road. "You'll get trodden on if you stay there."

"I've lost my mummy," Katy whimpered, rubbing the heel of her hand at the most realistic tears of woe that a child could possibly manufacture. "Have you seen her?"

The old man frowned as he peered around the busy market square. He removed his threadbare cap and scratched at his thinning scalp with chipped fingernails. "I don't know. What does she look like?"

"My mummy," Katy volunteered not-very-helpfully.

The man frowned. "Look, you can't stay there. Why don't I help you get up off the road?" He bent to take her by the arm.

Then the screaming began.

Immediately, concerned heads turned in their direction.

The man froze in panic. "What? What's the matter?"

Still the child screamed.

"Here, what you doing to the kiddie?" demanded a rather large woman with ruddy cheeks and a somewhat grating voice.

"Well, nothing," the poor man protested.

"Then why's she screaming?"

Katy cracked open an eye and peered up at her elderly helper then proceeded to crank the volume up even further.

"What's going on?" came another voice.

"This old man's hurt this little one."

"Well, I never."

"But I only asked her what was wrong."

"Some people…"

From the corner of the square, Bobby carefully crept behind the mass of people fighting to see what was causing such a fuss. When he was sure that no one was looking, he swept handfuls of fruit into his tunic. When it was full to overflowing, he stuck two fingers in his mouth and blew a sharp whistle that rose above the hubbub. From between the legs of the mob baying for the blood of the unfortunate Good Samaritan, Katy crawled on her hands and knees.

"Come on," Bobby whispered. "Time to go."

It almost went without a hitch.

Almost.

"Hey!"

Bobby turned and saw a group of older boys running towards them, across the market square.

"Teller," he moaned. "Quick, Katy. Run!"

So they did.


The feet of the two youngsters squelched and splattered through the muddy streets. They didn't dare look back for fear of losing ground. Not that they needed to check if they were still being pursued; the sound of Teller and his gang of thugs echoed through the empty alleyways, informing the young thieves as to exactly where the older boys were.

After a short while, Bobby could feel his lungs start to burn and he could see through the tears of exertion in his eyes that Katy was also fit to drop. "Quick! Down here!" He yanked his little sister through a series of small alleys until they reached a shadowed courtyard. "If we're lucky, they might run past."

However, luck had decided not to favour them that day.

"They went this way!"

The older boys turned the corner and stood across the entrance to the dead end. Bobby and Katy were trapped. Teller swaggered up in front of his three cronies, his wicked smile looking even more vile in the gloom of the side street. "Nowhere to hide, *Normal*," he leered.

"Don't call me that," Bobby managed through gasps of hot air as he tried to regain his breath.

"I'll call you what I want, street trash," Teller spat, his chest puffed up like a sail on a barge that has caught a strong tailwind. "You're *normal* and there's nothing you can do about it. Now come here and get the thrashing you deserve." He reached into his belt and drew out the evil-looking whip that he always carried on his person.

Bobby pushed Katy protectively behind him as he frantically looked around them for a means of escape. There were a few old boxes and some battered barrels by a wall, but they were both exhausted and, by the time they had started to climb, Teller and his cronies would be upon them.

He felt the purloined apples in his tunic jiggle about against his chest. He pulled one out and held it up threateningly.

A harsh bray of confident laughter burst from Teller's narrow lips. "Seriously? You're gonna defend yourself with a piece of fruit?" Shaking his head, he drew his whip hand back. Bobby did likewise with the apple.

Just as the older boy was about to let the whip fly and inflict serious harm on Bobby, there was a twanging noise and the bully crumpled down onto one knee, dropping his whip and clutching at his temple that was now miraculously oozing blood. He shouted out in equal amounts of surprise and pain.

"Up here! Now!" came another voice, a female one this time, from behind them.

Bobby spun around and saw a figure atop the wall by the boxes and barrels. He did not need telling twice. He hefted Katy onto the pile of wooden packaging and helped her scramble upwards. He clambered up in her wake as another twang rang out from above, closely followed by a second scream of agony from down below.

"In there." Their saviour motioned to an open window, its shutters rotten and fallen away. "Run through the building. I'll follow."

They did as they were directed and emerged on a neighbouring street.

Their companion joined them and Bobby saw their face for the first time, surrounded by a brown hood, trimmed with purple. It was a girl, not much older than him. She winked and stowed a small catapult away in her belt. "Let's keep walking," she instructed and guided them away from the building.

Away from the alley.

Away from Teller.

## Chapter Two

A short while later, Bobby and Katy were warming themselves in front of an impromptu fire in one of the many abandoned buildings of Irlingbury as they and their new friend tucked into their well-earned haul of juicy apples.

"What did you say your name was again?" Katy mumbled around a mouthful of half-chewed fruit, watery juice dribbling down her chin.

The other girl smiled. "Persephone," she replied for the third time.

The youngster frowned. "Funny name," she said.

"Katy!" her brother scolded. "Don't be rude. Especially after she saved us from Teller."

The youngster gave a sigh that demonstrated just how often she suffered her older sibling's despair. "Sorrrrrryyyy…" she apologised half-heartedly.

"That's okay," the redheaded girl smiled. "It *is* an unusual name for these parts."

"You're not from round here then?" Bobby asked, curiosity getting the better of him. Normally, his and Katy's existence was a simple one of feeling hungry, stealing food and being chased until they either escaped or were caught and punished. Now, this newcomer had burst into their lives, altering that mundane balance, and he just had to know more about her.

Persephone shook her head. "No. Just passing through, really."

Bobby gave a small laugh.

"What is it?"

"No one ever comes to Irlingbury. We never see travellers."

The girl looked sad. "*Nowhere* sees travellers these days, Bobby. It's not safe."

"But *you're* travelling," he pointed out.

"I'm supposed to deliver something." She absent-mindedly poked at the fire with a charred stick, causing small embers to spit and the flames to jump around like living creatures. "Why were those older boys chasing you?"

"Because they smell!" Katy piped up.

Bobby rolled his eyes. *Sisters.*

Persephone giggled. "I'm sure they do."

"It's actually because we're orphans," Bobby explained. "Teller and his gang come from whole families, which is so rare these days. They see themselves as better than everybody else."

"That's awful. Is that why they called you *Normal*? Because they see themselves as special? Privileged?"

Bobby nodded. "They see us as beneath them. They are the high and mighty ones. We are just oxen to be whipped into pulling their carts and do the jobs that they find undesirable. Nothing special. Normal."

"One of these days," Katy grumbled, "I'll show Teller what's for."

Bobby rolled his eyes once more at her eight-year-old ire.

Persephone frowned. "It strikes me that they have a very skewed view on life, but then that's not surprising these days. The things I have seen on my travels…" She drifted off momentarily before focussing once more on the fire. "To me, being normal seems like a wonderful thing. What I wouldn't give to have a touch of normality in my life right now." Then, without the slightest warning, she started to cry.

Katy opened her mouth in shock and the piece of apple she had been eating plopped out into her lap. Bobby crossed the room and lay a hand on the older girl's shoulder. "Are… are you okay?"

Persephone sat up, rubbed the heel of her hand into her eye and pulled herself together. "I'm sorry. It's just that… Oh, I can't pull you into this. It's not fair on you."

"I'm sure it's not *that* bad," Bobby said reassuringly.

Persephone gave a deep sigh, looked him square in the face and said, "Actually, the fate of the world might depend upon it."

For a moment, Bobby was fearfully quiet. Here was a girl that he and his sister had only just met. True, she had saved their skins from Teller and his thugs but to be told that they were being drawn into fate of the world stuff…

Eventually, he said, "Well, we owe you. So, whatever it is, I guess we're in."

"Really?"

"It's not like we've got anything else to do," he shrugged.

Katy just sat oblivious, munching on another apple.

Persephone reached into a faded leather pouch which was attached to her corded belt and pulled out a small wooden token. "This," she explained, "is the Eternal Talisman." She passed it over for Bobby to take a look at. It was about the size of the palm of his hand and on one side was a burnt etching of what looked like a fancy cup and a sword.

"What's it for?" the boy asked, turning the artefact over in his hands. "It doesn't look very special."

"It needs to reach a man in the next village, Orchester," Persephone continued. "For the likes of you or me, it has no use, but for him…" She trailed off and Bobby saw tears start to form in her eyes once again.

"What will he use it for?"

"It will help him kill Kanor."

Bobby's eyes widened to the size of dinner plates. "You know *Kanor*?" His voice was no more than a whisper, as if even the walls around him were not supposed to hear the name.

Persephone shook her head. "No. I don't. No one does. You know that. You also know what that monster has done to our land. The dragon has ravaged it, burnt it to a husk and trampled upon those that remain. It wasn't always like this, you know, Bobby? Once, there were fields as far as the eye could see where people grew an abundance of crops. There were majestic cities with buildings that rose into the sky.

"And even the sky was not the limit," she continued. "People fashioned powerful craft that could take us away from here, out into the darkest of nights to visit other planets and far off places.

"Then the Divergence came and Kanor stole this world from us overnight. He devoured our dreams like a hungry monster that had been lurking under our bed; biding its time, waiting for the right moment to strike."

Bobby sat and listened quietly. His father had told him tales of times long, long ago. Tales that echoed what Persephone had just described. Bobby had just discounted them as funny bedtime tales; men flying through the air, buildings the colour of which could be changed at the touch of a button. These were surely just things of fancy? Things with which to entertain a five-year-old boy as he was tucked into bed at night.

Or perhaps they were real?

"The constructs are his creations, aren't they?" Bobby asked, already knowing it to be the truth. "They're not of the natural order."

"That's right. He fashioned them from clay and sent them across the globe in the shape of normal human beings. They dwelt amongst us for thousands of years. We were unaware of their existence. We never knew that they lived next door to us and laboured with us at our places of work.

"That was how they were able to slaughter almost everyone in one single, crushing blow.

"When the Divergence came, Kanor rose and called out to his children. They took their true form and butchered without mercy all those that they saw until humanity was reduced to a pitiful remnant. Now all we are good for is to provide sport for Kanor and those that have thrown their lot in with him.

"He has to be stopped."

Katy finished munching on her stolen fruit. "Why can't you take that thing to Orchester?"

Sadness clouded the older girl's face. "My father is sick. Very sick. I have received word that he has but a few days left. I have my duty to deliver the Talisman, but the need to see my father before he dies is calling to me in a louder voice. I fear that I will not make it back in time."

Bobby looked at Katy. She shrugged.

"We'll do it," he said. "What is the name of the man that we should find?"

"His name is Jason." Persephone lay the Eternal Talisman in Bobby's palm and gripped his hand tight. "You must not let anyone know about this. No one at all. Kanor has spies everywhere. Remember that. Also re-member that constructs can change shape. They may not all look like the abominations we see around from time to time. They can look just like you or me…

"Until it's too late."

They stayed there that night: Bobby, Katy and Persephone. Katy drifted off to sleep within minutes and the older girl was not far behind. Bobby, however, found it much harder to switch off. His life had been changed in an instant. This morning, it had all been about simply sur-viving and finding the next meal whilst avoiding bullies like Teller. Now, it was the fate of the world and the powerful monster known only as Kanor.

He tossed and turned next to the fire, trying to achieve some level of comfort. When he did finally nod off, the few hours he grabbed were filled with dreams of being chased, not by Teller, but by staggering constructs, their clay-like arms reaching out to grab at him.

In his dreams, he ran out of the city onto a great plain of grass. In front of him lay a huge lake that stretched a great distance. In its midst was an island and, on that, an old building with a spire that reached up to the heavens. He had to reach the building, he knew he must, but how could he cross the lake?

Then the constructs were upon him. He heard them shuffling up behind him and he ran for the lake but, as he did so, the sound of cruel laughter drifting across the water from the island reached his ears and overhead, above the ruined building, an immense obsidian shadow spread its vast wings and rose into the sky.

Bobby woke with a start. His heart was pounding and his mouth was dry. Persephone was already awake and frowned at him. "You okay?" she asked. "You were dreaming."

Bobby shook his head violently from side to side. He wanted rid of that image of the dark shadow. It did not belong inside of him.

"I'm okay," he reassured her. "When are we leaving?"

"As soon as your sister wakes up."

Bobby glanced over at Katy who was snoring loudly. "I'd better wake her then, or we'll be here all day."

# Chapter Three

"So how will we know where to find this man called Jason?"

The three youths were approaching the edge of the village. The buildings were even more dilapidated out here. Once, it had been a thriving suburb where proud parents had happily watched their beloved and cherished children play in neat, well-tended gardens; now it was just a haunt for thieves and beggars who would grab you from the shadows, slit your throat and make off with the rags on your back. It was a perfect symbol of what the land had become post-Divergence.

Persephone pondered the question. "I was told that there is a small house on what is left of the main road into the village. It bears a white door upon which there is a green mark, a face of some kind. You need to knock there and say that you have come to deliver the goods. Those inside will know what to do."

Bobby frowned. It all sounded very vague, not to mention dangerous. He cast his eyes back down the street along which they had walked. True, Irlingbury was not much, but at least he knew it like the back of his hand.

He had never left its borders before; the world outside was a strange and unfamiliar place.

Persephone could clearly see the hesitation in his face. "If… If you don't want to do this, I'll understand."

Bobby sighed. How could he refuse? The sadness in her voice was heart-breaking. She had a sick father to whom she desperately needed to return. *His* father was dead. How would he feel if he had just one final chance to say goodbye? It was right that he and Katy do this for her.

"No," he said. "I'm okay. We'll be fine."

He felt an insistent tug on his sleeve. Looking down he saw a concerned look on Katy's face. "I'm not so sure we will be." She pointed down the road that led out of the village and Bobby groaned.

Teller and his gang were stood on the perimeter of the village.

"I thought we'd lost them," he groaned. As he whipped his head to and fro, looking desperately for a place to hide, he heard an excited shout go up from the older boys. "Quick!" Bobby said, darting into the ruins of the dilapidated buildings. "This way."

The three companions ran away from the main road and started to jink left and right through the run-down suburbs. All the while they were aware of the clattering of footsteps and whoops of excitement from Teller and his crew. The tumble-down housing was a rabbit warren, with holes and rubble to dart behind and hide underneath, but the thugs were persistent and it was soon apparent that they were not going to lose them easily.

"What are we going to do?" Persephone whispered in an agitated voice as they caught their breath in the remains of a small house. "We need to get out of here."

Bobby shook his head. "I know. I know. I just don't

know how we can shake them."

"What about the tunnels?"

Bobby turned to his sister. "That's an excellent idea!"

"Tunnels?" Persephone asked. "What tunnels?"

"There are tunnels under the village," Bobby explained. "Dad told us that their old job was to take waste water and other stuff..."

"Poop!" chipped in Katy.

"Yeah, poop," Bobby continued. "They used to take all that stuff away from the village. Sometimes, when we have nowhere else to go, we hide down there because Teller and his crew won't go down there. They see themselves better than that. It's not pleasant, but it does from time to time. The best thing is that the tunnels lead out of the village. They should get us past Teller."

"How do we get into them?"

Bobby cautiously craned his neck around the rotten doorframe of the old house. "I can see a way in just up the street. It's a metal plate in the road." Then he frowned. As he looked down the street, he was sure that he had seen something, or was it some*one*, moving in the shadows of another rundown house. Then he snapped back into his hiding place as he heard the sound of running coming in the other direction.

"But we've got to get to it without being seen," he grumbled.

Then the most curious thing happened.

A shout went up in the street. "There he is! There's Normal." At first Bobby felt chilled to the bone. He had been spotted and Teller was going to capture them, but then the sound of running clattered past and he heard a voice call out, "There he goes! Around that corner!"

The three listened to the sound of Teller and the others running away from their hiding place.

"We'd better go," Persephone insisted and crawled out from the ruined house. Bobby and Katy followed. She pointed to a round metal object in the surface of the road. "Is that the way into the tunnels?"

Bobby ran up to the disc and slid his fingers into an eroded gap at the side. He heaved and lifted its covering up. The three of them peered down into an uncertain gloom. "We'd better hurry," he said. "I don't know who Teller's chasing, but when he finds out it's not me, he'll be back.

"And he won't be happy."

One by one, the three companions climbed down a rusted metal ladder that was vaguely fastened to the side of the access hole. Bobby was the last one to descend and, as he did, he slid the cover back into place, plunging them into complete darkness.

There was a flash of sparks and he blinked as a fire blossomed in front of them. Persephone had pulled a small torch out of her backpack and had ignited the cloth around the end. "I hope this passage isn't too long," she frowned over the flickering source of light. "There's not too much life in this. I just keep it for emergencies."

Bobby looked off into the all-encompassing gloom. "It's not far. The tunnel will run down the main road then out of Irlingbury." He pointed off into the darkness. "We just need to head that way to reach the main tunnel then turn right and keep going."

"Just look out for rats," chipped in his kid sister. "They're really big and they bite."

The children edged their way cautiously along the

side tunnel, the glow from Persephone's torch doing an adequate job of highlighting any obstacles that lay in their way. "You say these are left over from long ago?" the older girl asked as she picked her way over a fallen stone.

Bobby nodded. "Dad said that they were built before the Divergence, before society fell to bits."

They sidled around a hole in the floor of the tunnel. Bobby tried not to think about what creatures might be lurking down there; creatures that could see a lot better in the dark than he could.

"There's so much that we lost," Persephone said. "So much knowledge, so much society. It has to be put right."

"You think that this man called Jason will be able to do that?"

She nodded, vehemently. "He has to. He is special. He's the Virtuous Man." She turned and saw the look of incomprehension on Bobby's face, so explained: "There is a prophecy, from before the Divergence. *'He who rose like a dragon of old will be slain by the man of virtue.'* You see what that means? Jason is the one who will free us. He will slay Kanor."

Bobby frowned. "How can one man slay a dragon? Surely, he won't be a match?"

The tiniest of smiles on Persephone's lips was illuminated by her flickering torch. "First, Kanor isn't *really* a dragon. Those things have never existed. They were myths and legends from millennia ago. He is just a man, a powerful one albeit, but just a man. He's referred to as a dragon because of the fear that he strikes in our hearts. Second, Jason *will* be victorious because that is exactly what he does not feel: fear. He is full of virtue and lives his life for the sole purpose of freeing us from this tyranny."

Bobby shrugged. He remained unconvinced. "If you say so, I guess. But it all just sounds like words to me."

"Well, don't forget that it's not just the prophecy. There's the talisman too. If the talisman exists, then the prophecy must surely be true."

Bobby saw the logic in what she said. Words were, well, just words. Anyone could make them up and spread them around. But for there to be something physical, something tangible to back them up, that made them far more real. "I suppose it gives us something to believe in, doesn't it?"

He saw Persephone nod her head above the flickering light as they reached the junction where their offshoot joined the main tunnel. They turned around the corner and paused as something caught their attention.

"What was that?" Persephone asked.

They listened and the unmistakable pattering of tiny feet rose from a faint echo to an oncoming rush.

"That'll be the rats," Katy explained, her eyes wide in the half light. "We should run now."

So they did.

As the thousands of tiny feet crescendoed into a roar, the children chased after the glowing torch, dodging as best they could the random pieces of fallen stonework and discarded detritus that lay around the main tunnel of the sewer. Every now and then, the torch would flicker as the rushing air brushed against its flame. They held their breath as it burst anew into life and guided their way along the tunnel, away from the following swarm of rats.

And what a swarm it was that was pursuing them.

Once, just once, Bobby allowed himself a hurried glance over his shoulder and wished that he hadn't. It was close to pitch black behind them but, in the glow of the torch, it was as if the floor and the walls were moving. The surface of the rock seemed to undulate in the shadows and from the midst of the pattering feet a new noise could be heard; an unmistakably hungry squeaking. He snapped his head back to the front and almost tumbled as Persephone yanked him sharply to a halt. He tottered and swayed as his arms pin wheeled and his eyes boggled at the sheer drop in front of him. Part of the floor had collapsed and he had almost plummeted into a dark void.

"We're trapped!" Katy screamed out.

Bobby frantically looked around. There had to be a way across. There had to. Then, in the glimmer of the torch he saw something lying against the wall. He ran over and grabbed it. It was an old piece of wood. He had no idea what it was doing here, but it looked like it would be their saviour. "Help me!" he called out.

Persephone and his kid sister helped him drag the plank of wood to the hole. Between the three of them, they swung it out and over the chasm, so that it sat flat on the far side.

"Quick!" Persephone bounded across the wood to the other side. "Just don't look down!"

Katy looked up at Bobby, fear in her eyes.

"Go on," he reassured her. "I'll be right behind you."

She inhaled a small courage-gathering breath, then scampered across the plank.

The noise behind Bobby was getting even louder. He snuck a quick glance behind him and saw that the rats were almost at his ankles. He turned and bolted for the plank, but the light was poor and he hadn't judged his route as carefully as the others. Just two steps in and he felt his body lurch to one side. He was aware of Katy screaming out to him and his arms flailing around in an insane manner as he forced his feet to continue one after the other. He had to get across; he could not leave Katy on her own. Focussing his eyes on his sister, who stood beneath the glow of Persephone's torch, he levelled himself up and ran straight ahead. He ignored the bouncing of the plank beneath him and flew off the wood onto the other side, collapsing in a heap at his sister's feet.

Turning his head, he watched in horror as the rats reached the makeshift bridge. They crowded onto it and began to traverse the chasm. Persephone screamed out in a shriek of rage and heaved against the wood with all her weight. Bobby and Katy joined her and they watched as it tumbled down into the dark, taking the rats that were running along its surface with it.

The three sat for a moment catching their breath.

Finally, Katy let out a deep sigh and said, "Do you have any more of those apples? That made me rather hungry."

The ladder up to the surface was not far along from the chasm. The three of them blinked repeatedly as their eyes adjusted to the bright light of day.

"I never want to see another rat as long as I live," Persephone muttered.

Bobby and Katy nodded in agreement. They peered down the road and Irlingbury was now away in the distance.

"Well, I guess this is where we part company," the older girl said as she extinguished her torch. "Remember, you mustn't tell anyone about the Talisman and Jason is in a house with a white door on the road into Orchester. There will be a green face painted on the woodwork and you need to say that you have come to deliver the goods."

"We'll make sure that he gets it."

Persephone smiled. "Well, I wish you luck. Walk well and stay safe."

"Walk well and stay safe," Bobby and Katy replied together.

The girl turned and looked back at Irlingbury. "I'll skirt around the edge of the village. I don't want another run in with our *friends*. Thanks again," she said.

They watched as Persephone made her way back down the road before turning North when she reached the outskirts of the settlement.

"Well, it's just you and me now," Bobby said to his sister.

"It always is," she replied as they walked away in the opposite direction.

For a while, they walked in silence, the tattered buildings falling far away behind them and the barren countryside stretching out in front. Eventually, Katy piped up, "What do you think Orchester will be like?"

Bobby pondered this for a moment. He had never left Irlingbury before and had very little information about the wider world. "I'm not sure," he eventually replied. "I guess it'll be a bit like home, perhaps a bit busier."

"Why do you think it'll be busier?"

"*Anywhere* will be busier than home."

The two children laughed.

That night, the two siblings slept out in a field. The air was warm and there was no sign of rain, the black sky clear above. They hunkered down beneath a wiry hedgerow to make sure that they were unseen by any un-friendly passers-by and allowed themselves time to relax after the excitement of the day.

Bobby looked over at Katy and saw that her eyes were fixed on the full moon, high above. "What are you thinking?" he asked.

"Do you think the moon is a long way away?"

"Definitely."

"Further than Orchester?"

Bobby smiled. "Oh yes."

"What about Wellington?"

"The moon is so far away that we could never get there."

The small girl pursed her lips. "Do you think people have *ever* got to the moon?"

Bobby rolled onto his back and gazed up at the white orb with its mysterious patterns etched into its pale face. "I don't see how. It's not as if we could fly, is it?"

"I know… But what about *before*?" The word was filled with childish awe. "Weren't people supposed to do all manner of incredible things? Persephone said that they went to other planets. Perhaps they flew to the moon back then?"

Bobby continued to stare up at the lunar land-scape. It looked so peaceful up there. Was it so fantast-ical to think that people had once walked up there, back in the time before the Divergence? "Perhaps, I guess."

Katy sighed. "Bobby, does the moon have a name?"

"What do you mean?"

"Well, does it have a name or is it just called *the moon*?"

Something moved, back in Bobby's memory. "Dad used to tell me old, *very* old stories about times when people thought the planets were gods, creatures that influenced the lives of humans. They all had names. I think he said that some people called the moon Selene."

"Selene." The name rolled around Katy's mouth. "That's a pretty name. I like that. I think, when I'm a grown up, I'll be called Selene."

Bobby chuckled. "Don't be silly. It doesn't work like that. People don't change their names. The name we're given as a baby is the one that we keep." He turned to watch his sister as tiredness started to creep across his weary limbs. She lay there, still gazing up at the moon which cast its pale light down on her young, innocent features. He couldn't help but feel that it made her appear deathly white. Bobby shuddered. It was as if it wasn't his kid sister lying there right now, but someone else. Someone a lot older. He sighed and pushed the thoughts from his head. He had too many other things to worry about right now. "You do say silly things, sometimes."

But Katy didn't reply. She was fast asleep.

Bobby closed his eyes and joined her.

## Chapter Four

The next day, the weather was rather pleasant. As a result, Katy was in a surprisingly good mood when she awoke.

For once.

"How long do you think it'll take us to get to Orchester?" she asked as she smacked a few innocent weeds around the head with a random stick that she had discovered by the roadside that morning.

"Not long," Bobby replied, dodging around a deep rut in the road. The last thing he wanted right now was to be ankle-deep in mud. "It's only the next village along. The sun shouldn't have travelled too far across the sky. Perhaps mid-afternoon."

There was a sharp snicking sound as Katy's stick sent a yellow flower hurtling off into a ditch. "Whoa!" she exclaimed. "Did you see that?"

Bobby chuckled. "Great shot, but we'd better keep the pace up if we want to make good time. I think Persephone would want us to get this talisman delivered as quick as possible."

Katy quickened her pace, catching up with her

brother and leaving the offending weeds behind her. She didn't abandon her stick though. Instead, she waved it in front of her as if it were a sword. "Take that," she shouted, lunging forward with a quick jab before swiping it across an imaginary foe. "And that!"

Bobby turned and watched. "And just who are you saving the world from right now?"

"Who do you think?" Katy glowered.

Bobby frowned. "Katy, you can't let Teller get to you like this."

"But, he's horrid."

"I know, but we've left him behind in Irlingbury. He's of no matter to us now."

Katy harrumphed in a manner unsuited to a small girl. "I think I'd rather keep practicing, just in case," and she continued to swipe and jab at her unseen enemy.

"Careful with that. You'll have your eye out."

The two children stopped still and looked for the source of the voice.

"Who... who's there?" Bobby stammered, trying to sound a lot braver than he felt.

"Show yourself, or I'll stab you with my sword!" his little sister cried.

The voice chuckled. "But how can you stab what you cannot see, little one?"

Katy frowned. The disembodied voice had a point.

"Don't worry. I mean you no harm." There was a rustling from some overgrown hedgerow by a copse of withered trees near the roadside and a man appeared from the undergrowth. To the children, he seemed terribly old, simply by the fact that his hair was white and his skin was incredibly wrinkled. His clothing was fashioned from patches of rags and furs that had been crudely stitched together and he was hunched over, using a hefty staff to support his bent frame as he carefully eased himself up onto the road.

Bobby positioned himself between the stranger and his kid sister. The man was smiling, but that did not mean he wasn't dangerous. "You startled us."

"Well, please accept my apologies," the elderly man said. "It was not my intention." He limped closer, until he was but a short distance from the children.

Katy wrinkled her nose. "You smell," she noted.

"Katy!" Bobby hissed.

The man just laughed. "I'm sure that I do, as do most things that have not dwelt in civilisation, or what is left of it, for a good number of years. Now what are two children doing, straying far from home?"

"We are going to visit family in the next village," Bobby lied, before Katy could blurt out their real mission. There was no way that he wanted to tell anyone who they did not know what they were *really* doing.

The man closed one eye and peered at them with the other. "Are you now? Are you now?" he mused.

Bobby shifted uncomfortably under the perceptive stare and there was an awkward moment when no one said anything, not even Katy.

"Well," the stranger finally said, gripping the tip of his staff between his gnarled hands. "I'd better not keep you. Just be careful on your journey.

"You never know who you'll meet." With that, he turned to head back off the road.

"Wait a minute," Bobby called out to the old timer's hunched back. "Have you eaten today?"

The man paused, seem to consider the question, then replied, "Well, come to think of it, I don't think that I have."

Bobby reached into his tunic pocket and drew out one of the remaining apples that they had stolen from the market. He handed it over to the strange man. "My father once said that we should never see anyone go hungry, even if they were not known to us."

The man smiled as he took the apple. "Why, thank you, youngster. Your father must be a wise man. What is his name?"

"He was called Howard. He was a wood carver in Irlingbury, but he has been dead some years now."

The man stowed the apple away in a deep pocket and continued to stare at the youngsters. "A terrible thing to lose one's father, especially when so young. Tell me, how did he die?"

Bobby took a deep breath as he recalled the awful day. He and his father had been at market as usual and everything had seemed very pleasant to start with.

Until the Shadow Wraiths had descended on the village.

Dressed in their obsidian robes, the servants of Kanor cantered into the village marketplace on their giant black horses and dismounted right in front of his father's stall. Riding with them was Teller and his own father. The other man whispered something to the leader of the Wraiths and then pointed down at the woodworker. Two of the Wraiths grabbed Howard and hauled him out into the town square. Bobby screamed and tried to stop them, but another Wraith grabbed him and snatched him off his feet, holding him tight. To this day he could still feel the hard, unmovable arm wrapped around his chest. It had felt more like a fired pot than human flesh. There was no give, no movement to the flesh as he strained and struggled to try and reach his father.

The woodworker called out to him, "Bobby! No! Stay there!"

The leader of the Wraiths lowered his black hood, revealing a face that was truly unforgettable: skin impossibly smooth, as if fashioned from glass, and hair slicked close against his scalp. "This is what happens to traitors!" he declared to the startled villagers that had been shopping for their goods as he held his hand out in front of Bobby's father. In a quick stabbing motion, the hand transformed into a long, stake-like weapon and plunged deep into the man's chest.

Howard was dead before he hit the floor.

As Bobby screamed and cried, the commander of the Wraiths just peered across at him with a curious look in his eyes.

Then the Shadow Wraiths simply climbed back up on their horses and rode out of town, leaving Bobby and Katy behind: orphans.

"He... he was executed by the Shadow Wralths," Bobby summarised. Not wanting to relive the details any more than he had to. "They said he was a traitor, but he was just a woodworker. He had never done anything wrong."

Bobby turned at the sound of a wet sniff from his kid sister. He shook his head and held out his arms. She threw herself into his side and buried her face into his clothing. He felt his own tears start to burn at the sides of his eyes.

The old stranger sighed. "Many evil things have been done in the name of the law, child. Perhaps, one day, the law will change."

Bobby nodded, forcing back the tears. He did not

want to cry, not in front of this strange man, not in front of Katy.

The man lay a disfigured hand on the teenager's shoulder. It felt incredibly heavy, far heavier than one would have expected. "I wish you well, Bobby. Walk well and stay safe."

"Thank you, sir," the boy replied. "Tell me, what is your name?"

"The name I use is Cutter, and I hope that we meet again." With that, he turned and vanished once more into the undergrowth.

Bobby sighed and turned to his kid sister. "Come on," he said. "Let's get going."

As the two children carried on along the bumpy road, Katy asked her brother. "Bobby, how did that man know your name?"

# Chapter Five

Bobby was deep in thought as he and Katy trudged along the ill-maintained road to Orchester. The encounter with the man called Cutter had left him deeply unsettled.

First, there was the memory of his father's death at the hand of the Shadow Wraiths. The boy could not get his final image of his father out of his head as he called out Bobby's name. That alone was enough to tie his stomach in knots.

Then there was the mysterious Cutter. How had the old man known his name? Bobby kept going over the conversation in his head to see if he had forgotten something. Perhaps Katy had said his name? Perhaps he had introduced himself and had forgotten?

"Perhaps he already knew us?" Katy suggested, stepping carefully between rank, festering puddles.

Bobby considered this. It was possible. The old man could have met them before.

But surely he would have remembered him?

The older sibling shook his head with a fair amount of hesitation. "I don't know, Katy. I didn't recognise him at all, and I think he has a face that we would remember."

He thrust his hands in his pockets and his fingers latched onto the small wooden talisman. He rubbed his thumb over the engraved surface and felt the distinct shapes of the sword and the cup. He needed to keep a clear head if he was to fulfil his promise to Persephone.

It was then that he heard the sound of horses' hooves pounding up the road behind them.

"Katy! Quick! Hide!"

Bobby grabbed his sister's arm and pulled her off the side of the road into the brush and thicket that grew in the parallel ditch. For once, she didn't protest. She could hear the alarm in his voice. Their feet squelched in the filth and the mire and Bobby felt the ground give way beneath him, causing him to slide unceremoniously down into a stagnant pool of scum-covered water. As he was holding onto Katy, he could not help but drag her down with him but, to give his sister her dues, she didn't shout out in surprise.

They righted themselves and hunkered down in the dirt and the weeds, pulling the undergrowth around them to keep them shielded from unwelcome eyes, but allowing enough space to see who was riding along the otherwise empty road.

As the two children crouched down in the thick, unwelcoming undergrowth, Bobby curled his arm around his kid sister desperate to protect her from the one thing that the sound of horse beats could mean: trouble. He kept his breathing shallow as four horses cantered to a halt right in front of them. Someone dismounted and Bobby peered through the scratty undergrowth to see who it was. Nausea rose in his gut as he immediately recognised the rider.

It was Teller.

"What do you see?" came a voice from one of the other riders. Bobby couldn't make out who it was, but he was guessing that it was one of the bully's cronies.

"I'm not sure," Teller replied, bending down to peer into the dirt where Bobby and Katy had been walking just a short moment ago.

Bobby's blood ran cold as his hand instinctively slipped into his pocket.

His *empty* pocket!

Oh no! This was definitely not good.

Teller stood up, dusting off his discovery. "Look at this," he instructed his companions. "What do you make of it?" The four riders peered down at the talisman. "You think that's a sword and some sort of cup?"

"You think it's Normal's?"

"I doubt anyone else has been along here."

"What do you think he was doing with it?" one of the others asked.

"Not got a clue, but my bet is that traitorous little piece of pigswill was up to no good."

Teller pocketed the artefact and remounted his steed. "Come on, there's a field up ahead where we can camp and rest for a bit. They're on foot. We'll soon catch them up, so there's no immediate hurry."

And, with that, the four rode off in possession of the one thing that Bobby had sworn to keep safe.

Once he was sure that Teller and his gang were at a distance from where he could not be seen, Bobby clambered up out of the ditch. His garments were muddy and his hands were cut. What was worse, his heart was weighted down as if with a handful of lead. He had failed. Persephone had trusted him and he had failed.

He felt a small hand slip into his and he looked

down at Katy. "What are we to do?" he asked.

"Simple," she replied. "We need to get it back."


True to their word, Teller and his companions camped in the field that they had mentioned. They tied their horses to an old tree and set a campfire close by. For fuel, they burnt hunks of decayed wood that they had scavenged from the remains of a rotten tree after igniting some scrubby bits of dried bracken for kindling. The remains of an overgrown hedge traced the perimeter of the enclosure and it was through this that Bobby and Katy spied on the thieves, working out what they should do to recover the precious talisman.

"What's the plan?" the younger sibling asked the older.

Bobby thought about it for a moment. "Well, we can't just walk in and take it, can we? We'll have to wait until they go to sleep and grab it then."

"How will we see? It'll be pitch black!"

Bobby shook his head. "No, it won't. Think about the moon last night. It was full. Once it rises, we should have enough light to let us find the talisman whilst it being dark enough to conceal us in the shadows."

Katy nodded and they continued to observe the four riders who seemed to be deep in conversation. Bobby watched them hand the talisman around and turn it over, studying it, trying to discern its purpose. In the end, they apparently gave up and Teller stashed the wooden artefact in his saddlebag which lay next to him on the grass by the fire. He pulled a bottle out of the same saddlebag and there was the sound of cheers from his companions as he unstoppered the cork and took a long, thirsty swig before passing it around.

Eventually, the sky turned dark as the stars and the moon rose above. Teller and his companions started to stretch and yawn. Bobby watched anxiously as they unrolled their beds and settled down to sleep. Within minutes, the sound of drunken snoring reached the ears of the children.

Bobby pried his way through the hedgerow. "Come on. Now's our chance." Carefully, he tiptoed his way into the makeshift camp. The only sounds that he could hear were the loud snoring, the crackling of the fire and the pounding drumbeat of his heart. If Teller or one of his companions were to wake...

Bobby shoved that thought out of his head. He had to concentrate on retrieving the talisman. He could not let it stay in the possession of this cruel thug.

Easing himself around the fire, he approached the sleeping Teller. The older boy was flat on his back with his mouth wide open. Bobby winced at the rank breath that came from the bully's mouth. Then he paled when he realised where the saddlebag was. Teller was using It as a pillow!

This was not good. How on earth was he supposed to reach into the bag's pocket and grab the talisman? Quietly, he crouched down onto his haunches and looked closely at the bag. It was well and truly lodged under his enemy's head and there was no way of reaching into it.

Just as he was considering this dilemma there was a noise. The horses gave a brusque snort and stamped their feet. Teller's mouth closed and reopened as vague words were mumbled through his sleepy lips. Bobby felt as if he were going to be sick. If the older boy woke up right now, he would be done for! Instead, Teller grimaced, drew his blanket up tight and rolled over to his left. As he did so, his head rolled off the pocket of the saddlebag.

Bobby seized the opportunity. He darted forwards and quickly unclasped the buckle. Before the older boy could roll back, his hand snaked inside the depths of the leather bag, rooted around and found something small and hard. His face grinned in the moonlight as he snatched the talisman out and stashed it back into his pocket.

He was just about to move away into the night when an almighty crash came from behind him. His head snapped back to see Katy flat on her face with a piece of food in her hand. By the looks of her, she had been following the demands of her stomach and had been rifling through a promising saddlebag before promptly tripping over its treacherous long straps.

Bobby winced then blanched as he turned back to be confronted with the furious face of the now wide-awake Teller. The last thing he saw before a painful blackness grabbed him was the older boy's fist hammering towards his face.

# Chapter Six

*"Bobby! Bobby!"*

Bobby had been dreaming. He wasn't sure what he had been dreaming *about*, but he realised that he didn't like it much. It was mostly shadows and silhouettes, as if the subjects of the dream were standing in front of a very bright light. There was a cup, a sword and something his mind would not let him recognise. Something with large black wings. This last thing filled him with a terrible fear that twisted the very base of his stomach.

Its mouth was moving, but Bobby was unable to hear any discernible words. It was as if the voice of the creature was coming from a long, long way away; as if the sounds were travelling from a place either far in the past or the future. There was just the *feeling* of words, a three-pulse pattern repeating over and over like an erratic triple time beat of a heart.

*"Bobby! Bobby!"*

The creature had lurched closer now and the light behind it was blindingly bright. Bobby could make out gnarled claws at the end of its powerful black arms. As the light streamed between the outstretched talons, they opened and shut in hungry, grasping motions, reaching out desperately for the cup and the sword that remained tantalisingly out of its avaricious reach.

*"Bobby! Bobby!"*

It was closer still. There was a smell from the creature that made Bobby want to roll over and vomit the contents of his gut onto the floor. It was rank and sulphurous. It was the odour of a thing that shouldn't be, that was completely unnatural. The three-fold sound increased in pitch and volume, screaming through his tortured ears. It was dry and sibilant, passionate and desperate.

He strained as best as he could to make out the words that were sliding from the gaping maw of the monster that so desperately wanted the cup and the sword. He screamed out into the dream that he wanted to hear what was being said, that he *needed* to hear what was being said.

"We… are… one!" came the cruel voice. "We… are… one!"

And the monster was upon him, its head to his. Bobby continued to scream into the nightmare as all the world around him began to dissolve away. He looked left and right, seeing fields and villages put to the torch. Armies of constructs marched across the barren land, slaying all who stood before them.

*"Bobby! Bobby!"*

"We… are… one!" the voice insisted once more, before the beast opened an obsidian eyelid and its snake-like eye peered deep into Bobby's heart, judging whether or not he should be consumed like the rest of the world.

*"Bobby! Wake up!"*

Another voice, closer this time. Right next to him, in fact. The boy opened his eyes and immediately regretted the move as pain erupted down the side of his head. "Ow," he murmured.

"Bobby? You okay?"

Bobby Normal groaned as he inched his head up into a position to look at his sister. She was sat on the ground next to him, concern on her face. He tried to reach out to her but discovered that his hands were tied firmly behind his back.

Then he remembered Teller and groaned again.

"I'm okay," he managed to say. "You?"

Katy nodded.

"Well, well, well," came a mocking voice. "The food thief is awake at last. What happened, Normal? Take a little tumble?" Teller's cronies cackled in response to the pathetic joke. However, it made Bobby realise something and he tried to rub his leg against the inside of his trousers. He felt something small and hard inside the fabric. Yes! The talisman was still there. The idiots had assumed that they had just been raiding the camp for food, so hadn't bothered to search him.

Now, if only they could escape...

However, escape was far from Teller's plans. "Well lads, I think we need to make an example of these two. Make sure that they remember that thieving is a crime."

The teenager's cronies chuckled darkly as Teller unfurled his prize possession, his vicious whip. He made a great show of stretching it out and flexing it this way and that. In the still dark, the sound of the creaking leather was all that could be heard.

Then there were three sharp cracks as he flicked it left, right, left, grinning cruelly as he did. It was intended as a demonstration of his mastery of the weapon, to show that *he* was the one in complete control here.

Bobby didn't move a muscle. In his head he re-called the images from his dream: the large dark creature that hungered ravenously for the cup and the sword. He remembered the feelings of pure terror that it had brewed inside of him. That was something to *truly* fear, not some bratty teenage upstart with a whip and an inflated ego.

Teller frowned at the lack of response from his captive. "Playing the hero, Normal?" he sneered, coiling up his whip. "You think you're just going to walk away from this? Think you're better than us? Than me? That's what your father thought and look where it got him." He flicked his whip out and a sharp snapping sound echoed first through Bobby's left ear, then his right. "You are nothing, Normal! Nothing, I say!"

Again, Teller cracked the whip either side of Bobby's head.

Still Bobby did not flinch. This was nothing to fear. The creature in the dream was *something* to fear. He saw it reaching out, grasping for the cup and the sword. The cup and the sword that were engraved onto the surface of the Eternal Talisman. As Teller ranted and raved unimportant words in front of him, Bobby withdrew inside. The nightmare and the talisman must be linked; the imagery was the same. But what was the creature? Why did it want the cup and the sword? What were they to it?

Bobby's left cheek stung as the whip nicked the skin just below his eye.

Still he did not respond. His mind was still concentrating on deeper, more important things. The creature had been speaking in the dream. "We are one," it had said, over and over. What did that mean? It had to be important. If he could figure that out...

It was then that three other words snapped Bobby

back to the here and now.

"Bring the girl."

Katy kicked and bit as two of the thugs dragged her over to their grinning leader.

Bobby tried to lunge forward to save his kid sister. However, the other goon kept a firm hand on his shoulder to prevent him from interfering as Teller drew out a huge hunting knife that glinted wickedly in the unnatural white light of the full moon.

"Aha!" Teller crowed with delight. "At last we have our guest's attention. Fun at last!"

Katy fell terribly silent while he ran the flat of the blade across her smooth cheek. "What do you think, lads? A nice big cross to show the world just what a horrid piece of work she is? That okay, Normal? Every time you look at it, you can remember just how insolent you were to me."

Bobby struggled to break free but only managed to receive a sharp blow to the head for his troubles. All he could do was watch helplessly as Katy wept in fear, the wicked point of the blade approaching her face.

It was then that they all heard the long, mournful howl from out in the dark.

Teller froze, the knife still poised a breath away from the girl's cheek. Bobby watched as the bully's eyes widened and scanned the perimeter of the camp. "What the hell was that?" he snapped. "Find out what it was!" he barked at the other older boys.

The three exchanged glances, obviously not wanting to be the first to wander off into the surrounding night.

"Now!" Teller yelled, waving the hunting knife in their direction.

As a trio, they edged towards the point on the perimeter of the camp from where they thought the noise had originated. Then there was a stomach-churning roar and something large and hairy flew through the air, flattening two of the hoodlums. The third gave off a falsetto shriek and ran back towards the fire.

Bobby turned as best as he could to watch the beast. It paced slowly forwards on all fours, its grey hair bristling in the flickering light of the fire, malice in its dark eyes as it stalked towards Teller who was waving his knife towards it. A knife that, in Bobby's opinion, now seemed incredibly ineffective.

Then something miraculous happened.

The beast spoke.

"You harm so much as a hair on that young girl's head and I will make you watch whilst I slowly devour your pathetic entrails." It padded further into the camp, it's head low and menacing. It was now so close that Bobby could actually feel the heat from its immense, muscular body. "You will get on your horses and leave this place. Now!"

Teller and his companions did not need instructing twice. They launched up onto their horses and galloped off into the night, not once looking back.

The beast sat down on its haunches and gave what seemed to be an amused grunt of satisfaction. It turned its head to face Bobby, who was desperately trying to wrench the bonds from his wrists. He had no desire for him and Katy to be this creature's supper. Then he stopped as the animal seemed to laugh.

"They may have been cowards but they seem to have tied rather good knots. Wouldn't you say so, Bobby?" Then, right in front of the boy's amazed eyes, the beast's features seemed to melt and transform until there

The Adventures of Bobby Normal

on the ground sat the old man from before, Cutter.

# Chapter Seven

A short while later, Bobby and Katy were devouring a simple broth that Cutter had produced from some of the provisions that Teller's party had left behind as they had fled for their pitiful lives. As he spooned the tasty meal into his mouth, Bobby kept glancing over the top of the bowl at their saviour. Rather than joining in with the food, the old man was sat quietly, drawing deeply on a long, hand-fashioned pipe, its fragrant smoke drifting up into the night-time air.

When he had finished his food, Bobby lay his bowl down next to him and spoke. "Thank you."

"It was the best that I could do with what those cowards left behind," Cutter shrugged.

"That's not what I meant. You saved our lives."

The old man shrugged again.

Bobby continued to stare at him, the moonlight making his face appear pale, mystical.

"What are you?"

"I am an old man."

"I've never met an old man who can turn into a wolf."

"So, I'm a *special* old man," Cutter smiled as he blew a smoke ring into the air.

Bobby's eyes never left him.

Katy produced a small, ripe belch as she finished her food. "Does it hurt?" she asked.

Cutter raised an eyebrow for her to explain.

"When you change like that. Does it hurt?"

The old man shook his head. "No. There is no pain."

"But surely all your bones get bent and twisted? That must hurt a lot."

Cutter chuckled as he tapped his pipe in the palm of his hand in thought. "How much do you know of long ago. In the time before the Divergence?"

"Not much," Bobby admitted. "Dad used to tell us bits and pieces, but they were only fragments." He noticed a certain sadness cross the old man's face.

"Did your father ever tell you about the Bloodline of Abel?" Cutter asked, the sadness quickly dissipating, a harder look forming on his face.

Both children shook their heads.

The man took a long draw from his pipe and continued. "They were a group of people with special abilities that enabled them to become wolves. They were powerful, strong. But they were also greedy. They thought only of themselves."

Katy frowned. "But you're not greedy. You just saved us and fed us."

"I am not of the Bloodline," Cutter shrugged, "but those morons before did not know that. No, the Bloodline died out many, many years ago. Before the Divergence. Before Kanor."

"How did they die out, if they were so strong?" Katy

asked.

The fire cracked and spat up into the air.

Cutter watched a mote of singed wood spiral up into the night.

"They crossed the wrong man," he growled.

"Then who are you?" Bobby asked.

Cutter watched the fire dance in the dark. "Just an old man who has made too many mistakes. But right now," he smiled as Katy let out a huge yawn, "I believe that you two should be getting some sleep."

The next morning, Bobby awoke with a stiff crick in his neck but, aside from that, he felt relatively refreshed.

There had been no nightmares.

As he lay on his back, gently rocking his head from side to side in an attempt to loosen his protesting muscles, he gazed up at the lightening sky and watched fluffy clouds drift across the wide blue above him.

*Had the skies been the same before the Divergence?* he wondered to himself. He knew that the land had changed dramatically when Kanor had risen and unleashed his merciless constructs. Before, there had been huge cities and machines with people travelling up and down the country as well as up into the skies beyond the planet. Now there was barren countryside and the occasional ramshackle village. The Divergence had changed the very ground upon which people walked.

But had it changed the skies?

Before the decimation of the human race, had people been able to lie back like he was doing right now and look up at clouds dancing lazily in exactly the same manner?

Bobby did not know. There was so much that he

did not know of the time before the Divergence. Cutter's tale last night of men being able to turn into wolves had whetted his appetite. What else had there been?

Speaking of Cutter.

Bobby sat up and looked around for the curious old man, but he was nowhere to be seen. There was just Katy, snoring loudly under her grey blanket.

What was the old man? People could not change shape like that. He claimed to not be of the Bloodline, but surely he had to be something else. Something special. Also, was he following them? First, he had appeared out of apparently nowhere on the roadside, then he miraculously turned up last night to save them. Then Bobby recalled a memory from when they had left Irlingbury. Teller had called out to his companions that he had seen Bobby down the street. They had gone running off in the opposite direction. Who had they seen? If Cutter could change shape…

Then there was that nightmare, the creature that wanted the cup and the sword that were on the Eternal Talisman. Bobby slipped the artefact out of his pocket and traced the engraving with his thumb. What did it stand for? Were they actual things? Were they weapons to help this Virtuous Man defeat Kanor?

So many questions for so early in the day.

Bobby shrugged as his stomach rumbled. It was time to eat and time to wake his kid sister.

She would only be pleased at one of those two facts.

"So, how far is Orchester?"

Bobby sighed. "Like I said just yesterday, not far?"

"I know. But *how* far?"

"We should be there soon."

"But how long is *soon*?"

Bobby took a deep, steadying breath. The petulant questions had been non-stop since Katy had finished filling her mouth with breakfast. "I should think, by the time that the sun is at the top of the sky."

Katy peered up into the blue sky. "That's *ages*."

"No, it's not."

"Is. My feet hurt."

Bobby groaned and turned to face his whining sibling, but when he looked into her brown eyes he saw that she was telling the truth. Her mouth was turned down, her shoulders sloped and her face sad. "How bad?" he asked.

"Lots."

He studied his sister's feet - clad in a pitifully cheap pair of home-made leather boots that they had scavenged a few weeks back. The thinning material was scuffed and torn, her small toes poking through.

Bobby sighed as the guilt of dragging his sister along washed over him. "Let's take a break," he suggested.

"I want to go home," Katy whispered.

"We can't. We have to deliver the talisman, remember?"

Katy flumped down onto the side of the track, dust pluming up around her. "I don't care about the stupid talisman. I don't care about Orchester. My feet hurt. I'm hungry. I want to go to sleep in a comfy bed. I don't want mean boys trying to hurt me..." She trailed off as the tears came.

Bobby felt his heart crumble and, seating himself next to his kid sister, he wrapped her in his arms. "I'm sorry," he apologised, his voice brimming over with remorse, "I truly am. But people are depending on us."

"But why us?" she sobbed into his shoulder.

The image of the beast in the nightmare slunk back into his head.

"Because there is no one else," Bobby replied.

He pushed the dark creature away and instead let his mind drift back to some years previous. A happier time when there had been three of them. He thought about playing with Katy and their dad in the fields on a long hot summer's day.

"Do you remember playing *horse* with Dad?"

Bobby felt his sister's head rub against his shoulder.

"I've got an idea."

Sometime later, Bobby's feet were red raw, his back ached and he was fit to drop, but his heart was soaring to the sound of Katy giggling and laughing up on his back. It had been incredibly awkward helping her up there (he wasn't as tall as their father and she was all elbows and knees), but once he had worked out the intricate balancing act, he had found himself quite adept at dodging the ruts and potholes in the road to the neighbouring village.

As the sun reached the pinnacle of its daytime journey, the children started to once again observe signs of habitation and they galloped into their destination: the village of Orchester.

# Chapter Eight

Bobby hadn't really known what to expect from Orchester. All he had ever known, as far as villages were concerned, was Irlingbury. He had been born there, grown up there and, like the majority of its residents, had never ever left its not too sizeable boundary.

He had to admit that, as they walked into the neighbouring settlement, he was somewhat disappointed. It looked identical to his home village. The streets were muddy and rutted, the houses patched together with whatever random materials the townsfolk could scavenge and the inhabitants wore the same look of tired despair as did those from just a few miles down the road.

"Looks like home," Katy observed.

Bobby nodded. "I know."

"So, where have we got to go?"

Bobby's forehead creased as he recalled Persephone's instructions. "We're looking for a man called Jason. She said that he would be in a small house on the main road entering the village and that there would be a green mark on the door. Some sort of face."

"A happy one or a sad one?"

Bobby shrugged at the random question of an eight-year-old. "I have absolutely no idea. Let's go and find out. It shouldn't take too long, we're already on the main road."

The two children walked slowly down the centre of the street, their eyes scanning each door as they passed them by. Like in Irlingbury, they were all made from wood and each one was shut, unwelcoming, barring out any passing horrors or servants of Kanor.

As they reached the end of the road, where it opened out into the bedraggled market square, Bobby was aware of two things.

The first was that they had not found the door with the green face. They had studied every single door that they had passed, both on the left hand side and on the right. All had been distinctly faceless.

The second was that he had a strong feeling that they were being followed. He turned and peered down the high street. It was a straight passage out of the village and there was nowhere to hide, yet he was sure that there was someone there, lurking in the shadows. When he had been younger, his father had once taken him hunting for rabbits. They had found what his father had considered a suitable spot and had set up three snares, then retired behind the crest of a small mound and waited. In time, a diminutive rabbit had hopped out into the open and had started to sniff around, its tiny nose flicking its long whiskers this way and that. Bobby had felt his father's large hand come to rest on his shoulder. Peering up, he had seen the tall man place two fingers to his lips – an order for total silence. Yet, even with this silence, the rabbit had paused in what it was doing. It had stood up on its hind legs and peered around and about. Then without any warning, it had turned tail and scarpered. Bobby had asked his father to explain how the rabbit had known they were there, even though they hadn't made a sound. His father had mulled this over for a moment then had said, "Sometimes, it doesn't matter just how careful you are, just how many precautions you take, the little critter that you're following will simply, intuitively *know*. Something deep down inside of it will start tingling and ringing out like bells used to hundreds of years ago. It will sense this alarm and know that, right now, it ought to be somewhere else sharpish."

Right now, Bobby felt just like that little rabbit. He couldn't explain it, but he just knew, deep down, that he and Katy were not alone.

And this made him incredibly uneasy.

He was about to take Katy by the hand and lead her back down the street on another attempt at locating the green face whilst keeping an eye open for anyone who might be following them, when he realised that she wasn't there. His head snapped this way and that as his heart began to thump in his chest and his panic rose. All around were villagers going about their usual routine, milling around the few stalls that occupied the market square. They were bartering and haggling with stall vendors, oblivious to a worried teenage boy having lost his kid sister.

Bobby took a step towards the crowd of people, desperate to try and spot Katy in their midst, but all he could see was a mass of browns and greys of ragged homemade clothing identical to that which he and Katy wore. He ran his fingers through his brown hair and bit down on his lower lip. Tears were starting to well in the corners of his eyes.

Had someone snatched Katy away from him when he wasn't looking?

Why had he agreed to come here?

Why had he agreed to bring the talisman to a man he didn't even know?

He had put his and Katy's life in danger and now he was going to have to pay the price.

He heard the familiar crunch of a purloined apple, followed by, "What's the matter?"

Bobby stared down at the grubby little face that was merrily munching away on a freshly acquired piece of fruit. "Katy! Where have you been?"

"Getting food. Want an apple?" She offered one up to him.

Bobby saw red. "I have been worried sick! Don't you dare run off like that! Anything could have happened to you."

His kid sister swallowed and paused her munching. "But… I was only over there. I could see you."

"But *I* couldn't see *you*."

The eight-year-old harrumphed and crossed her arms. "I'm perfectly capable of taking care of myself," she grumbled.

No explanation, however, was going to stop her older brother. The stress and the strain of the last couple of days welled up inside of him and began to overflow. "No. No you can't. You're too young. You're my responsibility. I have to look after you. You're all I've got left!"

"I am *not* too young," Katy stormed as she stamped her foot. "I am perfectly capable of looking after myself. I got these, didn't I?" She thrust the apples up in her brother's face.

"But that's just apples. What if there was something

more serious? More dangerous?"

"I'd work something out."

"Oh, really? You'd be able to take on a construct? Perhaps a Shadow Wraith or even one of the Fallen?"

"Yes, I would!"

"No, you wouldn't. They were the ones who killed Dad, remember? If he couldn't escape them, then neither of us stand a chance."

And then he realised that, in letting his deepest fears spill out from his mouth, he had overstepped the mark.

Katy's lip began to tremble and tears welled up in her brown eyes. "You know I don't like it when you talk about how Dad died."

Bobby ran his fingers through his hair. "Oh, Katy, I'm sorry. I just..." He reached out to hold the sobbing girl, but she pushed him away and darted off into the crowd of shoppers.

The boy swore under his breath and ploughed in after her.


It was like pushing his way through a vertical sea of mud. Numerous market-goers and vendors shouted abuse and yelled insults at the apparently rude teenage boy who shoved at them and heaved them away as he desperately tried to keep sight of his kid sister. She, being smaller, was having a far easier time of dodging around the irate villagers of Orchester. Katy nipped under their arms and darted between their legs as she kept a consistent distance and pace ahead of her pursuing brother.

When they reached the opposite edge of the market square, the throng of people started to thin out and Katy made a break for a wide road that was situated on the far side. She glanced over her shoulder and hurtled along the broken, uneven road surface, heading for a stone bridge that rose up in front of her.

She never saw Teller step out of the dark side alley.

She couldn't even scream as he wrapped his arm around her mouth and dragged her up onto the bridge.

"Don't come any closer!" the older boy shouted down to Bobby, who had finally managed to extricate himself from the crowd. "Remember, I have a knife!"

Bobby skidded to a halt as Teller drew the familiar weapon from its scabbard. The sunlight glinted on its highly polished surface as the thug pressed it close to Katy's neck. The frantic brother held his hands out in front of him in a pacifying manner. "Okay, okay! I see it. I see it. Now, what's going on?"

Teller continued to back up onto the bridge, Katy clasped awkwardly in his arm. "I want to make you suffer, Normal, that's what. I want it so that every time you look at your brat of a sister, you'll know that I won."

Bobby shook his head. "What… what on earth do you mean? Won? Won what? This isn't a game!"

"But it is to you, isn't it? It's all a game. You flaunt the rules. You beg, you steal. You consort with those who would overthrow the power that rules us."

Bobby blanched. Instinctively, his hand darted into his pocket and felt the Eternal Talisman safely tucked away. Teller hadn't mentioned it before. Yes, he had found it on the road to here, but he had had no idea as to what it was or what Persephone had asked him to do.

He had to be talking about something else.

"What do you mean?"

The older boy let out a bray of laughter and

tightened the wicked knife up against Katy's neck. "You seriously expect me to believe you have no idea what your father was up to?"

"My f… father," Bobby stammered, "was a woodworker."

"Your *f…father*," Teller mocked, "was a dissident. He plotted against those above us. He planned to overthrow Kanor himself!"

Bobby's mouth hung open. It wasn't true. It couldn't be true.  How on earth could there be any truth to this?

Teller chuckled to himself then grinned maniacally as he raised the knife to Katy's grubby cheek.

His laughter was cut short in a scream of pain as the young girl bit down onto his other hand. He drew back in shock, waving his bleeding hand in front of him. Katy advanced and shoved him as hard as she could in his midriff. Normally, due to her comparative lack of size and weight, this would have been a completely ineffectual move, but two things played to her advantage. First, Teller was already off-balance, his concentration centred more on the bleeding hand than the enraged eight-year-old girl. Second, as he had backed up along the bridge, he had inadvertently edged closer and closer to the low parapet. As he flailed his arm around in pain, the minimal force of Katy's hands caused him to stumble and catch his hip against the crumbling stonework which immediately broke and gave way beneath him.

Teller tumbled over the side.

Bobby charged up to the crest of the bridge and joined his sister at the point where the older boy had fallen. They looked down and saw no flowing river but a dried-up bed of mud and stone. Across one of the larger boulders lay the broken body of Teller, his neck at a most unnatural angle.

"I told you that I could look after myself," Katy whispered.

Bobby turned to his sister, a look of horror on his face.

She, in turn, peered along the road that led past the bridge. "Look," she said, "this road leads out the other end of town. Come on. That house we're looking for might be along here."

It didn't take the two children long to find the door with the small painting of a wild-looking green face painted towards its top. Bobby, however, wasn't exactly concentrating on the task at hand.

His kid sister had just killed someone and was showing no remorse whatsoever.

How? Just how could this be?

Was it Katy? Was she some sort of hardened killer now? No, he refused to believe that.

Was it shock? That seemed more likely. Perhaps her mind was shutting down any reaction to what she had done, concentrating on another task to protect her.

Was it something bigger? Was it the world in which they were growing up? Had they grown up in a different time, they would have lived as children, been loved by their parents and been able to spend their time playing games. Here, however, they were on their own. A cruel monster ruled the world and they were considered the lowest of the low. Death was an everyday occurrence in this world. Was the atmosphere in which they lived fashioning them? Would *he* be the same as Katy was right now, should he have to kill someone to survive?

He did not know which of these was the correct answer.

"Well?" his kid sister asked as she stood before the door. "Are you going to knock?"

Bobby snapped back to the task at hand and nodded. He lifted his right hand to the wood and rapped three times with his knuckles. There was a short wait and they could hear the sound of movement behind the door. Then a high-pitched, reverberating squeal came from the creaking, unoiled hinges as the door swung inwards and the face of an elderly woman peered around its edge. "Yes?" she asked.

Bobby took a deep breath and repeated what Persephone had told him. "We have come to deliver the goods."

Immediately, the woman's face seemed to become twenty years younger. Her mouth rose in a beautiful smile and delight twinkled in her grey eyes. "Oh, bless you! Bless you. You seek Jason."

Bobby nodded. "Persephone sent us."

The woman glanced up and down the street.

"Then you had better come in and I will take you to meet the Virtuous Man."

# The Adventures of Bobby Normal

# Bobby Normal
## and the
## Virtuous Man

## Previously...

Bobby was a teenage boy from Irlingbury. He lived there with his eight-year-old sister Katy. Like most people in the Divergent Lands, they existed in a life of abject poverty. Many years ago, a being called Kanor rose like a black dragon over the entire world and decimated the human race by use of his creatures forged from clay, the constructs.

To make matters worse, the children's father had been executed for treason, leaving them to fend for themselves in this inhospitable land. Not only this, but they were frequently singled out and tormented by an older boy by the name of Teller whose family were allowed privileges as the bully's father was a quisling of Kanor's regime. This made Teller feel superior and, looking down on Bobby with derision, he labelled him "Normal".

Bobby and Katy met a girl named Persephone whose father was dying. She asked them to deliver a wooden token called the Eternal Talisman to someone called the Man of Virtue in the neighbouring village of Orchester. She claimed that it would aid him in destroying the vile Kanor, thus liberating their world. On their journey they were harried and subsequently captured by Teller and his gang of cronies before being liberated by a strange shape-shifting old man who called himself Cutter.

Upon reaching Orchester, they were tracked down once again by the vengeful Teller who abducted Katy and threatened to kill her. The small girl fought back and pushed him to his death over the side of a bridge, an action for which she showed no apparent remorse.

We rejoin them on their adventures just after they reach the house of the Virtuous Man…

## Chapter One

Bobby was nervous.

He realised that this seemed to be a perpetual state of affairs at the moment. As he and his eight-year-old kid sister Katy entered the small ramshackle house in the village of Orchester, he thought back to a few days ago, to what now seemed like a different lifetime. They had been living as street urchins in the unimportant, mostly forgotten village of Irlingbury, a settlement like so many in the ravaged Divergent Lands of the mysterious dark overlord, Kanor. The two of them had been impoverished orphans, living off scraps they could scavenge or food they could steal. It had been a hard life, but it had also been a simple one. They had known what to expect, be it a swift kick from an irate trader or a hurried escape through the derelict streets of a dying village.

There had been no drama, so to speak. The worst that they could have expected was the unwanted attention of the obnoxious bully Teller, a boy a few years older than Bobby, and his doting little band of cronies.

But now, as of a short while ago, Teller was dead.

Katy had killed him, pushed him over the crumbling

side of the bridge in the main street of Orchester.

And she had shown no remorse. None whatsoever.

Bobby's stomach knotted double then triple as he recalled Katy simply standing, peering over the side of the broken bridge at the distorted body of the boy she had just killed. He couldn't just let this matter slide. He was going to have to talk to her at some point.

But not right now.

Now they had to tend to the matter that had dragged them out of their simple routine of sleep, steal, run, eat.

Pushing his hand into the pocket of his ragged, dirty trousers, he wrapped his fingers around a small, hard object. His thumb traced a pattern that had been meticulously carved into the wood: a cup and a blade. This was the Eternal Talisman. Back in Irlingbury, he and Katy had encountered the girl named Persephone and she had entrusted them to take the talisman to the next village, Orchester, where they were to deliver it to an individual named Jason, the Virtuous Man.

He was going to use it to kill Kanor.

Bobby's stomach rolled again. Kanor was the being who had brought about the Divergence, who had used his constructs, his animated clay golems, to reduce the human race to a mere remnant. Known as the black dragon, no one had ever seen his face. Well, no one had seen his face *and lived*. And this small piece of engraved wood was supposed to help destroy him.

Bobby sighed.

He wanted to go back to his simple life. This was just not for him.

He wasn't a hero, someone who went on quests to slay unseen monsters.

He was *normal*.

The teenage boy thought about how Teller had labelled him with the moniker as an insult, saying that he was a nobody, no one special. But now he realised that normality was something that he desperately wanted back in his life. They would hand the Eternal Talisman over and go, return to Irlingbury and forget that this had ever happened.

But there were questions, weren't there?

Before he had died, Teller had said something about Bobby's and Katy's father, who had been executed by Shadow Wraiths when Katy was just an infant. He had said that Howard had been a traitor, that he had been plotting against Kanor. A part of Bobby wanted, no *needed*, to know more about this. Perhaps this Virtuous Man would have some answers?

"Are you okay, sonny?"

Bobby snapped out of his deep reverie and looked up at the elderly woman who had greeted them on the doorstep, a look of concern touching her grey eyes. "I'm okay, thank you. Just tired."

She nodded. "I imagine so. I'm guessing you've had a long journey."

"Not particularly," he shrugged, "just eventful." *And that is a true understatement*, he thought to himself.

"Well," she smiled benevolently, warmly rubbing his shoulder, "why don't you come on through and meet Jason. While you're doing that, I'll rustle up some food."

Bobby nodded, swallowed his nerves and accompanied her through to the back of the house, Katy following on his heels.

They emerged into a small room. The windows were tightly shuttered, allowing neither light nor inquisitive eyes to penetrate from the outside. It was illuminated by a collection of candles that were dotted around in the corners and by a roaring fire that burnt furiously in the ancient stone hearth. There were two old chairs positioned facing the fire. Bobby recognised them as wingbacks. He recalled his father Howard, who had been a skilled carpenter, manufacturing such items of furniture, taking great care in shaping the precious pieces of wood into ornate sides that allowed the head to rest at an angle when the sitter had dozed off.

The man that was seated in the wingback on the right was far from asleep. He was sat staring intently into the flickering tendrils of flame that were dancing in the fireplace. The waltzing red glow illuminated his face as he smoked slowly on the long pipe that was clasped between his lips. His hair was long and dark. Along with an accompanying beard, it framed a pair of eyes that were currently not in this room; they were staring off into and through the fire to somewhere far and distant.

Bobby had a feeling that he did not wish to know what those eyes were looking at.

"Jason," the elderly woman whispered as the logs in the fireplace crackled and spat. "It has arrived."

For a moment there was no movement from the quiet, bearded man. Then his head rose just a fraction, as if his mind was processing what it had been told, before he turned, looked at the children and nodded. "That is good." His speech was simple, plainly stated. "Please," he gestured to the other chair, "join me." Then to the woman, "Thank you, Joyce. Could you please let the others know?"

The woman nodded, smiled at Bobby, then left him and Katy with this curious man.

Bobby looked down at Katy. The eight-year-old looked fit to drop. "Go on," he said. "I'm okay."

She climbed up into the chair, curled up and promptly fell asleep.

"The little one must be exhausted," Jason observed, taking another draw from his pipe. "Have you come far?"

"Only from Irlingbury," Bobby explained. "But..." His words just drifted off, not wanting to recall the journey again.

The man's dark eyes held him, exploring what he had just said, then nodded. "I see."

There was an awkward silence as the two remained there a moment, just watching each other over the popping and hissing of the fire. Bobby thought that he was a strange individual, not what he had expected. But then, what *had* he expected? Some sort of brash warrior, clad in shining armour? Or perhaps a well-spoken general, a leader of troops? He wasn't sure, but he knew that it hadn't been this odd man who hardly spoke. He sighed, dug his hand into his pocket and pulled out the Eternal Talisman. "I believe that you need this?"

As Bobby passed the small wooden token over, he saw, for the first time, a change in the man's expression. Excitement filled his eyes and the corners of his mouth turned up underneath his ragged beard. He began to shake his head as if it was hard to believe what he was actually holding and then small tears edged their way out of his eyes. He turned to Bobby, gripped the boy's arm in a firm hand and whispered breathlessly, "Thank you. Thank you so very much."

"That's okay," Bobby shrugged, trying to feign a certain amount of casualness, "Like I said, we didn't exactly have to travel far."

The Virtuous Man settled back into his wingback chair. "But, that is not so. Sometimes, what seems like the smallest of feats can have enormous repercussions. The fate of the world can often hang upon the action of one man, or," he pointed to Bobby with his pipe, "one boy. So never underestimate anything that you do. All is connected." He turned the mouthpiece of the long pipe back around to his lips and took a long draw before blowing fragrant smoke up into the air.

Bobby tried not to cough. His father had not been a smoker. Howard had seen it as a frivolous, pointless and noxious act of self-indulgence. "It weakens the lungs and dulls the senses," he had stated bluntly one day when they had been watching local women gathering herbs for drying. "Imagine all that smoke going down into your body. It isn't good for you. Would you stick your head in a fireplace and gobble up woodsmoke as if it were a broth? Of course not. Mind you, it used to be worse." He had paused, sighed and continued. "People used to smoke something called tobacco. They knew it was dreadfully bad for them; it coated their lungs with tar and killed thousands. Yet, still they did it. Just like people accept their lives as they are now: drudgery, pointlessness and enslavement. It is all they can remember, so it is all they will accept.

"Somebody needs to change it."

A small cough escaped through Bobby's contorted lips and the smoker smiled. "I see you are not a fan. I have to admit, it is the one small vice that I have. I find it helps me think. It clears my mind." He paused, then continued. "Tell me, lad, what is your name?"

"Bobby."

"And the young one?"

"She is my sister, Katy."

"I was told that a girl named Persephone was sup-posed to be bringing me the Talisman. Where is she?"

"She received news that her father was gravely ill. She had to return to see him before he died and we volunteered to bring the Talisman the final length of its journey."

The man took another draw from his pipe and nodded. "I see." He held the Eternal Talisman in his hand, his thumb running over the carved engraving of the cup and the knife. "My family is dead, as I am guessing is yours?"

Bobby nodded.

"Death, Bobby, is a natural part of existence. With life, it forges a duality that balances all the universe. We cannot have one without the other. If everyone lived, life would be misery because there would be no space, no food. If everyone died, then life would again be awful as our species would be extinct within a generation. This is something that Kanor knows and uses well. He keeps humanity just at the brink of death, breathing in the occasional spark of life to rekindle us and sustain us in a weakened state to use us as tools in the field or as hunting practice for his minions of clay. Death, as life, is to be expected. It must be accepted and endured so that we can forge onwards for the greater good.

"Sacrifices must be expected."

Bobby frowned. "Are you saying that Persephone should have ignored the news of her father and carried on with her mission?"

"What is the life of one man compared to the life of the world? Persephone knew of that when she agreed to bring me the Talisman." He sighed. "They should have entrusted it to someone older."

Bobby felt something burn deep down in his gut. Back in Irlingbury, Persephone had saved Katy and him from Teller. She had helped them escape. The older girl had been incredibly torn with regard to her duty and returning to her ailing father. For this man who had never met her to sit here and criticise her… It felt incredibly unfair. Bobby opened his mouth to say something, when he heard Katy stir in her armchair. "Is it dinner time yet?" she yawned.

# Chapter Two

Bobby thought that Katy's eyes were literally going to pop out of their sockets when they sat down to eat. Her mouth hung open and, for once, she was devoid of all comments as she surveyed the feast that had been lain out in the dining room of the small house. He had to admit that his stomach was also enjoying the sight and smell of the home-cooked food. It was expressing its anticipation by roaring louder than a stampede of horses.

"I take it you're hungry, then?" Joyce chuckled as she finished setting the table.

Bobby settled himself down. "Definitely. I can't remember when we last had a meal like this. It must have been when our father was still alive. We've really had to scavenge for scraps since then."

"Bless your souls!" the woman exclaimed. "How long ago has he been dead?"

Bobby shrugged. "I've sort of lost count. Katy was still a babe."

Joyce intently studied the features of his face. "You're from Irlingbury, you say?"

The boy nodded.

"Was your father a carpenter? Howard?"

Bobby started. "You knew him?"

Joyce smiled sadly. "Indeed, I did. You look just like him, you do." She paused, as if there was more that she wanted to say. "I... I was saddened to hear what happened to him, with the Shadow Wraiths. We all were. He was a good man."

Bobby opened his mouth. Did this kind woman know more about his father? Could she shed light on Teller's revelation that he had been some sort of covert conspirator against Kanor? However, at that moment, Jason entered the room, followed by six people, all adults. Bobby studied the newcomers as they came and seated themselves at the large table. They seemed well acquainted with each other, talking quietly amongst themselves, so he supposed that they were residents of Orchester. Their clothing was simple, homemade; the attire of village folk. Four were men; two were women. As they seated themselves, the villagers gave quick, inquisitive glances towards the two strange children. One of the two women sat next to them and greeted them with a friendly smile. The other woman sat on the opposite side of the long table, next to one of the men. She gave his hand a quick, affectionate squeeze as she settled herself down. Bobby guessed that they were a couple. One of the men sported a wild shock of ginger hair. He seated himself down at the far end of the table, where he fiddled constantly with the tips of his fingers as he kept glancing up towards Jason then over to Bobby and Katy. The woman who had seated herself next to Bobby reached across and gently squeezed his forearm, offering him a reassuring smile. The final two, slightly younger than the rest, sat together just between Jason and Katy. Bobby noted the similarity in hair colour and facial structure. He guessed that these two were brothers. In all, the group looked just like any other collection of people that one would encounter in the street: some were related, some not; some took matters in their stride, others worried over the minutiae of details. They certainly did not look like a group of people who were intent on overthrowing the dark power that had enslaved their world.

But then, neither had his dad. Perhaps looks could be deceptive?

Jason took the head of the table. He seated himself down, waited until everyone else had settled themselves and spoke quietly, "Friends. Today is a momentous day. As I am sure you have noticed, we have been joined by two new young friends: Bobby and Katy."

The six villagers gave greetings to the children before Jason continued.

"But, more on that later. First, we dine and discuss matters of the day. Please, bow your heads."

Bobby frowned and glanced at Katy. His sister just shrugged back as perplexed as he was, so they both lowered their heads as asked, keeping one eye on Jason.

"Father," Jason continued. "We thank you for this bounty of food on our table and for the hands that have crafted and cooked it. We thank you for the arrival of our guests and your wonderful gift that they have brought to us. We praise your holy name. Amen."

The six others and Joyce replied, "Amen," and began to help themselves. Katy didn't need to be asked twice and dived in herself, piling her plate high.

The woman who had smiled at them as she had sat down laughed. "It would appear that your sister has an appetite larger than her stature."

Bobby shrugged. "Tell me about it. She's constantly hungry."

"I guess she is growing."

"I guess." Bobby helped himself to what he recognised as chicken and some sort of green vegetable whose identity was a mystery. "I'm Bobby and my sister is Katy."

"Pleased to meet you, Bobby. May our hearth be warm for you. I am Rose. Have you travelled far?"

"Just from Irlingbury," he managed around a mouthful of roast fowl. "Can I ask something?"

Rose nodded.

"Who was Jason talking to just then? Before the meal."

The woman lifted an eyebrow in curiosity. "You've never heard anyone say Grace before?"

Bobby shook his head.

"Jason is a priest. You know what one of those is?"

"Sorry, but I don't."

"Well, a priest is a man or a woman who serves God and ministers to His people here on Earth. The priest guides them and teaches them the words that God's son taught us thousands of years ago, before wicked men put him to death."

Bobby chewed his food thoughtfully. "Why was he killed? God's son, that is."

"Because he spoke the truth that the rulers of his time did not want to hear," came Jason's solemn voice from the head of the table. He sat, his dark eyes framed by his hair and beard. "It was a very, very long time ago. His name was Jesus. He lived in a distant land, far away from here, across the sea, across another continent."

Bobby became aware that everyone, even his sister, had stopped eating and all attention was now focussed on Jason.

"He spent his life tending to the sick and giving people hope that, one day, the tyrannical rule of man would be overthrown and that God would enter people's hearts, illuminating them with His love and bringing peace to the world."

"But why would the rulers want him dead?" Bobby asked. "Surely what he was teaching was a *good* thing?"

Jason gave a small, rueful laugh. "Not to those who control their people in a hand of fear. Those wicked men had their subjects exactly where they wanted them. Whatever they said was law and that kept them in power, making them incredibly wealthy. The common populace was no better than slaves as the power of the rulers spread out over the face of the known Earth. They demanded taxes and tribute to strengthen their armies and expand their greedy empire. Their subjects either gave willingly or were put to the sword as an example. There could be no opposition. Dissent was quickly and brutally quashed. They would take those who spoke against them and nail them to crosses of wood, leaving them to die an excruciating death before their withered bodies were devoured by carrion birds.

"Such was what happened to Jesus."

"So, he failed?"

"So the rulers thought. So they thought. But, three days later, a miraculous thing transpired. He rose from the dead and appeared to those who were closest to him. He instructed them to go out into the world and spread his message of peace and love, to minister to the poor and the protect those who were powerless."

"But he hasn't stopped Kanor, has he?"

A hush fell across the table at Bobby's words.

"For all his words, the Divergence still came and Kanor rose. I don't see anyone rising from the dead to stop him."

Some of the diners muttered amongst themselves, annoyed with what they saw as the impertinence of the boy. Jason lifted a hand and they fell silent again. "What Bobby says is true. The words of our saviour did not prevent the rise of Kanor. We cannot deny that. When the black dragon emerged, the world was unprepared, at peace. It is even said that angels had walked amongst us."

"Was this after the Battle?" one of the two brothers asked.

Jason nodded. "Yes, the great Battle on the plains of Megiddo, when the angels defeated the army of constructs."

"Wondrous day," the woman opposite whispered.

"Wondrous day," her husband echoed.

Bobby frowned. This was all far too complicated for him. They were talking about things of which he had never heard and certainly did not understand. "You're saying that an army beat a whole bunch of constructs? I've seen one up close, when I was younger. Those things are indestructible."

A smile touched Jason's lips. "Not at all. In fact, that is why I have summoned you all here tonight. We're going hunting."

The plan, according to Jason, was simple. Actually, it was so simple, that the creations of Kanor would never expect it. As the diners continued to eat, he spoke about how the constructs did, in truth, have a weakness; their physical make-up. "As we know, they are made from clay. Kanor drew them up from the very ground itself by the use of some arcane magic which breathed life into their inanimate bodies. So it is, that when people have tried to attack the golems in the past, what has happened?"

"Their weapons plunge into the abominations' bodies with no effect," answered the man on the opposite side of the table.

"Even if you cut off their head, the creature will just grow another," said his wife. "It is the same for any of their limbs. They are indestructible."

Jason popped some bread into his mouth and chewed it in a thoughtful manner before picking up the plate upon which it had been sat. "Clay, is a most useful material, is it not? It can be hewn inexpensively from the riverside and moulded or shaped to whatever the potter or craftsperson desires. Look at this plate for example. It is a simple, utilitarian device that is intended for us to eat our food from. It is made from the same substance as those creatures out there that stalk the land and destroy our families, is it not?"

There were tentative nods from around the dining table.

"Yet, it is decidedly different in its physical properties." He knocked a knuckle against the plate's surface, creating a dull thunking noise. "Why is that?"

"It has been fired," Bobby said. "My father took me to a potter once, when I was little. We needed a new water jug. I watched the potter take a tray of identical jugs that he had made from soft clay and place them in an incredibly hot oven. They baked and became hard. I was fascinated."

Jason smiled his appreciation. "Very good, young

one. And did you acquire a jug on your shopping trip that day?"

Bobby nodded, remembering the day well, walking home with his father, being allowed to carry the bright red jug in his small hands. "Yes, we did. My father let me carry it home. It was the most beautiful thing: a vivid scarlet, and its glaze shone brightly in the sun."

"Ah! And I guess your father gave you a very special piece of advice as you carried that jug. A warning, perhaps?"

Bobby chuckled. "Oh, he certainly did. He told me not to drop it."

There was an almighty crash as the plate tumbled from Jason's hand and smashed to pieces on the hard floor.

"Constructs," he growled, "are no different to the pottery that we make on a daily basis. In their current state, they are soft, pliable and able to be repaired. However, if we fire them, we can break them!

"For too long now, we have cowered in our houses, in our hovels, terrified at the creatures that stalk the highways and byways of our land. *Our* land, not *theirs*. We have considered them to be super-human, unstoppable. Yet, they are no different to the very plates off which we eat, to the cups from which we drink. I have received word that, in a few days' time, a party of three constructs is due to pass by this village. We are going to lure them into a trap, bake them solid and grind them into dust. We will show the people of this land that the time has come for us to rise up against our oppressor and throw off the shackles into which he bound us, enslaved us. If we destroy his army, then he will be defenceless and I will be able to walk into his lair unhindered and do what needs to be done."

Jason paused, took a moment to compose himself and continued. "This brings me onto the most joyous news and the reason why we have to strike now. As you know, I am tasked with the mission of slaying the vile Kanor, that black dragon, which is why I have journeyed here from my own home, a home that was ravaged by his soulless monsters. Well, the last few days have proven to be most auspicious. Just yesterday, I was walking in the old cemetery on the outskirts of the village, taking in the air and searching my soul for answers. I wanted to know how I was supposed to defeat a monster like Kanor. As I wandered, I saw a crypt that stood out from the others. It was incredibly plain, but upon its lintel was an emblem that struck me as unusual. It was of a cup and a knife."

Bobby's ears pricked up at the reference to the same image that was upon the Eternal Talisman.

"As you know, there has long been whisperings of two things known only as Eternals: one a Cup, one a Blade. Things older than time itself which Kanor craves for some mysterious reason but, as yet, has been unable to find. So, I was drawn to enter this tomb and inside I found, under a loose slab of stone, a box. Inside, was this." In a swift movement, he drew a long knife out from under his cloak and lay it reverently on the table. It was bright silver in colour and its blade was wavy in shape. There were gasps of amazement from the rest of the diners. Jason just nodded. "I know. I have told you before of the stories I have heard that there is one weapon that can kill Kanor: the Eternal Dagger. It was forged centuries ago by a very wise, holy man who knew that, one day, the man of virtue would rise to take arms against the Black Dragon. It was imbued with the grace of God himself, giving the Virtuous Man, me, the ability to end this Divergent Land in which we live."

The table sat in awed silence until Katy swallowed her current mouthful of food and said, "It's incredibly shiny. It looks like new, not old."

Bobby felt the atmosphere in the room become somewhat awkward as all eyes turned to his outspoken kid sister.

"I had a little spoon once," the girl continued, oblivious to the attention. "Daddy gave it to me. It was made from metal, so he said it was very precious. It was so shiny that I could see my face in it. That was because it was brand new. I can see my face in that shiny knife too. Also, it's a funny-looking shape. You couldn't cut anything with it. Ow!" She turned and glared at Bobby, who had just kicked her under the table.

A deep chuckle came from the head of the table. "From the mouths of babes," Jason smiled. "See how the child recognises the pureness of this dagger, how it is so different to any other mortal weapon. This is why it will destroy Kanor when I plunge it deep into his cancerous heart."

"But how will you be able to reach him?" asked the woman sat next to Bobby. "His lair is surrounded by the lake that he created in the middle of Wellington."

Jason reached out and lay the Eternal Talisman on the table. "Because, thanks to our young guests here, I now have this. The Eternal Talisman will bring me safe passage across the lake. All I have to do is to present it to the ferryman, and he will carry me across.

"As you can see, God has not deserted us. He has provided us with the means to destroy this evil for good. All we need to do now is to stack the odds in our favour by thinning Kanor's vile army."

## Chapter Three

The next few days were a flurry of activity. Jason decided that the best place to confront the constructs would be in the old cemetery where he had found the Eternal Dagger.. "It is out of town, so we will not run the risk of others being wounded or killed by Kanor's creatures. Plus, it is a rabbit warren of old tumbledown buildings, which will serve our purpose well."

The plan, he explained, was simple enough. They were to cause a commotion as the three constructs approached the village and then lure them, unsuspecting, into the cemetery. "They are mindless beasts, so they will undoubtedly follow, their main directive being to kill all those who cause trouble." Once they had the constructs' attention, they were to get the pursuers to chase them through the cemetery and into the old chapel.

Bobby stood and frowned at the derelict building. The roof was long gone, destroyed by wind and rain, and the timber from which the walls were fashioned looked frail and brittle. "It doesn't look capable of holding one construct, let alone three," he said.

Jason smiled. "Ah, well that's all part of the plan.

The beasts will see it the same way that you do and will blithely charge in. Once in, there will be no escape. We will spend today ensuring that every hole in the walls is filled in and packed tight with timber to make sure that it is escape-proof. After that, we will gather dry timber from what wood we can scavenge in the locale. We will pack it into every corner of the chapel as more fuel for the fire, along with the dry wood from its walls."

"But surely it is too large a space to trap them in? Three constructs do not take up much room. They'll be able to move freely and avoid any fire."

The Virtuous Man chuckled. "That is where our final surprise will come into play. After they have charged blindly into the chapel, we will make sure that they have congregated into its narrowest part, the sanctuary." He pointed to the far end of the old building. "You see how it is a fraction of the width of the rest of the building? Well, we will take what is left of these old pews and make a wall to barricade them in. It will be hefty enough to prevent them from escaping. Then, when they are secured in that tight space, we shall rain fire down upon them and they shall bake."

Bobby frowned. "But how can we be sure that they will enter the sanctuary? What is to stop them from just turning around and heading back out?"

Jason pointed out a small hole at the base of the wall behind the ruined high altar. "You see that space up there? Well, someone will have acted as bait and will have lured them in on a fruitless chase. Then, when the constructs are close enough to almost catch their prey, that individual will duck down and bolt out of that hole to safety before the wall of pews is thrown into position."

"But, that hole is tiny. Who do you think would fit

through it?"

Bobby's heart sank as Jason's eyes alighted on his sister, Katy.


"I really don't think this is a good idea."

Katy huffed and rolled her eyes as she carefully filled another clay pot with vegetable oil and placed it in a row with twelve others. "You just think I can't do it because I'm a girl."

"No. That's not it at all. I just think you can't do it because it's suicide." Bobby rolled his thirteenth fuse from a bundle of dried grass and inserted it into Katy's pot of oil. "The whole thing sounds crazy." He carefully cast his eyes around to make sure that they couldn't be overheard. The other villagers were either hard at work nailing old pews together to make a hefty looking barricade or were bulking out the walls of the sanctuary with kindling and straw, materials that would instantly ignite on impact from the fiery pots of oil that they intended to hurl in from above. "I just don't think that the constructs will buy it. Jason says that they are mindless, but that's not my experience." The image of the construct in the village square at Irlingbury drifted into his mind. Its wet laugh still filled him with dread. "I'm worried that they will catch you."

Katy shrugged as she filled another pot ready for Bobby's fuse. "Not a chance of that. Teller couldn't hurt me, so neither will some heavy-footed clay monster."

Bobby watched his kid sister methodically filling her pot with oil. What had happened to her on that bridge? She still showed no remorse in her killing of Teller. Last night he had watched her drift off to sleep. There had been no nightmares, no twitching or sleep talking. She had rested peacefully all night. Surely she should have been disturbed? This just didn't feel natural.

"How's it going?"

The children glanced up. It was Rose, who had sat next to them at the dinner table. Her hair was bound behind her head and her forehead was drenched with sweat. Her clothes were covered in wood shavings and splinters.

"I think our job is easier than yours," Bobby observed.

Rose's mouth turned up in an easy smile. "Ah, but it'll be worth it, won't it? Imagine what people will say when we destroy three of those creatures?" She knelt down next to Bobby and began to help him roll more fuses for the makeshift incendiary devices. "It will be the dawn of a new day."

"You really think so?"

"Of course. Jason has it all planned, doesn't he? He is the Man of Virtue. He will lead us to victory over Kanor."

Bobby's eyes fell on the bearded man as he wandered around the cemetery, watching over those who were going about their work on his master plan. The man nodded in approval at bundles of dry kindling, he smiled as he pulled at firmly constructed scaffolding that rose up behind the sanctuary. Bobby watched as Jason supervised and praised, yet didn't actually do any of the manual work himself.

And that worried him. It worried Bobby a great deal.

# Chapter Four

Eventually, the day came. Bobby and the others had laboured incessantly at their preparations until Jason was satisfied with their work. The decaying walls of the church were now packed with timber and kindling. The makeshift barricade of ancient pews had been assembled and placed next to the sanctuary. Neat rows of incendiary pots were lined up along the near non-existent roof of the old church.

Jason nodded in satisfaction as he surveyed the work for the final time. He tugged at patched up holes, pushed against solid pews and peered into oil-filled pottery. "Excellent," he nodded. "Excellent, indeed. The constructs won't stand a chance."

The villagers smiled, albeit somewhat wearily. They appreciated the thanks for their hard work.

"Do you all know what tasks you have?" he asked them.

They nodded and listed off their allotted roles. One group, the couple and the brothers, was to cause a disturbance to attract the constructs before darting into the shadows of the chapel, behind the makeshift barrier. Katy was to go along with this group and was to split off from the others, leading the constructs down the central aisle and up into the sanctuary. Once the barrier was in place, the second group, consisting of Bobby, Rose and the ginger-haired man, were to throw down the incendiary devices from the roof as Katy crawled through her small bolthole in the wall.

"A simple but effective plan," Jason smiled. "I am sure that, with God on your side, you will not fail."

Bobby frowned. "*We* will not fail? Will you not be fighting alongside us."

Jason gave a mocking laugh. "Bobby, someone has to let you know when the constructs are coming. That will be me. You see that ridge over there?" He pointed to a rise to the north of the cemetery. "I will lay in wait, watching the road for when they approach. When they do, I shall catch the light of the sun with the Eternal Dagger. It will glint three times to say that the enemy approaches. It is by far the most dangerous task of all. I will be on my own and at risk of being spotted by these creatures. I will need to time my signal precisely so that you know of their imminent arrival and so that they are not forewarned."

Bobby's frown refused to be parted from his forehead. It made sense, sort of, but there was something deep down that he did not like about this plan. Something he could not put his finger on.

He had a terrible feeling inside that it was all going to go wrong.

A while later and the sun was rising into the morning sky. Bobby had heaved himself up onto the roof of the church, taking his position on a makeshift scaffold that the villagers had constructed over the previous days. He grimaced as it creaked ominously under his weight.

"You doubting my handiwork?"

He looked up to see Rose grinning at him as she lifted a sackcloth off the pots that contained the highly flammable oil. It had been lain across them the night before to prevent dew settling on the wicks, rendering them damp and useless.

Bobby couldn't help but smile back. Over the last few days, he and Katy had spent more time with the amicable woman than any of the others. The rest of the villagers had been welcoming, but not over-friendly. It was as if they had too much on their mind, were too preoccupied with the task at hand to get to know the newcomers as well as they should. Rose had been different. She had chatted away to them quite happily, asking them about their life in Irlingbury, enquiring about their father, marvelling at their adventures on the way to deliver the Talisman. "I'm just not used to being this far off the ground," he said.

"You'll get used to it." Rose checked a fuse over and nodded in satisfaction. "Plus, it's not like we're going to be up here long."

"I suppose."

The woman eased herself into a seated position and her eyes studied the boy's face. "You seem somewhat unsure. What's the matter?"

"It's just... I don't know. I have my doubts about the plan."

"Really? It seems quite simple. We lure them in then bake them. Job done." She watched his eyes flick towards the small hole in the back of the sanctuary wall. "You're worried about Katy?"

"What if something goes wrong? What if the constructs catch her?"

"They won't. Bobby, look at me."

He lifted his eyes and gazed into her smiling face.

"Everything will be fine. You're not on your own now. Should anything... *untoward* happen, I've got your back. Okay?"

Bobby looked into those trusting, hopeful eyes for a moment, then nodded. "Okay," he finally agreed. "Okay."

The other villager on the scaffold patted Rose on the shoulder. "There's the signal: three flashes. It's time."

It all happened so quickly. One moment, they were stood atop the scaffold, waiting for the signal, the next...

The first thing of which Bobby was aware was a noise. It seemed to be coming from far off, but he knew that that wasn't really the case. He knew it had to be the other villagers catching the attention of the constructs. He listened carefully and could start to make out shouts and cries, before a raucous cheer drifted up to them from the road and was followed by the sound of running feet. Human feet.

The feet of the constructs made a very different sound altogether as they took up the chase.

*Thud, thud. Thud, thud.*

Precise and in time. Marching together in a slow, methodical beat. They pursued the humans, safe in the knowledge they were at no risk from the frail mortals. They would hunt them down, kill them, carry on with their journey. Unemotional. Unstoppable.

*Thud, thud. Thud, thud.*

"I can see them!"

Bobby followed Rose's gaze and spotted the party

of villagers running as fast as they could, off the road and through the cemetery. He looked frantically for Katy, terrified that she would not be there, but swallowed his nerves as he saw her dart out in front of the pack towards the church.

And there, just entering the boundary of the old graveyard, came the three constructs.

Impassive. Relentless.

*Thud, thud. Thud, thud.*

The villagers down below reached the chapel and darted inside. Bobby carefully peered over the parapet as he watched the adults hide themselves behind the improvised barrier that had been made to appear as if it were just a pile of old wooden furniture. Katy, however, took centre stage in the middle of the ruined building. There was no look of fear about her person as she pulled back her shoulders and began to shout out all manner of things in order to keep the attention of the constructs, who had now reached the threshold of the building.

Bobby chewed on his bottom lip as he moved around to his station, readying himself to throw down the incendiary devices. As he eased himself around the scaffold, his eye line shifted and, for a moment, he caught sight of the road coming towards the cemetery. For the tiniest moment of time, he thought he caught sight of a figure on a horse riding towards them, but then he was pulled back to the here and now as the constructs bore down on his sister.

Katy played her role perfectly. She teased and taunted the clay creatures, all the time backing up towards the killing room of the sanctuary. She eased herself up against the back wall and continued to hurl abuse at them.

"She's good," Rose smiled at Bobby.

"She's practised lots on me," he replied.

The constructs followed, just as Jason had insisted they would. They took the steps up into the sanctuary.

*Thud, thud.*

They were no more than five arm lengths from the small girl.

Bobby felt as if his heart had stopped beating and his lungs were no longer drawing breath.

Then there was an almighty crash as the walls of the chapel shook when the barricade was forced into place. Bobby and the two villagers actually had to steady themselves against the decrepit wall of the church as their scaffolding swayed slightly. The constructs realised that something was amiss and turned to confront the wooden wall that had not been there just a moment before. One reached out and its arm transformed into a lance, piercing the wooden structure which shook precariously from the impact.

"Now!" the ginger-haired man shouted as he started to hurl his ignited pots down onto the constructs.

Rose did likewise, but Bobby halted as the pots struck, causing flames to rise up the walls of the sanctuary.

Katy was still down there! She was tugging frantically at a piece of timber that had slipped down the insides of the wall. The force of the barricade must have caused it to come loose. She was trapped in a burning room with three constructs!

"Katy!" Bobby yelled across the rising inferno, but she couldn't hear him. She just continually tugged in vain at the wedged timber.

The eyeless head of one of the constructs swung

around and up towards the source of the shout then across to Bobby's sister, its thick tongue slithering across its lips as if scenting the air like a predatory serpent. There was the unmistakable sound of transformation and the boy screamed frantically as one of its clay arms snaked out and whipped itself around the small girl, dragging her across the rough floor.

"Katy!" Bobby screamed again. This could not be happening. It just couldn't! That monster had her! It was going to kill her. He watched in vain as Katy kicked and screamed against her assailant while the other two constructs continued to lance the barricade across the front of the sanctuary.

Then Bobby was aware of movement to his left as Rose vaulted over the side of the wall and clambered down the loose woodwork. At the last moment she leapt from the wall and launched herself into the construct that was holding Katy. Her impact caused it to lose its footing. It stumbled backwards, disoriented, and its grip on Katy slackened, allowing the girl to run towards the hole in the wall once more.

"Katy, go!" Rose screamed as the small girl tugged at the piece of now burning timber, prying the weakened wood from its hole and scampering out.

They were to be the woman's final words.

Bobby gaped in horror as he saw the prone construct reach out and plunge a lance into her back. Rose gazed down in confusion at the point sticking out through her chest before she fell limp, dead. The mindless golem paid her no more attention and rose, turned towards the barricade and joined its companions in battering at the wood.

The wood that was now aflame from the burning

oil.

It was then that Bobby realised the major flaw in the plan that had been niggling away at him.

There was an almighty crash as the barricade gave way, its improvised structure weakened from the fire. It was like the logs over a fire pit when they have reached a critical point of burning; there is no more strength left in their crumbling structure and they just collapse.

The constructs strode through unimpeded, framed in a curtain of fire.

The four villagers let out a terrified shout and turned to flee, but they found their way blocked by a stranger dressed in black, his hair unnaturally smooth against his scalp. Bobby thought back to the lone horseman from before and his stomach lurched. It was a Shadow Wraith; the villagers were doomed.

The three constructs did not attack the panicked villagers, instead they worked their way around them, their arms outstretched, corralling them into one single spot, then the Wraith struck. He was so much more fleet of foot than the other creatures. A wicked smile spread across his face as he leapt from the floor, spun in the air and reached out with an arm that transformed into a sharp scythe-like blade. Bobby was aware of a wet cutting sound then watched in blood-chilling horror as the villagers' heads parted company from their necks and tumbled to the floor. Their bodies stood headless for a moment, as if in shock and unable to comprehend that they were now dead, lifeless, before they too fell to the floor of the chapel.

The Shadow Wraith withdrew its scythe back into a hand, flexed its fingers, then looked up at the wall where Bobby and the last remaining villager stood. It smiled once more and turned to walk out of the church, the three constructs following.

"We need to get out of here," the man whined, partly to Bobby, but mostly to himself as he ran his shaking fingers through his ginger curls. He snapped round and began to frantically clamber down the rickety scaffold. Bobby dragged his eyes away from the carnage in the burning church and followed suit. The improvised footholds and ladders swayed terribly under the weight of the two fleeing humans, but they made it down in one piece. Bobby turned to ask the man where they should go, but the villager was already running away, around the side of the church, back towards the village, towards the safety of his home. All Bobby could do was watch dumbfounded as he was left abandoned to fend for himself. Then, as the man passed out of sight, Bobby heard a dreadful scream and a sickening ripping sound. The fleeing man came back around the side of the church, impaled and writhing on the end of the Shadow Wraith's arm. His hands slapped helplessly at the clay lance and his legs kicked spasmodically as blood flowed out of his mouth, until he fell limp and lifeless off the simple but effective weapon.

The Shadow Wraith peered without emotion down at the dead human before flaring his nostrils, catching the scent of its next intended victim.

It looked across the churchyard, straight at Bobby.

Bobby froze. This was it. He was going to die. He had no hope. There was nothing he could do. He should just stand there and accept his fate. He would let his legs go weak and motionless. He would give himself to this superior creature.

The Wraith nodded and smiled as if it knew what

the teenager was thinking, but then it frowned as a scream echoed across the churchyard.

It took Bobby a second to snap out of his reverie, to realise that the screaming human voice was aimed at him, but then the words seeped into his confusion, pulled away at the fabric of the clouds that were smothering his will to live and a familiar voice reached his ears.

"Bobby! Bobby! This way!"

At once, he was snapped back into his true senses and he saw Katy standing in the shadow of a grove of trees waving frantically, beckoning for him to follow her.

As the three constructs appeared round the corner of the burning church to join their superior, the boy, needing no further encouragement, rammed his legs into gear and shot after his kid sister.

# Chapter Five

*Don't trip! Don't trip!*

These were the only words screaming through Bobby's head as he and Katy crashed and ripped their way through the undergrowth of the all-surrounding, claustrophobic woodland. To trip was to fall; to fall was to die. They had size and agility on their side. They could leap over fallen tree trunks and dive through narrow gaps which were too small for their pursuers. However, they were only human and eventually their muscles would tire and they would have to stop to rest and recuperate.

Constructs, being monsters fashioned from clay, did not have this problem.

They may have been slower, but they were relentless, unstoppable.

Bobby did not dare to glance over his shoulder for even a split second. To do so would be to take his concentration away from the task at hand — staying alive — yet he knew in grim detail what was behind him. It was the slow, methodical beat of heavy clay footsteps grinding down all that stood before them, confident that, in the end, they would catch and dispatch their quarry.

The outcome was inevitable.

Already, Bobby could feel his lungs starting to burn and his calves beginning to tremble as exhaustion began to take hold of his mortal frame. The constructs would know nothing of this. They were the ultimate killing machine.

And then there was Katy.

She was just eight, still in single figures. What must she be feeling right now? Without looking, Bobby knew that she was right beside him. He could hear the snapping of twigs and the harsh, erratic gasping of her breath as she, like him, dodged and wove her away around the densely packed trees. Surely she couldn't sustain this frantic pace for much longer? She would stagger, trip, fall...

*No! Don't think it! Don't give in!* There had to be a way to escape. There had to!

"When you think that all is lost," their father had used to say when life was even harder than normal, "something will always present itself. You just need to keep your eyes and ears open, your senses alert, and be ready to follow the new path that life presents."

Hot tears of exertion streamed down Bobby's face as he recalled his late father's calm, philosophical voice. A path! What he would give for a path right now! In the last few days, his life had presented him with just problem after problem. They had ranged from a hoard of rats to a sociopathic bully; from a fanatical leader of an underground rebellion to questions about his father. Not to mention the worries about his kid sister that continually gnawed away inside of him.

But it had most certainly not provided so much as a simple path through a forest!

The branches and twigs whipped at his face, scratching him, causing his skin to sting. Reflexively, he lifted a hand to protect his eyes, obscuring his line of sight for just a split second...

And then the unthinkable happened. Bobby's hand fell away and he watched helplessly as the world around him slipped up over the horizontal. The ground came crashing up towards him as he instinctively stretched his hands out in front to soften the blow of the ground hurtling towards his face. His feet parted company with the treacherous woodland floor and he was aware that they were now higher than his head as he tumbled forward and landed in a heap on the ground.

Ground which was incredibly wet, sticky and stank abysmally.

*Something will always present itself.*

His eyes snatched around him, taking in his situation in an instant and he quickly called out to his sister, "Katy! Here! Quick!"

The small girl ran over and joined him then tried to protest as he rapidly began to cover her with the putrid filth from the stagnant pond. "It might just save us," he explained. "Quick! Cover yourself!"

And all the time, he was waiting for the twofold beat of the relentless footsteps of their inhuman pursuers.

In less than a minute, the two children were covered from head to toe in black, foul-smelling filth. Bobby caught his sister's hand and dragged her down to a secluded point of the pond that was overshadowed by a fallen and decaying tree. Quietly, they edged their way down, out of sight.

Just in time.

*Thud thud.*

*Thud thud.*

*Thud...*

The heavy footsteps ground to a halt just on the other side of the tree trunk. The two children held each other tight as they shivered in the cold stagnant water. They clenched their teeth tight to prevent even the slightest noise of chattering. The slightest noise and they were dead.

"Well?" came a harsh, commanding voice. "Nothing?"

Bobby and Katy held their breath as the Shadow Wraith climbed up on top of the fallen tree to survey the surroundings. They were aware of the creaking of the damp wood above them as the creature turned around, trying to locate them with its eyes that they knew were blacker than night. Bobby kept his arm tight around his sibling and they remained motionless, petrified.

Never before had they been so scared.

Eventually, the Wraith leapt off and landed heavily on the ground behind them. "We've lost them," it said and the distinct sound of the constructs marching off through the woodland resumed.

Bobby and Katy waited.

They waited some more.

They continued to wait.

When they could bear it no more, they crawled out from under the tree and emerged into the forest. They eased themselves upright to see the light of day above them and were confronted by the grinning face of the Shadow Wraith who was sat nonchalantly against a tree by the side of the pool.

"Patience truly is a marvellous thing," he grinned as he rose gracefully to his feet, his limbs languid and supple, clearly not made from flesh and blood or bound by the mortal constraints of hard, rigid bones. The children didn't have a chance to run as his arms snaked out beyond any humanly possible length and grabbed them tight around their necks.

The siblings thrashed and slapped helplessly at the long, clasping fingers that held their throats tight. They gasped and gaped as they tried to breathe but could only flounder like perch on the end of a long line, dragged out of the water. The Shadow Wraith reeled them in. "Humans are just so predictable," it mused, its dark eyes glistening in the half-light of the woodland, the water from the pool reflecting in the inky, soulless blackness. "You really think you could evade me by hiding in this filth? If your scent suddenly disappears then, where else would you be? I just had to wait here until you emerged from your pathetic little hidey-hole."

It swung its arms around and threw them onto the forest floor. Bobby felt shards of broken wood and treacherous twigs dig into his skin through his ripped clothes as he fell down heavily, winded. He pulled himself onto all fours and crawled over to his sister. "Katy," he barely managed through his bruised throat. "Katy?"

She nodded back. She was shaken but relatively unharmed.

"So touching," the Wraith sighed. "But now, to business. Tell me who organised the attack on the chapel."

"It was nothing to do with us!" Bobby protested. "We were just passing and got caught up in it."

The Wraith raised a disbelieving eyebrow in a mockery of human emotion. "Really? You just got caught up in the affair and happened to end up on top of a scaffold? Or was that another boy who looked just like you?"

He slapped his forehead in mock anguish. "Don't tell me I've been chasing the wrong pair of meddling brats!" His face turned into a vicious scowl and he whipped his left hand out. It shot towards Katy who was still prone on the floor. His hand parted at the end and forked around her neck. The small girl screamed out in shock but even then she wouldn't give up, hitting and smacking the arm with all the strength she had in her small, fatigued body.

The Wraith smiled. "A feisty little thing, isn't she? Tell me, boy, how much energy do you think she'll have when she has no air?" He grinned as his forked hand contracted around Katy's neck. Her eyes started to bulge and her fingers desperately scrabbled at the deformed hand.

Bobby made to lunge towards her but found himself staring at the business end of a construct lance.

"Don't be stupid. Tell me who was in charge of the attack!" roared the Wraith. "If you don't, she dies.

"Followed by you."

Bobby looked on in paralysed horror as Katy's face seemed to start to turn an awful shade of blue and her movements became weaker and weaker. He couldn't let her die. He couldn't. She was all he had.

There was only one thing he could do to save her.

Bobby opened his mouth to speak.

An anguished scream filled the clearing.

The Wraith was staring at the suddenly truncated end of his arm. Bobby darted to his sister and wrapped her in his arms, holding her preciously close. He looked in awe at the severed hand of the Wraith that now lay on the forest floor, withering to dust, and the sharp metal disk that lay next to it. His head snapped up at the sound of a loud shout and his brain struggled to comprehend just what it saw occur next.

Someone had burst into the clearing. They were swinging a long, heavy stick that connected with the head of the distracted Shadow Wraith, sending it tumbling to the floor. The attacker swung the stick, clubbing it again and again onto the Wraith's head which crumpled under the repeated blows.

But this did not stop the creature. It rolled to one side and, as it rose fluidly to its feet, its mangled features expanded outwards, creating a freshly grown face from which it snarled at its attacker, a man dressed in filthy rags.

A man whom Bobby and Katy recognised.

Cutter.

The monster opened its mouth and Bobby watched in horror as its jaw dropped far lower than was possible for any creature. An incredibly long prehensile tongue snaked out of the wet, drooling maw and whipped towards Cutter's staff. It circled around the stick and the Wraith yanked back with its powerful neck, forcing the old man to surrender a few paces. Cutter, however, continued to move with the momentum of the attack and dived onto the ground, rolling across the forest floor. This caused the tongue of the beast to lurch sideways, yanking its head round at a completely unnatural angle as Cutter lunged to his feet behind the monster whose head was now facing completely backwards. With a skilful flick of his wrist, the old man snatched his stick out of the grip of the momentarily confused creature as it turned its body around to face the same direction as its head. He then proceeded to advance on the Wraith, dodging from side to side, repeatedly striking its head from first one side, then the other.

The monster raised its damaged arm to protect itself and finally crumpled under the continuous, unrelenting blows.

Within moments, the grizzled old-timer was standing over the vanquished foe, his staff raised and aimed in deadly fashion at the creature's forehead.

"Leave the children be," the children's saviour growled at the fallen Wraith. "They are nothing to you."

The Wraith winced as it flexed its left arm, miraculously sprouting a new hand from the severed clay. Its face glowered ominously like a wild dog that had been soundly kicked with a heavy boot. It was desperate to retaliate but knew that it was beaten. It opened its mouth to speak but Cutter threatened once more with the stick. "No more words; not from you. Just leave."

So the Shadow Wraith did as it was told. It rose elegantly to its feet as if it had risen from a summertime picnic in the woods, casually brushed the leaves and twigs from its clothes then turned and simply walked away into the dense undergrowth.

Cutter turned to the two children. "What on earth have you two gotten yourselves into this time?"

# Chapter Six

Smoke rose from a campfire that Cutter had built in a small secluded clearing. They had moved, on his insistence, to another part of the forest. Also on his insistence, Katy and Bobby had taken a bath and had washed their foul-smelling clothes in a clean pool. They were now sat swathed in blankets as their clothes, hung between two trees, were drying next to the warm fire. Suspended above the same fire, a pot bubbled and spat. The delicious aroma emanating from a rabbit stew almost masked the less than pleasant odour of the steam that rose from their clothing.

Cutter poked inquisitively at the contents of the pot, gave a satisfied grunt, and removed it from its hook. He divided the stew between two wooden plates he had produced from his pack and handed it to the children.

"Eat," his gruff voice commanded them. "I don't want you wasting away before your clothes have dried." He then eased himself down onto the forest floor, sat against an old tree and proceeded to fill and light up his long pipe. The fragrant smell of his homemade smoking material drifted up into the air of the clearing and combined with that of the stew.

Katy and Bobby exchanged concerned glances before tucking into the delicious meal. The old man had hardly said two words since he had rescued them from the Shadow Wraith. He had just told them to follow him, which they had gratefully done, then had instructed them to clean themselves up as he wandered off into the undergrowth before returning in a short while with a rabbit that looked like it had been caught with a spear.

Not once had he enquired as to how they had come to be captive of the clay monster.

"It is important that your bellies are full before you explain how you have been so stupid," Cutter said as if reading their minds, speaking around his pipe. "A content body is more likely to be truthful. It has no need to lie." He blew a smoke ring up into the air.

"Are you not going to eat?" Katy asked as she paused her ravenous consumption. "There is plenty here. I don't mind sharing."

The old man looked across at the small girl and Bobby saw a distinct amount of affection touch his face. "It's okay, little one. I am not hungry. You eat it all up. It'll help you grow... as long as you don't do anything stupid like, say, annoy a Shadow Wraith."

Katy and Bobby smiled. They finished their meals in contented silence.

After the meal, their clothes had dried sufficiently in order to be worn, so they dressed themselves and Bobby washed up the pot and plates in the small pond where they had bathed. As he did, Katy sat herself down next to Cutter and stared intently at his pipe.

The old man raised an eyebrow at her in question.

"I like the smell of your pipe."

"So do I. That's why I smoke it."

"What is it you burn in there?"

"A mixture of herbs and tree bark." He looked down at the girl. "Want to try it?"

"Am I allowed?"

Cutter shrugged. "Who's stopping you?"

"No one."

"Then why do you ask if you are allowed?"

She paused. "Because there are certain things we shouldn't do."

The old man held her eyes for a moment then nodded. "It would be wise to remember that, young one."

Bobby walked over and joined them under the tree. "Our father wasn't a fan of smoking," he said.

"That's not what she was talking about." Cutter turned to Katy. "You had no choice, child. Teller..." He shook his head. "He was sick, like a mad dog. He needed putting down or he would have killed you both.

"He was like his father. Some things run in the family. Madness is one of them."

He held the two children with a steady gaze.

"Honour is another."

Bobby let the words sink in. "You knew our father."

Cutter nodded, his face suddenly sad, tired.

"How?" Bobby asked. "I don't remember meeting you before the other day," he said, referring to their encounter on the road from Irlingbury to Orchester as they had journeyed to take the Eternal Talisman to Jason.

The old man took a thoughtful draw on his long pipe. Bobby could tell that he was carefully choosing the correct words. He had seen his father do the same whenever an awkward customer had made a complaint about something that they thought was wrong with an item that Howard had fashioned for them. Once, there had been a woman who had kept goats. She had ordered a chair upon which she could sit whilst milking her animals. His father had fashioned her a plain, three-legged stool but the woman had complained that it was boring and not to her liking. She had said that she wanted something fancier, something more pleasing to the eye. Howard had asked her what she had in mind. She said that, for starters, she wanted four legs, not three. She also wanted a back to the stool. Not just a plain back, either. It had to be intricately carved with birds and ivy. Howard had held the woman carefully in his gaze before finally asking, "Your goats, do they clean up after themselves?" The woman had looked perplexed but had shaken her head. "The stool you are asking for will not last a month. Three legs are better than four because they help to spread the weight of the person milking the animal. This is important because the ground upon which it will sit will be soft from the waste and the trampling of the animal. You do not want the seat to sink into the ground as you are milking. Also, it needs to be backless or it will be unbalanced. Animals can be flighty, yes? They can decide to kick or wriggle, causing the person milking them to need to readjust themselves at a moment's notice. If you have an ornate back to the chair, it will topple over when you suddenly shift your weight. The carving in the wood will either become encrusted with filth or will break, making the furniture impractical and unsightly.

"Sometimes the simpler tool is the most effective."

"I was younger," Cutter explained. "I was a different person back then."

Bobby opened his mouth to ask more, but the old man held up a gnarled hand. "Later. Right now, I'd rather know about how you ended up in the state in which I found you."

So the children explained. They told him everything, about the Eternal Talisman, the Virtuous Man, the plan to destroy the constructs. And, as they spoke, Cutter just sat and smoked on his pipe, his eyes carefully studying the wispy patterns of the aromatic vapours that drifted up into the woodland air.

When they had finished, he studied the bowl of his pipe, tapped out the burnt ash and packed in new ingredients from a leather pouch that he magicked from the depths of his ragged clothes. Taking a steel, he struck a spark into the bowl and the mixture sprung to life. After a few long drags he was satisfied with the result and turned to look at the children.

"What an absolute load of nonsense."

Bobby and Katy exchanged confused looks.

"I assure you it's the truth," Bobby began to protest.

Cutter held up a hand. "Of that I have no doubt, Bobby. You, like your father, are as honest a person as I have ever met. What I mean is..." He shook his head. "A piece of wood and a knife to destroy Kanor? Corralling constructs into an old church and setting fire to them?" He shook his head once more and tutted disconsolately. "Absolute nonsense! I have garnered more sense from a mud-covered swine!" He made to smoke more from his pipe and paused. "This man, Jason. He claims to be the Man of Virtue?"

Bobby and Katy nodded.

"Yet he left all of you to face down those creatures on your own? Where was he when the fighting began?" He made a disgruntled noise of disgust. "No. He is either a fraud or a fool. When the Virtuous Man comes, he will lead his army from the midst of the battle, not cower at the back like a startled dormouse."

"But what of the Eternal Talisman and the Eternal Dagger?"

"What of them?"

"They are supposed to help him overcome Kanor? How can he not be the Man of Virtue if they have found their way to him?"

Cutter sighed. "If you give a hound a knife, does that make it a swordsman? If you give a rabbit feathers, can it fly? It is nonsense. I don't know what these things are or how they made their way to him, but they are not the things that scare the Black Dragon."

"Does anything scare him?" Katy asked.

Cutter nodded. "Child, everyone is scared of something."

# Chapter Seven

After their meal, Cutter suggested that they lie down and get some rest. "You have had a very busy day," he said. "Now is not the time for questions or discussion. Now is the time for recuperation."

"But I'm not sleepy," Katy protested as she stretched her arms and gave a huge yawn.

"I think your body says otherwise," Cutter smiled. "You two curl up here, close your eyes and rest. I will watch over you." The old man turned, rummaged in his pack and produced a small, hand-fashioned recorder. He placed it to his lips and began to play a light, lilting tune.

So it was that, to the relaxing tune of Cutter's lullaby, the children curled up on the soft ground next to the warm fire. Within minutes, they were asleep.

And, as Bobby slept, he dreamed.

His dreams were far from peaceful.

A cruel wind whipped around him as he stood on a high hill overlooking a deep valley. Down below, two armies were fighting. One he recognised immediately. Constructs, hundreds of them marched relentlessly forwards, their arms shaped as lances and scythes. Riding with them were Shadow Wraiths, their cruel faces hungry for battle. Facing off against them were an army of creatures the likes of which he had never before encountered. They were humanoid in shape, two arms, two legs and a head, but they possessed wings. Clad entirely in white, their eyes blazed with fire as they charged towards the creatures of clay. And there, in their midst, was a figure dressed entirely in black. Bobby frowned as he tried to make out the person's face, but it was shrouded by a hood and a material that looked like a thick black gauze swathed its visage.

This unknown warrior was amazing! It darted between the winged beings and shot into the army of constructs. It possessed a long whip which it cracked left and right, plunging its sharp silver tip through one construct then another, causing them to pause or stumble. Then he would vault and somersault and flicking his weapon out, wrapped it around their heads and pulled tight, making them part into two. The constructs, not yet dead, would stumble and try to pull themselves upright, but then the winged creatures were upon them.

The result was devastating.

From their hands, a green mist emanated. Every construct that the ethereal vapour touched withered and died. It was instant death to the creatures of Kanor.

Yet still the mindless beasts came, onward and onward. But the result was inevitable and at the end of the battle every member of Kanor's army was destroyed. A cheer rose up from the winged beings as they saluted their masked champion.

Bobby wanted to join in. He opened his mouth to praise the warrior, but a dread chill ran down his spine and he was aware that he was no longer alone on the hilltop. His stomach churning, he turned to see a man standing in a dark cowl. He was glowering out across the battlefield, his dark eyes, full of hatred, focussing on the hero of the hour.

He moved his lips and Bobby heard his low voice hiss a single word:

"Claw..."

Bobby woke with a start, his heart pounding against his rib cage. It was dark, early evening and the fire had started to burn low. Katy was still asleep and Cutter was nowhere to be seen.

*But that doesn't mean he isn't nearby*: Bobby told himself. He knew that the strange old man would be watching. He seemed to be some sort of enigmatic guardian spirit who appeared when necessary.

But who exactly was he?

The more he told them, the more questions it raised about him.

Bobby shook his head. Perhaps one day they would be answered. Right now, it was getting dark and they needed to find shelter. He gently rocked his sister's shoulder. "Katy. Wake up. We need to get going."

Having nowhere else to go, they decided to head back to Orchester. They could stay there the night and then, the following day, head back to Irlingbury, to normality.

"It'll be nice to go home," Bobby said as they approached the edge of the small village. "We can put all this behind us and go back to our lives."

Katy was curiously silent.

"What's up?" he asked.

She just shrugged.

Bobby sighed. More questions. Well, they could just wait. Right now they needed somewhere safe to shelter. "I think we're best finding an empty house on the outskirts. I don't really want to cross paths with Jason right now," he said.

"And why might that be?" came a familiar voice from behind them.

Bobby and Katy turned to the sound of the voice and gasped at the sight of Jason standing behind them with a group of villagers. The children didn't take the time to consider whether this was a good thing or not. Without a word, the two siblings did what they seemed to do best.

They ran.

*Is this to be our lot in life now?* Bobby wondered to himself as he and Katy sped down first one cluttered alley then another, leaping over discarded piles of refuse and dodging around broken and discarded household items. It certainly seemed to be that way as the angry shouts of pursuing villagers followed them through the unfamiliar passageways.

Had this been Irlingbury, he and Katy would have used familiar routes to escape those who wanted back their fruit that the street kids had stolen. They knew their home town like the backs of their hands, every nook and cranny: every dead end to avoid and every abandoned house in which to lay low.

Orchester, however, was a completely different story.

Time and time again they skidded around a blind corner to be presented with yet another cul-de-sac or a means of escape that was blocked, causing them to double back and seek another route. Consequently, with every wrong turn, any lead on their pursuers that their youth and swift feet had provided was gradually whittled away, until it felt like the baying mob were literally breathing down their necks.

But they knew that they had to keep running. Jason's voice had sounded far from friendly. He did not seem at all delighted to see them returned safe and sound from their doomed mission. In fact, he sounded just as dangerous as the Shadow Wraith that they had previously encountered.

"Bobby, it's another dead end!" Katy wailed as they found themselves once more facing a sheer wall at the end of a blind alley. "Do these people have no idea how to plan a village?"

The sound of running and shouting was now closer than ever. Bobby whipped his head from side to side and caught sight of a small door in a darkened corner of the back street. "Katy! Here!" He ran over to the door, his sister right behind him, wrapped his hands around the handle and pushed.

Nothing. No movement.

He pushed again, leaning forwards with all his weight.

Still nothing.

Anger and frustration consumed the boy as he physically threw himself at the door. They had to escape, they had to. Again he launched himself at the small door and still it remained resolutely shut. Tears of frustration welled up in his eyes as saw all the hardship they had suffered over the last few days personified in this rectangle of faded wood and he screamed at the top of his voice as he charged forwards, colliding with the locked door. But his onslaught did not stop there. He pounded against it with his fists, screaming inarticulately with previously suppressed rage into the cold night air.

He only stopped when the firm hand of a villager fell on his shoulder.

Bobby sank to his knees, defeated.

Bobby and Katy had barely any energy left and could only put up the vaguest of struggles as they were dragged into the village square.

Jason was stood there with more angry-looking villagers. Set up behind them were two stout poles which had wood piled up around their bases.

This did not look good.

"Citizens of Orchester," Jason called out those who stood around them. "You know me. You know what I stand for, how I bring society hope. We need to rise up and overthrow that vile dragon who has destroyed our world. You know that I will lead you in this.

"Yet there are those," he pointed at Bobby and Katy, "who would see us fail."

The villagers shouted and hurled abuse at the two children. Jason motioned towards the two poles and they were dragged over and tied roughly to the wood.

"You have all heard of your kindred's valiant attempt to destroy a contingent of constructs. They came so close to success. They had ensnared them and had set fire to them. But they were betrayed by these two incomers."

"That's a lie!" Bobby shouted. "Your plan was flawed. It failed. We almost died."

"You dare to accuse me of falsehood?" Jason screamed back at him. "You know who I am. I am the Man of Virtue. I have the Eternal Talisman and the Eternal Dagger. I am tasked with destroying Kanor himself. How dare you try to pin blame on me?" He paused and composed himself, running a hand through his glossy black hair. "No, these *supposed* children sabotaged my efforts and allowed the constructs to slaughter your friends and family. I say we test them. Show them for what they really are.

"Servants of Kanor."

It was as a villager stepped forwards with a burning torch that Bobby realised what the wood around their feet was for. "No! No! You can't be serious! We're human!"

"You are heartless beasts of clay. You are soulless denizens of Kanor and you must be destroyed." He nodded to the villager and the woman began to lower the torch.

There was a cracking noise and Bobby watched a whip lash itself around the woman's wrist, yanking it backwards, causing the torch to fall harmlessly to the floor. The rest happened faster than he could possibly perceive.

A figure strode into the midst of the villagers who were yelling, shouting and taking up arms. He was clad from head to toe in black and as they charged him, he leapt gracefully up into the night air. As he descended, his feet kicked out causing those close to him to fall backwards and his silver-tipped whip swung around in a wide circle, making others stagger backwards.

Bobby had just caught sight of Jason darting out of the village square when he heard a woman's voice behind him. "Hold still," it said as his bonds fell free. "Now hold your breath."

He felt a strong pair of arms encircle his middle and

suddenly the world flashed past him in a total blur. He gasped for air and blinked his eyes as he found himself being settled down at the edge of what looked like a field, but he was so startled, it could have been the moon for all he knew. The woman let go of him and pulled back, a lopsided grin on her face. By the light of the rising moon, Bobby saw a pair of sparkling green eyes and a shock of short red hair. He saw movement to his left and a blur transformed into a blonde-haired woman coming to a stop with Katy in her arms.

There was another flicker of movement as a third shadow transformed into the man with the whip. He pulled back his hood, revealing a concerned face. "Are they okay?" he asked the redhead.

"Absolutely fine."

The man nodded. "Hello Bobby," he said. "My name is Claw."

# Bobby Normal
## and the
# Children of Cain

# Previously...

Bobby, a teenage boy from the village of Irlingbury, and Katy, his outspoken eight-year-old sister, were entrusted with the Eternal Talisman by a girl named Persephone. On their travels to the neighbouring village of Orchester, they were hounded by Teller, a bully from their home village whose father was a servant of Kanor, the being that had brought about the Divergence which had decimated humanity, reducing it to a pitiful remnant that lived in constant fear of death. Things came to a head when Katy pushed Teller from a bridge, leading to his gruesome death — a death for which the young girl showed no apparent remorse.

Upon arriving in Orchester, the siblings successfully delivered the Eternal Talisman to Jason, the individual that Persephone had believed to be the Man of Virtue, the only person that could overthrow Kanor. Jason persuaded them to join his followers on a mission to destroy a group of constructs, the clay-based lifeforms that were the murderous servants of Kanor. The assault ended in tragedy with Katy and Bobby being the only ones to escape with their lives after the old man known as Cutter saved them from a cunning Shadow Wraith.

After Bobby had a dream about a shadowy warrior named Claw fighting an army of constructs, the children returned to Orchester where they found themselves accused of treachery. Jason claimed that they were in fact constructs and instructed that they should be burned at the stake. They were snatched from the jaws of death by three mysterious strangers, one of whom was Claw, the brave warrior from Bobby's dream.

We rejoin them as they travel away from Orchester and back towards their home village of Irlingbury…

# Chapter One

Right about now, Bobby was feeling decidedly un-sure of things.

It could have been any number of the weird and de-cidedly dangerous life-altering events of the past week that were causing him his current consternation, but it wasn't.

It was something far more immediate, far more ter-rifying.

With every pounding hoofbeat from the large brown horse beneath him, Bobby was convinced that he would soon be departing this mortal world in a terribly agonising manner, thrown from a great height and trampled over by the demonic beast upon which he was currently travelling.

"You're sure this is safe?" he asked the blonde wo-man around whose waist he had his arms tightly locked in a life-preserving grip.

She glanced over her shoulder, her long hair flick-ing to one side, and just smiled.

That was not reassuring to the green-faced teen-ager.

Bobby held on even tighter as the horse beneath

him steadily pounded its feet along the rutted and worn track along which he and his kid sister Katy had walked in the opposite direction just a week previous. Bobby, being the impoverished orphan of a widowed woodworker, had never before ridden on a horse. To Bobby, the large equine beasts symbolised just one thing: privilege. And with privilege came subservience to Kanor and his hierarchy of fear. The only humans he had ever seen riding horses had been Teller and his father or their cronies and associates. Aside from that, the only other individuals he had ever seen travelling in this fashion had been the merciless Shadow Wraiths. As a result, horses, for Bobby, were things to be feared, not trusted.

This lack of trust was reinforced with every precarious jolt that the beast took, threatening to tumble him to a bone-shattering impact on the road below, as they continued on their nighttime journey.

"Hey, kid!"

Gripping the blonde woman's waist and keeping the side of his face resolutely fixed against the long cloak that she wore, Bobby ventured to turn his head to the right. He peered over to the image in front of him that bounced up and down in an overwhelmingly nauseating manner. It was the other of the two women, the one with short red hair. She was grinning at him as Katy sat behind her bouncing up and down on the horse with utter glee.

"What?" Bobby squeaked.

"I told you earlier, Scorpion don't say much. No point asking her questions."

"Oh. Okay."

"But," the redhead continued, her green eyes twinkling in the moonlight, "in answer to your inquiry: mostly."

*Mostly?* What was *that* supposed to mean? Bobby gripped Scorpion even tighter and felt her body judder as she laughed silently to herself.

"Come on, Bobby," the redhead continued, obviously taking great glee in the boy's discomfort. "Lighten up. Your kid sister's certainly enjoying herself. Ain't that right, Katy?"

Katy nodded emphatically, "Yes!" she squealed. "Can we go faster?"

The redhead laughed. "Course we can!" She snapped her reins and yelled something unintelligible at her mount, causing the horse to whinny in excitement and bolt forwards. The eight-year-old girl on its back shrieked with utter glee as her long, knotted hair flew out behind her.

Bobby just squeezed his eyes tight shut and buried his face into Scorpion's fair hair as he prayed for the torture to end.

"Don't you mind Tigress. She's just trying to lighten you up."

Carefully, Bobby cracked open one tentative eye and looked over at the third and final horse rider of the party, the man who called himself Claw. "She's not succeeding," Bobby grumbled.

The sandy-haired man considered Bobby's words before replying. "I think they did things differently when she was your age."

The teenage boy frowned. "I can't believe things have changed *that* much since she was a child. She's only in her twenties."

Claw gave an amused snort.

"What?"

Again, the man seemed to carefully consider his

words before answering. "Looks can be deceptive."

Bobby definitely couldn't argue with that. In the last few days, he had encountered an old man who could turn into a wolf, a Shadow Wraith that could transform its arms into deadly weapons and now these three curious strangers who could run faster than he could perceive. "Tell me about it."

"How old do you think I am?"

Bobby eyed his companion up and down. "Somewhere between thirty and forty years or so?"

Claw's eyes twinkled amusement in the moonlight. "Bobby, I was born over two thousand years ago. Scorpion, with whom you are riding is over four thousand years old and Tigress… Well, we're not entirely sure because she was born before calendars were really a thing, but a good guess would be about five thousand plus."

All of a sudden, Bobby's primal fear of horseback riding dissipated into the night sky like steam from a pot that has come to the boil over a campfire. He sat up straight and looked Claw in the face, trying to discern whether or not the man was teasing him in an attempt to take his mind off the torturous journey. His father, Howard, had always said that it was a wise thing to look into people's eyes when they told you something that you did not expect to hear; it would give you an insight into the validity of their words and the truth of their intentions. As he stared into the brown eyes of the man who claimed to be older than Bobby could even comprehend, he saw no hint of mirth or deception.

"How?" he finally asked.

Claw opened his mouth to reply, but his attention was diverted to the sound of Tigress and Katy galloping back along the road towards them. Bobby followed his gaze and could not fail to see that a darkness had erased all traces of mirth from the woman's face.

"What is it?" Claw asked her.

"Trouble."

Until Bobby and Katy had been rescued from an irate Teller by Persephone, the girl who had entrusted them with the Eternal Talisman, neither of them had set foot outside of their home village of Irlingbury. Sure, they had known that there was a world outside of their microcosm, but it had not really interested them that much.

Irlingbury had been their home.

Katy, Bobby felt, had always had a simpler relationship with the place than he did. She had never known their mother plus their father had died when she was very young, so the majority of her life which she could remember had been spent with just Bobby. To his sister, Irlingbury was a place she existed with her brother. They lived by their wits, scavenging or stealing food when they could and running whenever was necessary.

For Bobby, his views on the place of his birth were more complex and fell into three distinct phases.

He remembered a period when things had been much simpler, when he had been truly happy and content in Irlingbury. This was the time when his mother had still been alive. His earliest memories were of helping her tend the neat vegetable patch that she had cultivated behind their small, homely cottage. He would toddle around the garden, picking weeds out from between the vegetables as his mother instructed him, then they would pull the fully grown produce that they would eat that evening. She would hold his hand in hers, soft skin with fingertips that had been roughened from constant gardening and housework, and she would lead him to the hearth where she would sing softly as she chopped the vegetables and cooked them in a pot over the fire, ready for when his father came back from market.

This stopped suddenly when Katy had been born.

His mother had died in childbirth. Bobby had listened as the midwife had explained to his father that the baby had been problematic, facing the wrong way. There had been a lot of blood lost, and the last thing that his mother had seen had been the child which she had just brought into the world.

She had held Katy in her arms, closed her eyes and fallen asleep as if tired from the exertion, never to waken.

This brought the second phase in Bobby's relationship with Irlingbury, one of hard work but a feeling of accomplishment. The first few months after his mother's death had been terribly hard. His father had needed to adjust to a new routine of life. He had become a familiar figure around town, carrying not only his handmade goods but also a newborn baby that had been constantly nestled in a sling on his chest. And, always by his side, was the young, serious-faced lad who was his constant companion and aide. However, even with Bobby there to carry what Howard could not fit on his back and to assist with small jobs and customers when Katy demanded his father's attention, it was obvious to all in the village that the widower was not coping with the sudden, dramatic change in his domestic arrangements. The young Bobby noticed that in the year following his mother's death, his father seemed to age considerably more than twelve months, his face becoming drawn and his skin slack.

Neighbours suggested to Howard that he take another wife, a young girl who would do as she was told and would look after the *young 'uns* while he went about his work. But the woodworker resolutely refused. He said that he had only intended to wed the once and he would not dishonour Ruth's grave by wedding again. So he would work his finger to the bone in his workshop whilst caring for and feeding his two children.

Things came to a head when Howard was taken ill. Bobby woke one morning to the sound of an infant Katy shouting for her father. He ventured downstairs and found his dad asleep in a chair in front of a dead fire, his skin chilled and clammy. Howard had fallen asleep there the previous night, too weak to make it to bed. Bobby guided him upstairs and helped him to settle under his sheets, watching fretfully as the man drifted off to a feverish sleep. The boy then took his sister by the hand and led her out into the vegetable patch that he had used to tend with their mother. It was wilder now; his father was not much of a gardener. Weeds grew around the garden, but there were still some persistent root vegetables there that could be dug up, cooked and eaten. So, Bobby set to, settling Katy down in a small patch of earth, letting her play with the worms and bugs, trying not to think about how many went in her mouth. A few hours later, he had prepared a hearty stew which he and Katy took up to their father.

"Did you make this?" Howard asked as he devoured the meal.

Bobby nodded. "Is it good?"

His father presented him the empty bowl, a weary smile on his fatigued face. "I think we need to have a rethink about how we do things around here."

And so it was that, for the next few years, whilst

Howard turned wood and created goods to sell, Bobby was the one that tended the garden, kept the house clean and watched over his infant sister as she continued to grow in both height and appetite. It became a time of contentment as the three of them settled into this new type of life. He found it immensely rewarding, making their little house a welcoming home once more.

Then the Shadow Wraiths rode into the village and his life in Irlingbury entered the third phase.

Howard was labelled a traitor and summarily executed. Teller's father had not hesitated to inflict even more cruel punishment on the newly orphaned children. When Bobby and Katy managed to get back to their cottage, they found their home aflame. All of their father's materials had been stacked up against the small house and had been set alight. The garden, which the two of them had meticulously tended, had been trampled over, the vegetables ripped out of the ground and pulverised under foot and hoof.

Bobby had just stood and watched the flames rise, smoke curling its way up into the air.

Just as he did this evening on the road that led into Irlingbury.

Bobby, Katy and their three companions stood at the edge of town and watched the flames rise into the night sky as the entire village burned.

## Chapter Two

Bobby did not sleep well that night. Claw had said that nothing could be achieved from him and Katy stumbling around a ruined village as sleep tried to drag them to their bed. "You would just hurt yourselves," he had explained. "There is nothing you can do for your village, so you must tend to yourselves." He had located a copse of trees on the outskirts of town and had sat down with them as they had settled down to sleep. The last thing Bobby saw as his eyes drifted shut was Scorpion and Tigress heading off towards the smoke and flame.

It was the smoke and flame that dominated his dreams that night. He found himself staggering around the back alleys of Irlingbury, coughing and spluttering as the acrid fumes from burning cottages filled his tortured lungs. In the distance, through the gloom, he could make out Katy running just ahead of him, almost out of sight. He made after his kid sister, but every time he found himself closing in on her, she darted around a corner, giggling and laughing, oblivious to the burning ruins that surrounded her. Bobby lurched forwards, his arms outstretched, in part as an attempt to grab his younger sibling, in part to stop himself from stumbling in the chaos of the devastated village. All around him, people were screaming as they ran from the flames, bundles of belongings grasped desperately in their arms.

Then, above in the night sky, Bobby heard something which chilled him to the core, even in the searing heat of the inferno.

A primordial screeching filled the midnight sky as the sound of long black wings clapped in the air. Bobby stopped running, turned to look up and saw the obsidian silhouette of a gigantic dragon soar in front of the pale, white moon. It circled above, turned its head towards the village and let loose a fireball from its screaming mouth. The villagers fell helplessly to their knees in terror and were immolated by the roaring breath from the monstrous creature. Bobby watched, sickened, as their skin blistered and peeled from their bones, before their skeletons were reduced to ash in the overwhelming heat.

Bobby made to run but found that he could not move. Thick arms of clay were bound around him, holding him fast to a stout pole set amid a pile of kindling and firewood. The arms of the constructs tightened as he tried to wriggle free and he could not escape as the fire crept up the base of the pyre and began to lick hungrily at his clothing.

As the flames started to catch at his skin, he saw Katy again across the other side of the village square. She was not alone. His sister was holding the hand of a tall, elegant, dark-haired woman. Bobby cried out from amongst the flames, begging the woman to save him, but the stranger smiled wickedly, turned and, taking Katy with her, walked away in the light of the full moon.

Bobby twisted and writhed against the immovable

arms of the construct that held him fast.

He watched in horror as the creature's arms baked solid.

Then the flames cracked, leapt up and engulfed him.

Bobby awoke with a start.

The sound of the cracking carried across the small clearing once more and he frantically patted at his clothes, his face, terrified that he was burning. Instead of fire and scorched burns, he just found cold, chilled skin. He shivered as he pulled his fraught mind together and seated himself up under his blanket.

"I'm sorry. Did I wake you?"

Bobby frowned as his sleep encumbered brain tried to drag itself up to speed with its surroundings. It was later in the day than he had expected, the sun having passed its zenith. Katy snored resolutely next to him. Across the other side of the copse, Claw was stood, heavily cloaked, a long whip in his gloved hand. A reasonable distance away from him, set upon a fallen tree were propped small pieces of wood.

"I was practising," the man explained. As if to demonstrate, he let fly across the clearing the silver tip of the whip and one of the targets shot off into the surrounding trees.

Bobby eased himself up from the floor. "Impressive," he noted.

Claw quietly nodded his thanks. In the depths of his cowl, his brow furrowed. "You were dreaming. Nightmares?"

The teenager forced the images of his disturbed sleep out of his mind and gave an approximation of a nonchalant shrug. "My waking time seems to be one long nightmare at the moment. Why should my sleep be any different?"

The cloaked man stood silently regarding him. His brown eyes peering intently out of the gloom of his hood. He nodded. "I know what you mean. There was someone I knew many years ago. His life..." He shook his head. "It was turned upside down. The day-to-day became a collection of the bizarre, the crazy. He suffered so much at night with dreams. He saw things that no one should see."

"What happened to him?"

The man slid his tongue over his lips as his brown eyes held Bobby.

"Would you like to have a go?"

Bobby frowned. "Pardon?"

Claw curled the whip up into his gloved hand. "It's quite simple," he explained, gesturing for Bobby to come and stand by his side. "It's all about acquiring the most speed at the tip."

Bobby frowned. "I don't know. The last time I got up close with one of those wasn't very pleasant."

The man nodded. "I find it is important to not let your past dominate your future." Once more he gestured to a spot by his side.

Bobby looked again at the weapon. His hand rose to a small scratch just below his eye before he stretched, ran his fingers through his unkempt hair and walked over to the cloaked Claw.

"Come and stand here," the man gestured to a spot on his left, "and watch what I do."

Bobby stood where he was told and observed carefully as the long whip was unravelled from its coil. Claw's hands expertly flicked it outwards in small movements until the long stretch of leather lay in a straight line behind him. He reached his arm out past his shoulder and flexed his gloved grip on the solid handle of the weapon.

"It's all about timing and momentum," he explained. He snapped his hand forward and Bobby let out a cry of excitement as the silver talon at the end of the leather cord smashed a piece of wood off the fallen tree. Claw began to wind the whip back. "Okay?"

Bobby just grinned in excitement.

Claw smiled and handed him the weapon, moving carefully to the boy's left-hand side. "So," he explained, "gently flick it out to extend the material. Feel the weight as you do so; balance it in your hand. Familiarise yourself with a weapon. You should never use a weapon that you don't understand. It will harm you more than those at whom you are aiming."

Bobby nodded as he studied the long weapon. He carefully ran his fingertips over the corded leather, feeling the tightness of its structure until he reached the silver barb at the end — a simple metal hook tied into the end of the whip. He winced as he prodded its curved tip. "It's really sharp. Did you make this yourself?"

Claw gave a so-so gesture with his hand. "I made the whip, but the barb I acquired on the day the constructs rose. It's what gave me my name."

Bobby's attention switched from the weapon to the man who was hidden under the deep hood. "You were there? When Kanor destroyed humanity?"

Claw nodded.

The boy swallowed. "What... what was it like?"

Even in the dark shadows of the hood the emotions on the man's face were clear to see. He was no longer looking at a teenage boy in a clearing in a wood. His brow was knotted, his lips compressed and his sight was focussed elsewhere.

"It was brutal," he eventually managed. "I was a different person before Kanor came. We all were." His shoulders rose and fell and his lips moved as if he were emitting a melancholy sigh, but Bobby noted that, even stood close to him, there was no sound of expulsion of air, nor the feel of the man's breath on his skin. "That was a long time ago," Claw continued, the corner of his eyes relaxing. "Let's concentrate on this whip, shall we?"

Bobby nodded silently and began to gently move his hand in a rhythmic flicking motion. He watched in fascination as the cord of leather seemed to take on a life of its own, the silver talon snaking like a stealthy predator through the grass. "It's really heavy," he said, noting the weight of the handle in his grip.

"That keeps it grounded," Claw explained. "And you, too. It makes you aware that you are holding something that can actually kill individuals, should you desire it." His brown, hooded eyes watched as the whip reached its full length. "Good. Now just give it a couple of gentle shakes. Feel how it moves."

Bobby did as he was instructed and watched the whip ripple through the patchy grass. Its long structure undulated, causing the silver tip to flick left and right. "It looks alive."

"Back when I was younger, before the Divergence, I knew this cat. He was black and malicious. His tail would flick like that before he pounced on you and drew blood."

Bobby's attention was drawn from the whip to the face of his tutor. "A cat? What's that?"

The shoulders of the hooded man rose and fell. "Sorry. I forget how much of the old world has disappeared, died out. It was a small creature that lived with humans. They were originally predators that humans domesticated to hunt down rats and the like, but being smart, they wheedled their way in front of the fireplace. This cat was one of the shrewdest creatures that I ever knew."

"I could have done with him a few days ago," Bobby said. "I had a rather horrid encounter with some rats in a sewer."

"Not pleasant," said Claw.

"Not pleasant," Bobby concurred.

"So, back to the whip. Stretch your arm backwards and be aware of the connection from the shoulder to your wrist. The strong shoulder muscles will give the whip power as you thrust it forwards, the wrist will give it precision and guidance. Go for it."

Bobby flexed his hand on the grip and rotated his shoulder to unkink the muscles that had knotted up from his restless sleep on the hard floor. He felt his heart begin to beat faster with excitement and his breathing increased in rapidity. He jerked the whip forward and watched its shining barb smack into the ground in front of the tree trunk. He grimaced.

"Hey, don't be hard on yourself," Claw smiled as Bobby disconsolately wound the weapon back into his hand. "It was your first go and a good effort. You just need to bear in mind two things. First, is the trajectory of the tip. It needs to flick around and be fully extended. That gives it the fullest momentum and speed. Rather like putting a starship into a slingshot manoeuvre around the sun." He paused as Bobby frowned in confusion. "Don't worry," Claw apologised, shaking his head. "It's an old reference. Just make sure that the tip comes all the way around.

When you threw it that time, it sort of snaked past your head. You were lucky you didn't take your ear off," he winked. "The other thing you need to be aware of is what your body is doing when you crack the whip. Time it so that you sling the whip between breaths. That keeps it steady. I forgot to mention that. It's not something I have to think about." Again, Bobby frowned and Claw motioned to the whip: "Go on. Try again."

Bobby let out a deep breath and concentrated on his breathing as he slid the whip out in small, gentle gestures. He felt the cool afternoon air seep down into his lungs and the warm recycled air expel through his mouth. Three times he repeated this until the whip was at full length then, pausing the breathing cycle, he flicked the whip round in a full, horizontal arc. A sharp crack filled the glen and a piece of wood flew off into the thicket behind.

The teenage boy whooped with exultation as he punched the air with the handle of the whip. "Yes!" he cried. "I did it!"

"Looks like you've been working up an appetite," came an amused voice from over his shoulder.

Bobby turned to see Tigress and Scorpion, both cloaked like Claw, enter the clearing, carrying packages in their arms. "Good job we found some food for you."

A tired yawn emanated from the small bundle that was a waking eight-year-old girl. "Did someone mention food?" Katy asked.

Bobby and Katy tucked into the simple meal with ravenous gratitude. They hadn't eaten since the stew that the old man Cutter had cooked for them after he had rescued them from the Shadow Wraith. There wasn't much in the way of variety in the ingredients. They were mainly scraps of meat, some fruit and a few vegetables that the women had managed to scavenge from the ruins of the village. "There wasn't much left unburnt, I'm afraid," Tigress had apologised. However, the two siblings were used to surviving on other people's throwaways, so the randomly concocted meal that afternoon was more than sufficient.

It was, however, as Katy was going back for her third attack at the small pile of apples, that Bobby lay a hand on hers and whispered, "You should leave some for the others. They haven't touched anything yet."

The small girl frowned but nodded in acceptance and drew back from the food.

"It's okay," Claw said from where he was sitting with his back to a tree, idly running the length of his whip through his gloved fingers. "You two fill yourselves up."

"But surely you need to eat something?" Bobby asked as Katy just pounced on two more pieces of fruit.

Claw's hood moved from side to side. "We're fine. Go on. Eat."

Bobby felt his stomach rumble and did as he was instructed, rejoining his sister in the consumption of the food. As he did, he let his eyes study the three strangers. There was something about them, something unusual. He didn't know exactly what, but something about them disturbed him. Claw sat quietly and methodically inspecting the cords of his whip, checking the weapon over for wear and tear. Tigress, the redhead, sat propped against another tree, deep in her own cloak. The blonde, Scorpion was laying with her own hooded head on the other woman's lap. Tigress' gloved hand slowly and affectionately stroked the thick material. Her lips moved rhythmically and, as he listened, Bobby could make out musical words drifting across the clearing, but they were none that he recognised.

What was it about them that troubled him? He thought back to things that Claw had said about their ages. Could they all be as old as he had claimed? Back in Irlingbury, the oldest person he had known was Old Agatha. She had been an elderly widow who had outlived not just her husband but also her three children. With no family to speak of, she had lived in a small cottage on her own, resolutely independent and accepting no charity from anyone. She was a regular sight around town, haggling the best deal from the market traders and chasing "young ruffians" with a heavy walking stick that was as gnarled and as grooved as the wrinkles on her deeply tanned face. Katy had once said that her skin resembled the texture of an apple that had been left in the sun too long, shrivelling up into itself as all its moisture left its flesh.

These three individuals were no Old Agathas! They appeared young and strong. Not to mention they were so fast. When they had rescued them from Jason's clutches, the speed at which they had travelled had been incalculable.

But, Bobby told himself, they have not harmed us. They rescued us and have cared for us.

So why did something inside of his gut feel like it had eaten a rancid piece of cheese?

"What are you singing?" Katy's question cut across his worried musings as she got up and sat next to Tigress and Scorpion. "It's very pretty but I don't know the words."

The redhead paused her tune and smiled from the depths of her cowl. "It's a lullaby for my loved one."

"You mean Scorpion?"

Tigress nodded, her fingers idly plucking a stray blonde hair from her partner's hood. "The words of the song are very old indeed. That's why you didn't understand them."

"Where did you learn it then?"

"My mother taught it to me when I was very little."

Katy sighed. "I never knew my mother. She died when I was born."

Tigress' green eyes fixed upon the small girl from the shadows of her hood. "I'm sorry to hear that. Mine died when I was young. The sun had passed full circle around the stones just seven times, I was told. It changes you, not having your mother around. It makes you more independent, but something is always missing. There's a gap in your heart that needs filling, isn't there? I was on my own for many years after she went to join my ancestors. I got into trouble." A mischievous grin spread across her red lips. "A lot of trouble. The clan despaired of me. But I found my way eventually. I met someone who was to change my life. He taught me so much about the world. You've," she inclined her head across the clearing to Bobby, "got your brother, haven't you?"

Katy nodded as she leant in closer and whispered, "But he's always telling me off."

Tigress roared with laughter. "Sweetie, from what I've seen in my long life, that's the main purpose of older siblings. There was this one time in Rome when Scorp and I were tracking down this construct that had gone to ground in the Senate. We came across this senator whose brother was spending far too much time with this cheap whore..."

A deep cough resonated from Claw's side of the clearing. "Anyway, I think perhaps enough of the stories for now. We need to get going."

"Another time," the mischievous redhead mouthed to the eight-year-old, and then, out loud, "So, what's the plan, boss?"

Claw stood up, brushed himself down and reeled in his whip. "You know the drill. We inspect the ruins, find out which way the constructs went, track them down and kill them."

# Chapter Three

The first thing that hit Bobby as the five of them stood at the edge of the charred ruins of his home village was the smell. When he was younger, his father had taught him that wood was a precious commodity, never to be wasted. The young Bobby would sit in his father's workshop, watching intently as the serious-faced Howard worked with sharp tools on the construction of a chair, a table or something else that he was crafting with the utmost care, and he would listen intently as the carpenter explained, "We are so used to wood being all around us. The trees beyond the village grow with no tending. They are not like the crops in our garden that need our constant attention and care. They are wild creatures that follow their own rules and will grow back time and time again as long as we only take what we need. This is abhorrent to Kanor and his soldiers. They control humans by making sure that we suffer and that we are..." pausing, he glanced at the boy with concern, "reduced in number. No matter how much they try, they cannot temper the forces of nature. They cannot fix a harness around its mouth and ride it like a tame stallion. Every so often, they will come by and torch the forests, reducing them to ash. I remember this from when I was younger than you, the Shadow Wraiths arrived with an army of those faceless beasts. They cut down the trees, stacking up kindling in the woods. Then, using pitch and flame, they burned it to the ground. Yet, within twelve months, fresh shoots were creeping up from the scorched earth. Within a year, there was wild bracken. Within two, there was a base of undergrowth. By my tenth year, young trees were once again reaching for the sky. By the time I was fifteen, we had a new, full forest ready for coppicing and trimming for wood that we could utilise once again.

"No matter what it thinks, evil will never beat back the forces of nature. However, we need to be ready for the times that it will try." He had shown Bobby how to salvage every last scrap of waste wood from his work: how to sweep the floor until every single mote of stray sawdust had been gathered; how to efficiently store every off-cut and every sliver of unused timber. "These are what we should burn for fuel," he explained, "not the prime wood that we must use to fashion those items that we need. And, as we burn it to heat our homes and to cook our food, we hope and pray that we will have enough stored and hidden for the day that those monsters return to try and impose their will upon the nature that surrounds us. For if we do not, we will be forced to eat food that is cold and tasteless and freeze to death come the long winter nights."

The smell that reached Bobby's nostrils this early evening, just after the sun had dipped down below the horizon, was akin to the aroma of the scavenged firewood that he and his father had set light to in their hearth that day, long ago. It told of wood that had blazed at incredible temperatures.

However, whereas the homely fire that he and his father had created had been intended to preserve life, the fire that had blazed in Irlingbury for the past day or so had been ignited for quite the opposite intention.

Bobby wrinkled his nose. "The smell of the burnt wood is wrong. Why is that?"

The three adults exchanged glances.

"It wasn't just wood that burned here," Claw explained in a low voice. He reached up and rubbed at the back of his neck, his hood now hanging down, as were those of the other two, between his shoulder blades. "Listen, perhaps you and Katy ought to wait here with the horses."

Bobby looked at the three horses that had been tethered to the remains of a scorched tree. The three beasts were innocently chewing at a patch of grass.

"If it's okay with you, I think I'd rather not."

"But, there will be things there you might not want to see."

Bobby thought about Katy shoving Teller to his death from atop a stone bridge. "There are already things in my life that I wish I hadn't laid eyes upon."

Claw looked unconvinced.

"We're wasting valuable nighttime," Tigress urged. "Besides, we can't leave them here on their own. What if there are patrols or scouts?"

The man nodded in solemn acceptance. "Very well." Then, to the children, "Just, be careful."

The five of them headed into the remains of the village.

Not one building that they passed remained untouched by the devastation. As they progressed down the main road towards the centre of Irlingbury, scorched ruins flanked them on either side like a grim honour guard at a funeral procession. Acrid smoke rose from the smouldering ruins. Ash drifted lazily in the air, settling on the ground so that the floor now resembled a pale grey carpet. Bobby found himself constantly rubbing at his eyes to relieve the tears that were welling up in irritation at the intrusive dust.

"Reminds me of Pompeii," Tigress muttered, half to herself, half to Scorpion as they constantly scanned the ruins and side streets for signs of life or danger.

The blonde replied with a taciturn shrug.

"I know, I know. That actually had a purpose, whereas this..." The redhead made a noise of disgust. "Damn animated lumps of clay."

Claw just walked in silence — his brown eyes peering intently through the gathering gloom, his feet placing themselves one after the other, his tread hardly raising any ash from the dusty road.

Eventually, they reached the market square. The last time that Bobby and Katy had been here, it had been bustling, full of the villagers of Irlingbury going about their business, buying food to feed their families.

This evening, it was once more full of the villagers of the small settlement, but not one of them would be buying or selling ever again. Bobby stood numb as he tried to take in the sight that greeted him. He had witnessed death before, violent death, over the last few days, but not on this sort of scale. All around the edge of the square, bodies hung from tattered remnants of burnt-out buildings. Some bore ragged holes in what remained of their chests, testament to the death inflicted upon them by the constructs. Others were missing body parts — legs, arms, heads. All were scorched and burnt, some completely down to the bone, most to a mass of runny, gooey pulp that was sloughing from their exposed skeletons.

He tried to turn away from the sight, but whichever way he looked, the macabre horror confronted him, nauseated him. He opened his mouth to say something but, as he did, he realised that Katy was missing. His head flicked left and right as his eyes scanned the local vicinity. She was nowhere to be seen. Nowhere at all.

The three adults were standing to the side of the square discussing something. They hadn't noticed that she was gone.

Bobby did what he considered to be the right thing. He turned and ran, retracing their steps through the burntout village. As his feet plumed up clouds of ash, he concentrated on two things. The first was listening for the telltale *thud thud* of any approaching constructs. The last thing he needed right now was to bump into one of the monstrous killing machines. The second was studying the path in front of him. Through the grey ash on the floor, Bobby could make out scuffed footprints left by his feet. The three adults had left barely a mark. After a short while, he came across a smaller set of prints that had veered off down a side alley.

Bobby frowned. Where on earth was she going? He twisted and turned through the charred remnants of back alleys and side streets until, after a few minutes, he had a feeling of recognition, of familiarity, as he chased through the scorched remains and realised where Katy was headed.

Home.

He found his sister sitting on a large stump of a tree

that their father had felled before they had both been born. It was on the edge of their property and had always been a place where they had enjoyed playing together. Little Katy had always giggled as she had clambered up onto the remains of the old tree and had squealed with delight as she had flung herself off into the waiting arms of her big brother. The big brother who found her now sat there, looking over the barren land where they had spent their earliest years. Her eyes were fixed on the overgrown plot of the house that had been destroyed years before the constructs had torched the rest of their village.

Her eyes snapped up towards Bobby as he gently called her name.

"Why are you here?" he asked, his eyes cautiously flicking from side to side. "It's dangerous."

"Everywhere's dangerous," she shrugged. "Why should here be any different?"

Bobby opened his mouth to answer her but found that there was nothing that he could say in reply. She had a point. He joined her on the stump and looked across the ruined patch of land. Where once crops had grown, there was wild, barbarous bracken. Where once had stood a house, there was just rough scrub, all usable materials from the demolished building having been scavenged and taken away.

"There's nothing left," the small girl finally said. "Nothing at all. Everything we ever had is gone. We are all that remains in our life now. First mum, then dad and our home, now our village. They've taken everything that was dear to us and destroyed it all, bit by bit.

"When will it all stop? *How* can it all stop?"

Bobby studied his sister's face, expecting to see sadness, tears rolling down her cheeks. What he saw, however, was much worse. There was a hardness to her young features, a cold resolve that he had witnessed once before. It was how she had looked the day that she had killed Teller.

This was not the face of a young child.

"Katy," he began, carefully searching for the right words, "we know that the world in which we live is cruel, vicious. We have seen what constructs can do and those that pay lip service to the Black Dragon. They make people suffer. They ruin lives. Yes, they have done so to us, too. But there is one thing that they have not done, that they *cannot* do."

Her small face looked up at him. "What's that?"

"They can't take you away from me. I will always be here for you and you will be here for me."

A touch of a smile curled her lips upwards and she nodded.

Bobby climbed down off the stump. "We'd better get back to the others."

As they walked away from their old life, Katy asked, "What do you think they are?"

"The others?"

She nodded. "I've never seen anyone or anything like them. They are so fast and strong. Do you think they are as old as they claim to be?"

Bobby shrugged. "I don't know. I don't see how they could be, but then I don't see why they should lie about it. They have been good to us and haven't tried to harm us, have they."

"I like them. They feel so… *confident*. It's as if they know how things truly are."

"I know what you mean. It's like when Dad used to tell us stories. We would sit there, listening to every word, wondering how it would end. Would the hero succeed? What dangers would he meet on the way? Yet, Dad obviously already knew. He had been told the same story by *his* father and he knew where it was headed, what the conclusion would be. Claw, Scorpion and Tigress are like that. They've already been told the story, but rather than telling it to someone else, they are living it out in their own lives."

"I think that's great!" Katy grinned. "Imagine how it must be, knowing how something was already going to end. I'd like that. I'd like that *a lot*."

As the two of them traipsed through the mud and the ash, Bobby pondered this. What would it be like to know the path that your life was going to take? Sure, it could be useful. You could plan ahead for certain things, be forewarned. However, surely the ending would always be the same, no matter what twists or turns the story took? Imagine living with that constantly digging away in the back of your head.

He decided that he would not like it. Not one little bit.

It was as they turned a corner onto the main road back into the village that they heard it. At first, it did not fully register. It was just another background noise, a monotonous beat that may have been just something or nothing. But then, as it drew closer, it became dreadfully apparent that this was not something from the day-to-day, something from the mundane.

Besides, in a village where all the inhabitants were dead, how could anything alive be moving?

*Thud, thud. Thud, thud.*

Making their way down the ash-strewn road, Katy

and Bobby felt the vibration of the construct's leaden feet before they saw the clay monster itself. The heavy pulse travelled up through the mud and the ash, along the muscles of their legs and into their stomachs, where it gripped their innards tight and squeezed.

They turned as one and watched the clay giant lumber slowly around a corner. Its slick skin glistened eerily in the rising light of the pale moon, casting a dull shadow on the path behind it.

It did not pause.

It did not falter.

It did not stop to observe its prey.

It just continued walking. Straight towards them.

"Run!" Bobby screamed, and the two of them turned tail and fled. "This way!" Bobby jerked his sister down a small alley, almost yanking her small arm out of her shoulder socket. "Follow me." He leapt across the collapsed timbers of what used to be a doorway into a small house. Katy scrambled across in his wake. The teenage boy hoped that the fallen debris would provide some sort of barricade or obstacle that might slow down the construct. They scurried across to the far side of the abandoned building and clambered up the ruined walls, gaining as much height as they could in an attempt to escape the soulless predator that pursued them.

As they pulled themselves out of the ruin and over into the next building, there was a deafening crash from behind them. Bobby glanced back and felt all blood drain from his face. The construct had stretched out one of its malleable arms, wrapped them around the fallen debris in the collapsed doorway and had just yanked it out of the way as a child would throw a twig into a stream. Its thick, black tongue flicked out from the ragged gash across its otherwise featureless face as it scented the air. It calculated its new heading, turned and continued in its pursuit.

Bobby grabbed Katy's hand and pulled her down into the next building. They jumped and landed with a clatter. Knowing that to pause and check themselves over would be certain death, they ignored any scrapes and bumps that they may have sustained and fled to the other side of the burnt ruins, climbing through the remnant of the wall into an adjacent room.

There was the unmistakable sound of the construct transforming its limbs again, like that of something being pulled out of wet, sticky mud. As Bobby and Katy turned a corner that led them back out into the street, they caught sight of the monster descending into the room into which they had jumped. It had stretched its legs out like gigantic stilts and was stepping with apparent ease from the top of one building down into the room of the next. As it touched down on the floor, each leg shrunk back into its body and not once did it break step, its pursuit unencumbered, relentless.

The children scrabbled their way through a broken doorway and hurtled out into the dead street. Behind them the steady, unstoppable pace of the construct continued to haunt their ears. In his terrified mind, Bobby kept expecting to hear the creature's body transform one more time and for him to feel a sudden jab of excruciating pain and look down at the tip of a lance jutting through his chest, just as Rose had done when she had given her life to save Katy.

He shook his head.

There could be no thoughts like that; they were a distraction that he could not afford. They just had to keep on running. They slid and skidded in the loose ash as they careened around a corner back onto the main street that led down towards the market square. The two children pumped their arms as they hurtled down the abandoned street, ash and dust pluming up from under their feet that slapped frantically on the rutted surface. Bobby's lungs began to burn from the continued exertion as they rushed past more burnt-out ruins before careering into the opening of the market square. They looked around for the three adults but saw just the dead remnants of the villagers of Irlingbury.

All the time behind them came the relentless, non-stop drum of the construct's march.

*Thud, thud. Thud, thud.*

Panicked, their hearts ready to burst from their chests, the two children searched for somewhere to hide — somewhere dark and small in which they could cower like a tiny rodent that wishes to escape the attention of the housewIfe chasing it with a broom. But there was nowhere, nothing. All the once-thriving marketplace could provide them with was the constant demonstration that a brutal death awaited them. The dead hung everywhere, choking the life from every corner.

And soon, Bobby and Katy were to join them.

Bobby flung his arms around his kid sister and dragged her eyes away from the sight of the construct marching unimpeded into the open. There was nothing more that they could do. They were exhausted, all the energy in their young bodies consumed, whereas the creature of clay had no such handicap. Bobby covered Katy's ears as the construct stretched out its arm, the transformation of the limb into a cruel lance accompanied by the all too familiar sound that was akin to wet mud.

It continued, unbothered, towards the two children.

Katy writhed in her brother's grip and tore her face away from his chest. She pushed at her stunned sibling, stepped towards the towering golem and screamed in unintelligible rage at the creature that's only concern was her imminent and brutal death.

Bobby shook his head and made to grab her, to preserve even the slightest fraction of a second more of her life, but she just shoved him away and continued to scream at the clay monster as it bore down upon her.

And then, sprinting out of the shadows, a dark blur crashed into the side of the construct at such a velocity, that it sent the killer cartwheeling head over heels across the market square, causing it to crash into the charred remains of a former building. Two more shapes, moving faster than the mortal brain could understand, joined with the first and the three of them seemed to pick the construct up from the ground and hurl it back across to the other side of the marketplace. It collided with a sickening *crump* into a heap of discarded bodies. Bobby watched in awe as the monster made to lift itself to its feet only to stumble and fall once more as a black whip cracked out across the night and lashed around its left leg. The construct tried yet again to walk but Claw pulled tight, yanking the whip high over his shoulder and the creature fell once more.

This time, Tigress and Scorpion leapt and landed on its arms, pinning them to the ground.

The construct made to struggle, but the grip of the two women was unbreakable. Their pale hands held it fast to the floor as Claw approached the fallen golem, keeping a tight rein on his whip as he did so. Then Bobby gasped in shock as sharp points thrust out from the construct's chest, jabbing upwards towards its captors in a desperate bid to harpoon them. But the women were too quick and, each time an improvised weapon lunged up towards them, they seemed to nimbly edge out of the way as if they had not been in its path at all.

Bobby continued to watch as the women glanced at each other before opening their mouths wide. What the boy saw chilled him almost as much as the monster itself. At the edge of their lips, they both bore a sharp pair of fangs that glinted in the moonlight, wet with their hungry saliva. In unison the two women plunged their sharpened teeth down into the material of the construct's arms and to Bobby's revulsion, they appeared to drink.

The construct writhed and flailed under them, a deep wail emanating from its wide mouth as its black tongue whipped back and forth.

It was in utter agony.

Never before had Bobby seen the like.

"Enough!" Claw's voice was sharp and commanding across the howls of terror from the dying creature. "We need it alive."

The two women raised their heads and glared at the male as he untied his whip from the creature's leg. Ignoring their annoyance, he took the tip of his weapon, the silver barb, raised it high then plunged it down into the chest of the construct. The monster shrieked in a high-pitched wail that turned Bobby's stomach over in his guts. He looked on in morbid fascination as the construct seemed to shake and convulse as Claw rammed his hand in after the tip of the whip, stern concentration on his face as he twisted the barb around inside his prisoner's flailing body.

Then, the impossible happened.

In front of Bobby's eyes, the construct's skin shifted

and melted. The huge clay beast was no more and there, trapped by the three captors lay what appeared to be a naked human woman.

"Let me go! Let me go!" the woman screamed, her head flailing from side to side. "Let me go!"

"Not going to happen." Claw's voice was calm and commanding. "You're going to tell us what we want to know."

"Go to hell, *vampire!*" she hissed. "Why should I tell you anything, you weak abomination? You're a pathetic little remnant and your days are numbered."

"Says the lump of clay with a claw in its chest." He twisted his wrist as a painful reminder of the fact.

The woman's agonised screams echoed around the market square.

"Who ordered this? Who said the village was to be destroyed?"

The prisoner gritted her teeth, seeming to muster up all her strength, then glaring at Claw's passive face, she hissed, "Why should I tell you anything? You are weak, pathetic. You couldn't even destroy the Bloodline of Abel. No, the mighty Children of Cain had to depend on a mere mortal to do their dirty work for them. Thousands of years and you did nothing, just lurking, brooding in the shadows and how long did it take him to eradicate the Bloodline from the face of the planet? A few months?" She slammed the back of her head against the cobbled floor and brayed in laughter. "Pathetic! Totally pathetic."

"Tell me," Claw persevered, "who ordered the destruction of the village, and why?"

The woman's eyes burnt with fire as she glared up at him, ignoring the questions. "Tell me, *vampire,* where is he now, your great saviour? Where is Sam Spallucci?

He's nowhere! He's gone, never to return. He's..." Her words cut out as she opened her mouth as wide as possible and screamed in agony.

Bobby's hand flew to his mouth as he watched Tigress wipe a knife against the skin of the woman, just above where she had severed the prisoner's foot from her leg. "You want to lose another one? Because I'm game. Answer the questions."

"Never," the woman spat through clenched teeth as she tried to control her breathing. "I'll never betray him."

Claw raised an eyebrow. "Which *him*?"

"Screw you!"

Claw nodded to Tigress.

The woman screamed again as, this time, she lost a hand.

Bobby watched in morbid fascination as both the foot and the hand began to grow back, plain stumps edging out from the traumatised limbs, stretching and expanding to fill the spaces that the foot and the hand had previously occupied.

Claw sighed and bent down to the face of the woman. "You know we can do this all night. We just cut things off and wait for them to grow back. Eventually, you will tire. Eventually, you will tell me what I want to know."

In total, the woman lost six feet, seven hands and a nose before she finally cracked.

"Asmodeus!" she wept. "It was Asmodeus. The Fallen gave the order."

"Why?"

She shook her head. "I don't know. He was angry. So angry. I think he had received a roasting from *higher up*."

The three vampires glanced at each other.

"Where is he now? How many constructs does he have with him?"

"He's not far. He's to the north, camped on the Rishton wetlands. He has about ten constructs." She closed her eyes and her head sank exhausted to the floor. It was a look of utter, total defeat.

Claw studied the woman's sunken face for a moment before nodding to his two companions. Scorpion and Tigress once more revealed their fangs and bit down hard on the woman's wrists. This time she only managed a feeble moan as they drank heavily from her.

In a short while, she was nothing but fine, powdery dust.

## Chapter Four

They climbed on their horses and left the smoulder-ing ruins of Irlingbury behind them as they rode out into the night. Not pushing their steeds, they proceeded cau-tiously along the old road which led north out of the vil-lage.

In an hour or so, they reined in outside a curious looking building. Unlike most other structures that Bobby and Katy had known, it was constructed from stone, not wood, and rather than composing of the usual four walls, it had just three, its base forming that of a triangle.

But, perhaps more unusual than anything else, it was almost perfectly intact.

Claw dismounted and walked up to the door of the building. He turned the large iron handle and, with a small amount of effort, it opened inwards. "We will rest here," he said. The other vampires climbed down from their horses, helping the children to dismount.

As the adults settled the horses and took supplies into the building, Bobby wandered around the other side of the structure whilst Katy followed after Tigress and Scorpion. He gazed up in wonder at the design of the building that appeared incredibly old but was in unbeliev- ably good condition. Everywhere he looked there was threefold symbolism. The building had three straight sides and he noted that there were three floors. Not only that, but most of the windows were fashioned from patterns of triangles. He walked back towards the main door and saw writing across the top of the stone lintel. He frowned, un- able to read it.

"*Tres testimonium dant,*" came a gnarled, familiar voice from behind him.

Bobby spun around and smiled to see the old man Cutter stood there, leaning on his staff.

Bobby made to call out to him but the elderly man raised a finger to his lips. "Not here," he whispered and he motioned that they should walk a short way to a thicket of undergrowth that hid them from the sight of the building.

"It's good to see you," Bobby smiled. "Shall I get Katy?"

The man shook his head, peering cautiously across the boy's shoulder. "No, there isn't time. I can't stay long."

Bobby felt disappointed. "Oh," he managed. Then, pointing to the building, he said, "It's quite amazing, isn't it? How come it's survived this long?"

"It is the symbolism of the place. The notion of three appeals to Kanor. Its original architect would have meant it to stand for something else, a long-dead religious belief, but to Kanor it means something completely differ- ent."

"That inscription. What does it mean?"

"*There are three that give witness.*"

Bobby frowned. "And what does *that* mean?"

"Probably not what it was originally intended to.

Possibly more than the soul who inscribed it could have fathomed." Cutter paused, his sharp eyes studying Bobby. "Are you well? I saw what happened to Irlingbury."

Bobby silently nodded, not wanting to talk about what they had seen.

Cutter tutted appreciatively. "Listen and listen well. You are in danger. You and Katy need to be extremely careful."

Bobby turned and frowned at the triangular building. "It doesn't appear dangerous. It seems quite solid."

Cutter shook his head. "I do not mean the structure; I mean those within it. You cannot trust the Children of Cain. They are ruthless killers and will draw you into their righteous war. You must not fight their battles. It will be the death of you."

Bobby made to ask what he meant exactly, when there was a noise. He glanced across to the building and saw Claw approaching. Turning back, he found that Cutter had slipped away into the darkness of the night.

"Are you okay?" the sandy-haired man called. "I thought I heard voices."

"Just talking to myself," Bobby shrugged as nonchalantly as he could.

Claw paused and Bobby watched as the adult sniffed the air before frowning in apparent puzzlement

"Come on. We've made some food. You'd better grab some before your sister eats the lot."

The night was starting to fade away as the five travellers rested in the curious triangular building. The two children ate as the three adults checked over their gear. Bobby watched the three intently as they went about their own individual chores.

Claw inspected every part of his long whip: pulling it taut between his pale hands to test its strength, examining the sharp metal talon at the end that he had plunged into the chest of the construct. Using a smooth cloth that he kept on his person, he polished it until its silvery surface glinted in the light of the small campfire that they had set in the room's hearth.

Tigress appeared to be carrying more knives than seemed physically possible. She pulled them out from concealed slots and pockets in her clothes, lying them out in front of her in three neat rows, before meticulously cleaning each one and running a sharpening steel over their already finely honed blades.

Scorpion sat with her back to the wall of the weirdly shaped room and just stared straight ahead into the fire. Unlike the other two, who were concentrating on matters of the here and now, she seemed to be far off in some other place. Her eyes danced with firelight as she sat motionless, as still as a corpse.

Cutter had insisted that these three individuals were dangerous. Yet twice now they had saved Bobby's and Katy's lives. The old man had never been wrong before, acting as some sort of gnarled guardian angel, yet how could these three bear them harm?

But then, he and Katy knew next to nothing about their apparent saviours.

*About the same amount as we know about Cutter.* Bobby pondered. It had been so much simpler when it had just been the two of them.

Katy finished off some cooked meat and let loose a huge belch.

The silent Scorpion cracked a slight smile and her partner slapped her thigh in amusement.

"I take it that met your satisfaction?" Claw asked as he twisted his whip into a tight coil.

Katy nodded, then frowned. "I have a question."

The three adults flicked a glance between themselves. Claw nodded for her to continue.

"The construct you killed. It called you vampires. What's one of those?"

Another look was exchanged. Scorpion tendered a small shrug, Tigress held out a hand towards Claw. "Take it away, Your Majesty," she grinned. "This is above my pay grade."

Claw seemed to blow out a puff of air as he considered what his reply should be. "As we have already said, we are all very old. Some of us," he winked at Tigress, "more so than others."

"Still feel like a hot young thing," the redhead jibed back.

Claw chuckled and continued. "We all used to be human."

"But you're not now?" Bobby asked.

Claw shook his head. "No. We may *look* human, but we were born to a new life. A life that gives us greater strength and abilities that would be impossible for a human. We do not age as humans do. Only a handful of things can kill us: decapitation, trauma to our hearts, fire and daylight. Hence these," he explained, picking at the edge of his dark cloak. "We were all made vampires by another vampire. They did this by sharing their blood with us. So, Tigress shared the blood of her father. Scorpion shared the blood of her mother."

Tigress stuck her hand up. "Which would be me."

"And I took the blood of *my* mother."

"Where are your and Tigress' parents now?" Katy

asked.

"They are dead. They have both been dead for a very long time."

The small girl frowned in thought. "Was your mother a queen? Our dad used to tell stories about kings and queens of old. They were called Your Majesty. Tigress called you that, so you must be a king, which means your mother must have been a queen."

Claw's eyes seemed incredibly sad for a moment before he continued. "Yes, she was and yes, I am."

"What was she like?"

"She was very kind. She cared for all of us. She was terribly, terribly brave."

"What did she look like?"

Claw dug deep into a pocket and pulled something out. "Here," he said, "look at this."

Katy and Bobby edged over to the vampire and peered down at the thing that he held. "What is it?" Bobby inquired.

"It is a photograph. Back when the world was as it was, people used small machines to capture  the likenesses of objects and people. You see there, on the edge of the group? That is my mother."

"She looks pretty," Katy smiled. "What was her name?"

"Nightingale."

Bobby continued to study the photograph. It showed a group of people wearing fancy-looking clothes standing around some sort of stone structure, a type of large basin on a pedestal. Around the rim of the bowl were engraved five words. "*Knaves are not our responsibility*," he read. "What does that mean?"

"A whole heap of trouble," Tigress muttered as she

balanced one of her knives on a fingertip.

Bobby peered back down at the photograph and frowned.

"What is it?" Claw asked.

The teenager pointed to two individuals who were standing next to the large bowl, a man in black and a boy who appeared a few years older than himself. "Who are these? They look different to the others."

An awkward silence fell across the room.

"They are of no importance right now," Claw mumbled as he tucked the photo back into his pocket. "That was a very long time ago."

"Do *you* have a child?" Katy asked.

Claw shook his head. "No. I have never taken a child. We are all that remains of our kind, the Children of Cain."

Bobby's heartbeat flickered upon his ears hearing the phrase that Cutter had used.

"Why?" Katy asked in response to Claw's answer.

The male vampire appeared to sigh. "The first vampire, Cain, was created thousands of years ago. He was given three tasks to perform, three duties to follow."

"Find the Eternals. Protect the Twins. Await the Divergence!" Tigress spat with venom in her voice. "And we sucked at all three. The Divergence came and wiped out humanity. We only found one of the Eternals. We lost the damned Twins." Bobby noticed her eyes lance Claw as she said this.

"We've been over this before…"

"Yeah, and it still sucks! Probably the greatest weapon we had to destroy Kanor and you threw it away!"

"Tigress," Claw's voice was tired, strained, as if he was sick of defending himself. "You know it was the right thing to do."

The redhead shot a word at her king in a language that the children did not understand before continuing her rant. "You sent them here, to this gods forsaken place on the basis of a dream. A dream!"

Bobby noticed Scorpion shift uncomfortably where she sat.

"You know what Scorpion saw. We had to act on it."

"Yeah, yeah, yeah. Spallucci. She saw Spallucci stood in a barren, scorched world."

"It was here. You know it was."

"For all I know it could have been the juice of a construct tripping balls on LSD! The fact remains you sent our only weapon to gods know where, leaving us utterly defenceless."

Claw shook his head. "We don't know that's what they are. They could be intended for something else entirely."

"Like what? Baking cakes?" Tigress let out a screech of frustration and hurled a knife so that it struck a wooden beam across the doorway. She shook her head. "And as for the Eternals… Gods alone know where they are now."

Claw stared resolutely into the fire. "We did what we could, but everything was stacked against us. Without knowing it, we were a hidden weakness of the very thing we were supposed to protect: humanity. We fought quietly for them in the shadows, combatting constructs and other threats when we found them. Humankind had no idea that we existed. Then, when Kanor rose and brought about the Divergence…" He shook his head despondently. "They were… unprepared."

The five sat and watched the fire crackle in its

hearth, each seeing something different in their own mind.

"I want to be a vampire."

Four sets of eyes turned to the small eight-year-old girl.

"I want your strength, your speed, your abilities. I could use them to change things. I would train to be the strongest vampire ever and I would go to Wellington and kill Kanor. I would make him suffer for what he's done to everyone. I would make the world right again."

Claw shook his head. "That cannot be."

"Why not?" she protested.

He ran a hand through his sandy hair before saying, "There was a story from my youth that told of a land a long time ago and far, far away, where a group of heroes, knights you might say, cared for society and righted all its wrongs. But they didn't know that their leader was, in reality, their greatest enemy. He created a huge army that fought alongside the knights in a terrible war, serving alongside them as brothers-in-arms. Then, on his order, that army turned and eradicated almost all those heroes who had pledged their lives to serve the weak of society. In an instant, they were but a pitiful remnant."

"That's awful," Bobby said.

Claw shook his head. "But that was not all." He looked straight at Katy. "There was one of these heroes who thought like you do Katy, that he alone knew what needed to be done, that he should gather so much power to make himself invincible to protect those that he loved."

"What happened?" the small girl asked, her eyes wide in the firelight.

"The greatest tragedy possible. The power corrupted him, blinded his conscience to darker and darker deeds that he began to undertake in the name of protecting the weak. He killed the one that he loved, betrayed his best friend. He…" Claw shook his head and Bobby was sure that the vampire wiped a red-stained tear away from his cheek. "He even slaughtered all the youngsters who were training to follow in the footsteps of the older protectors of the peace. Children, Katy, that were younger than you. He…"

"Oh, in the name of the gods!" Tigress exploded. "Seriously? You do realise that you are just describing the plot of *Revenge of the Sith*?"

A certain awkwardness fell across Claw's face. "Well, it does have an unusual parallel with our situation. I feel it has a strong moral that we can take away and…"

The redhead snorted in derision. "Idiot!" she snapped as she threw a stone on the fire, causing hot embers to dance up into the air. "Here we sit in a post-apocalyptic wilderness which hasn't even known proper sanitation for over a thousand years, let alone electricity, and you tell these baffled kids about a film from your childhood! Unbelievable. No wonder they wiped us out!"

"It's a very relevant story," Claw tried to explain.

"It's a complete fiction!" Tigress screamed at him. "Just like the idea that there is some honest soul out there that will take out Kanor and make this all right again."

"The Virtuous Man exists," Claw stated plainly.

"You mean Jason? From Orchester?"

Claw turned to Bobby and shook his head. "There was not a grain of virtue in that man's body. He was a fraud that had tricked even himself into believing the lie. The real Virtuous Man is still out there, somewhere."

"Oh, gods," Tigress moaned. "Here we go again. The bromance to end all bromances!"

Scorpion got up and gestured for her to calm down.

"No! No, I will not! It is a fool's errand. There is no Virtuous Man!"

The blonde set her fists on her hips and glared at the redhead.

"Yes, yes! I know. The *prophecies.* The damned prophecies. A fat lot of good they've done so far."

"He's out there," Claw insisted. "We will find him."

"No. We won't. Spallucci is dead. You hear me? He's dead. He died the day the bombs went off. Before Lucifer and Abaddon…"

"No!" Claw had sprung to his feet, flown across the room and now had Tigress pinned by her throat against the stone wall. "He is alive! I know it. I feel it. We will find him and he will save us!"

Bobby protectively drew Katy towards him but she shrugged him off once more.

Scorpion forced herself between the two arguing vampires and thrust them apart before glowering at each of them in turn. The pair sat down, both of them staring at the floor in disgrace. The blonde shook her head in frustration and came over to the siblings. Crouching down, she placed a cold hand on each of them and cocked her head in a question.

"It's okay," Katy smiled, "we argue too."

Scorpion nodded, turned to look at the others, and sighed.

# Chapter Five

They arrived at the wetlands of Rishton just before nightfall. It had been a very tense ride north with the three vampires saying very little to each other following their spat at the triangular tower. Scorpion was her usual taciturn self and the atmosphere between Claw and Tigress was practically tangible. The only real conversation had been when the children had watched a tall structure rise on the horizon to the west.

"What's that?" Bobby asked pointing across the flatlands to the thin shape that seemed to dart its way up to the sky. "It's so tall."

"That," Claw said without even troubling to glance at the building in the distance, "is Wellington. That is somewhere you never wish to go, you hear?"

"Why not?"

"The tall building you see used to be a church, where people used to pray to their god."

"Jason mentioned something about that. He said he was a priest."

Claw made a small annoyed tutting noise. "That man's god would be ashamed of him for what he did to you."

"So why should we not go to that place then? Are there more there like Jason?"

"No," Claw explained, guiding his horse away from the settlement. "It is now the lair of Kanor. If you were to go there, you would die."

As they continued north, Bobby watched the spire fade into the darkening landscape and, as the sun sank down behind its imposing silhouette, he imagined that he could see a huge pair of black wings rising from the descending fiery ball up into the night sky.

Nothing else was said until the vampires drew their horses to a stop. They settled their rides by a small stand of trees that grew next to a wide plain of lush grass. It appeared a richer shade of green than anywhere else that Bobby had ever seen. Tigress caught him staring out across the wide landscape. "There's a lot of water here under the surface. It's something to do with the ground below. It enables the grass to grow easier than in most places. Look." She dismounted her steed, walked over to a patch of grass and placed her foot upon it. A pool of water pushed up the sides of her boot.

"Is it safe to walk on?" Bobby asked.

"I would advise against you going out there. You could hit a soft patch and sink below the surface. We, on the other hand, are far more agile and can just bounce around like dandelion heads in the wind," she grinned. "Ones with very sharp teeth, that is."

Katy came and stood next to them, wrinkling her nose. "It smells awful."

"The water is stagnant," Tigress explained. "It can't flow so it just sits here and smells bad."

Bobby nodded.

"Where are the constructs?"

As one, the vampires peered out across the wetlands. They all nodded and Claw said, "They are due north, across the marshland. We can make out their encampment over on the other side. It's a good job we can see where they are as we can't smell them across this quagmire."

"Smell them?"

The vampire nodded. "It is one of our skills. It helps us hunt them, even when they are not in their natural form."

"Like the one at Irlingbury?"

"Back before the Divergence, that was how most of them were. They looked like you, me, your sister and they walked freely among society. Most of them didn't even know what they were until something triggered them. Then they would turn on families, friends, co-workers." He shook his head. "There were a few ways to discern them, but their scent was always unmistakable."

"They smell almost as bad as this foetid water," Tigress chipped in. "Totally unnatural, unhealthy. They could mask it with scent or use other techniques such as staying dirty and unwashed, but we usually got them in the end.

"Until there were too many of them."

A sombre silence fell upon the group, which was finally broken by Claw. "Well, that won't be an issue tonight. Ten is a nice easy number, I think we can all agree."

The two female vampires nodded. "A walk in the park. What's the plan of attack, boss?" Tigress asked.

Claw unhooked his whip from his belt and began flexing the long weapon as he pondered their strategy. "I say a pincer manoeuvre. I'll come at them from the left, you two from the right.

"But Asmodeus is mine. Remember that."

The two other vampires nodded. "Goes without saying," Tigress nodded.

Bobby saw the look of determination mixed with anger that fell across Claw's face. "What is it with Asmodeus?"

"It's revenge, pure and simple. He killed my mother."

Bobby didn't know what to say. Claw had said that his mother was dead, but the fact that the person who had been responsible for her death was so close… Finally, he asked. "The construct said that he was one of the Fallen. Who exactly is he?"

Starting to check over her knives, Tigress muttered, "He's a jerk."

"He's also incredibly dangerous," Claw warned. "The Fallen, there are two of them: Asmodeus, the male, and Asherah, the female. They are, or *were*, angels. They are both older than this planet and used to live in a realm called Heaven until they became restless and greedy, then they fell to Earth, where they have been ever since."

"With massive chips on their shoulders," Tigress interjected.

Bobby frowned. He didn't have any idea as to what she meant. "Are they powerful?"

Claw nodded. "Amongst other things, they can control elements. Asherah can draw water from the air around her and use it as a tool or a weapon. Asmodeus can produce lightning from his fingers. If he fires it at your kind, it would be excruciatingly painful or indeed deadly. We can tolerate it better than you can."

"Oh, I'm not so sure about that," came a smooth

voice from behind them. "My master is always happy to prove a Child of Cain wrong." A Shadow Wraith emerged from the trees. Following him were four constructs.

The vampires moved without hesitation. Any differences they might have been arguing over were discarded, forgotten as they attacked like a well maintained, regularly oiled weapon. Even before Bobby could blink, three of the constructs were suddenly lying on the floor, their legs amputated at the knees. Tigress was circling back around on them, a stout blade in her hand. As she advanced on the first, Scorpion had slid between the legs of the one that remained standing, levering herself upright, causing it too to fall to the floor before she latched down on its clay skin with her sharp teeth, her body moving fluidly from side to side to avoid the sharp lances that the downed construct shot up from its torso in a vain attempt to skewer her. Shortly, two constructs were nothing but powdery dust and the two females were draining the other two.

There was a loud crack as Claw flicked his whip out and coiled the end around the Shadow Wraith's neck. He yanked backwards, trying to pull the creature off its feet, but the Wraith moved with the motion of the whip and sailed through the air, landing lithely behind the vampire. With its pale hands, it gripped the taut cord and jerked it down, continuing to work with the momentum of the weapon. Claw staggered and almost lost his grip, but he became a blur and, in less than a second, the Wraith was trussed tight in the whip that was now snaked around his body. It began to writhe against the bonds, its skin taking on a softer, more viscous hue, but Claw screamed out in rage and effort as he pulled the weapon to its tightest. The Shadow Wraith seemed to lose its solid consistency and partially oozed through the coiled weapon. Claw reached under his cloak and, in one swift movement, produced a wicked-looking knife that he swung through the neck of the Wraith, causing its head to tumble to the floor, its eyes staring up in horrified shock. The vampire launched onto the decapitated body, sunk his teeth into the exposed neck and sucked loudly as the body withered and desiccated.

In less than a hundred heartbeats, the three vampires were stood over the remains of the dead creatures. Bobby realised that he could not recall having breathed during the whole process. He turned to look at Katy. The eight-year-old was stood enrapt, a broad smile filling her face.

"That was *amazing*," she breathed.

"It's what we do," Tigress winked. Then, to Claw, "A trap?"

"Definitely," he agreed, then turned and gazed out across the wetlands, an odd look on his face.

"What is it?" the redhead asked.

Claw frowned. "I'm not sure. I'm sure I have a memory of this place from a long, long time ago. But, so much has happened since. It's just a vague image of fighting." He shook his head. "Forget it." Then, to the other two vampires, "So, they knew we were coming. You want to pull back?"

The redhead glanced at her blonde partner who was staring out across the marshland, her sharp teeth still exposed. "Like hell we do," Tigress snarled.

Claw smiled and nodded. "My thoughts exactly. Bobby, you and Katy must stay here, you understand? Whatever you see or hear, you do not intervene. If you do, you will die."

Katy made to open her mouth but the vampire held up a silencing hand. "No. On no account do you set one foot on that marshland. You remain here and await our return. If we don't come back, then you run. You run for your lives. Do I make myself clear?"

The children nodded.

He turned to the other vampires. "Asmodeus is out there. We know what he did. Let's make him pay," and they set out across the open marsh.

Even with the knowledge that they were walking into a trap, the vampires stuck to their original plan, feeling that it was the most practical tactic. Claw circled left, his hood back and his taloned whip in his hand. His dark eyes were black against his pale skin in the cold moonlight. They flicked back and forth intent, waiting for the trap to be sprung. Every now and then his head tilted to one side, then the other, his eyes carefully regarding the wet ground upon which he lightly trod. Tigress and Scorpion progressed right, around the other side of the marshland. They walked side by side, a watchful confidence apparent about them. In her hands, Tigress carried two of her wicked-looking knives, their finely honed edges glinting delicately in the light of the crescent moon. Scorpion held a short sword down by her side. It looked like she was holding it loose, casually, but Bobby knew that was not the case. The blonde, like the other woman, was a trained killing machine. Her sharp blade would be thrusting, slicing, killing as soon as they came under attack.

As they did roughly halfway across the open marshland.

One moment, the vampires were stalking their way carefully across the wet surface of the land, the next they had frozen solid, aware of something that was beyond the mortal senses of Bobby and Katy.

Then the ground around the vampires began to move.

The surface of the marsh started to undulate as if it were being breathed upon by some unseen deity. Ripples radiated out from points all around the vampires and Bobby's jaw fell slack as he witnessed the rise of not ten, not twenty, but thirty constructs from the depths of the marsh.

It was like watching an army of tree trunks emerge slowly in unison from the ground. First there was the dome of the top of their heads, then the broad shoulders, followed by the rest of their bodies, including the long, deadly arms with cruel lances protruding from the end of the limbs.

The three vampires did not hesitate. As one blur of motion, they struck whilst the constructs were still sprouting from the wet marsh. They managed to dispatch half a dozen before they had fully formed.

But that still left them terribly outnumbered and they were now fighting for their lives.

They had speed on their side as the constructs were heavy, cumbersome creatures and struggled to march to their usual steady beat through the dank watery surface. Tigress and Scorpion lithely lifted themselves off from the ground and catapulted across the heads of the golems, slashing and skewering with their blades as they did. The children watched as, at one point, the blonde vampire used five constructs as if they were stepping-stones, slicing down beneath her as she travelled across them, deftly dodging side to side, outmanoeuvring their thrusting lances.

But slicing and incapacitating the creatures was only half the battle. If the vampires did not drain them, they just drew themselves together and reformed, reentering the fray with their unrelenting steady pace.

The two females adapted their battle plan accordingly. Scorpion continued to slice the clay monsters apart, causing them to fall to the wet surface of the marsh, allowing Tigress to latch on to the severed remains and quickly drain them dry.

It was a shrewd tactic but, as Bobby watched powerlessly from the side, he could not help but feel that the women were fighting a losing battle. As Tigress continued to drain construct after construct, Scorpion seemed to be slaying one after another quicker than her partner could finish them off. This meant that, in the intervening time between slash and despatch, a number of the golems were able to reform and reenter the battle. As a result, the number of constructs that Scorpion actually had to fight kept increasing, which meant one worrying thing.

She was getting noticeably tired.

Claw also had a Battle Royale on his hands. He was taking a different tactic, having to fight through swathes of oncoming constructs on his own as he ploughed his way towards his Ultima Thule, the revenge for the death of his mother. Streaking up the lefthand side of the battlefield, his whip continually cracked out across the fray, parting one construct after another from its head. However, rather than staying to finish the jobs, the male vampire had another target in sight.

Bobby peered across to the far side of the carnage where he saw two figures standing side by side. One with its smooth white hair was undoubtedly a Shadow Wraith.

The other was a figure that he did not recognise. It was male, of apparently average height, and wore a flowing black cloak over its shoulders.

"Asmodeus!" Claw screamed as he ran towards the two figures. "I have come for you!"

The Fallen said something to the Shadow Wraith and the slick killing machine at once darted across the wetland towards the raging vampire. The construct flicked out its arms and they formed into two savage curved blades which it swung at Claw as it leapt across the ground towards him. The vampire met the creature mid-air and they collided with a furious impact, causing both parties to crash to the floor. The construct came up first, raising its blade hands, preparing to thrust them into its downed enemy. However, its grin of malice vanished as a sharp crack echoed across the battlefield and the hook from Claw's whip dug into the side of its head. The vampire jerked his weapon to the right and the creature's head ripped across the middle as Claw bounced to his feet. In one fluid movement, he had pushed the severed form of the Shadow Wraith to the floor and had sunk his teeth into its clay flesh. When he raised his face from transforming the construct into powder, he turned to confront his nemesis.

That was when the battlefield was lit up with the crackling devastation of Asmodeus' lightning.

Bobby screamed out as Claw was lifted from his feet and dangled like a stringless marionette amongst the deadly electricity that poured out of the fingers of his nemesis. The Fallen advanced towards the helpless vampire, a cruel grin on his sallow features. He pulled his hands back, briefly relenting his barrage and allowing the vampire to crash limply to the floor. Then, when he was sure that the vampire would not rise to attack him, he resumed his assault, bright lightning crackling across the stricken victim, smoke rising from the vampire's singed clothing.

Bobby shook his head. This couldn't be happening. The Children of Cain were unlike any folk he had ever known. They were sharp, deadly, unbeatable, yet here they were, overwhelmed and failing. His eyes flicked back and forth from Claw being assailed over and over by the relentless lightning of the gleeful Asmodeus to the pair of Scorpion and Tigress as they doggedly took out construct after construct at a slower and slower pace.

Then he looked to his side, to his kid sister.

Who wasn't there.

"Katy! Katy!" he screamed, his head turning this way and that, desperate to locate his only living relative. Then he spied her. She was dodging across the battlefield, taking a circuitous route around the melee towards the fallen Claw. Bobby felt his stomach lurch and his skin pale as he couldn't believe his eyes.

There was only one thing he could do.

He followed her onto the battlefield.


The route across the marshland was treacherous. Bobby stumbled and fell to his knees several of times, swallowing mouthfuls of vile stagnant water, but he heaved himself up and continued to chase after his lighter, more nimble kid sister as she pelted hell for leather towards the light-show of Asmodeus torturing the prone vampire.

Fortunately, like the vampires, the children had agility on their side and were able to dance around the side of any constructs that stumbled and lurched at them through the clinging mire of the marshland. Twice Bobby had to roll to one side to avoid a thrusting lance, but he left the constructs behind him, concentrating on one thing and one thing alone, reaching his sister. He tried to cry out after her, but his limbs ached and his lungs burned. All his energy was being used to propel his legs on through the deepening, grasping quagmire. As Bobby felt his last reserves drive him onwards, he grasped at mud and clay as he watched Katy sprint across the final distance of the battlefield towards the lifeless form of Claw. He pulled himself towards his sister as he heard her scream at the Fallen in unintelligible rage. Asmodeus paused in his assault on his old enemy and turned his attention to the newcomer. His brow frowned and his eyebrow rose in amusement. Bobby watched in horror as the Fallen drew back his hand, electricity beginning to dance across his fingers. However, a black shadow fell across the would-be child killer as Claw summoned up the last of his failing strength to heave himself up and catapult his weakened body into the Fallen.

The two of them crashed into the mud.

Asmodeus was the first to regain his feet. A mask of entire fury consumed his face and he made to strike the final blow.

Bobby forced himself forward, pushing his feet in the marsh with all the remaining strength that he could muster and threw himself across the last remaining distance, ending up across the fallen form of Claw. He looked up into the face of Asmodeus and watched the electricity build and crackle.

And then there was nothing.

The assault, the agonising death did not come.

Asmodeus closed his fingers into tight fists and just

stared down at the mud-encrusted, pathetic little boy.

"You," he glowered, a frown of disbelief on his pale brow. He sneered in disgust, looked out across the battle-field, shook his head and disappeared in a loud cracking noise.

Bobby lay panting across the scorched body of Claw, unsure as to what had happened.

"Bobby! Bobby!"

He was aware of Katy rushing to his side and help-ing him sit up. Then, together, they tended to the injured vampire. Easing him up, they manoeuvred him into a seated position. He placed his hands on their shoulders and nodded before doing as his nemesis had just done and gazed out across the battlefield.

What met his and the children's eyes was an amaz-ing sight.

Not one construct remained standing.

There, in the middle of the marshland, Scorpion and Tigress stood barely upright but victorious. The two women grinned at each other and the redhead stepped towards the blonde to embrace her.

An unmistakable, horrific sound filled the ears of the onlookers and they cried out with Tigress as they watched the lance shoot out through Scorpion's chest. Tigress screamed louder and louder in words that Bobby and Katy did not understand as she desperately grabbed at her partner and dragged her limp form off the lance. Claw growled in a wrathful effort as he practically threw himself across the wetlands to where the remains of a near-dead construct were trying to pull themselves out of the marsh. He sailed through the air with his black cloak flapping behind him, giving him the appearance of a dark, ferocious flying beast and he landed solidly by the coagulating mess of clay, thrusting his face down into its midst, drinking heavily.

Bobby and Katy stumbled and staggered their way across the killing field to the inconsolable Tigress.

"Cassie! Cassie!" she wept, red streaks flowing down her cheeks. "No! No!" She buried her face into the neck of her dead companion and seemed to try to pull them close enough together in a vain attempt to forge them both into one.

"She's gone." It was Claw who spoke, quietly, accepting the dreadful thing that had happened. He lay a hand on the shoulder of the redhead who just gazed up at him with emptiness. She opened her mouth to speak, but nothing came. Tigress turned to look at the lifeless Scorpion once more, then back up to her king.

She did not move from her mourning.

Claw nodded in response to an unspoken request and rose to his feet. He limped over to the children. "Come with me."

Bobby and Katy followed him across the marsh, walking back to where they had left the horses, leaving the grieving woman with the body of her dead love.

"Is Tigress not coming?" Katy asked when they reached the stand of trees.

"No," Claw replied, collapsing on the dry grass, resting his forehead on the floor. "She is not."

"What will you do with Scorpion's body?" Bobby asked. "Does Tigress want to bury her?"

The male vampire was still for an uncomfortable moment, his face close to the green grass. Eventually, he rolled over onto his side, his eyes staring out across the marshland. Bobby saw the same red tracks coursing down his cheeks.

"That will not be necessary. We vampires are curious creatures," he whispered. "Daylight will eventually come."

Bobby frowned, recalling what Claw had said about their few weaknesses. "Then Tigress needs to come with us and we must get to safety."

Claw continued to stare out across the empty space. "When we are born to this life," he continued, "it is not an easy birth. We have a dream, a nightmare. We see the very moment of our final death. It haunts us through our long lives as we wonder to ourselves, *is this the day?*"

Katy knelt next to the vampire and dragged his cloak around him. "What was Tigress' dream?" she asked.

"I think you both know."

So the three of them remained in that place and watched the long night away. They sat there as the cruel rays of sunshine began to creep across the horizon in the east. The children covered the weak vampire as best as they could, leaving him a small gap in his cowl through which he could watch the terrible sight of a final lovers' embrace.

As the sun rose, bringing life to the plants upon which it shone, Tigress drew herself closer to her loved one. She did not make a sound as smoke began to drift up from her shoulders, from her short red hair. She did not cry out as her skin began to catch aflame and fire danced across her form. She did not scream as that flame erupted in a fierce fireball, consuming her and the woman in her arms, sending them both to their final fate.

## Chapter Six

The children and the vampire had to remain where they were for the best part of the next day as Claw's wounds healed themselves. Barely a word was said, just occasionally a member of the party would stare out across the barren marshland and sigh deeply before feeling the comforting weight of another's hand on their shoulder.

Bobby found the healing properties of Claw quite extraordinary. After Tigress and Scorpion had died, he had insisted that he check the vampire over. Claw had protested but, when Bobby's insistence was bolstered with that of Katy's, he had relented and they had carefully inspected his wounds, wincing at the savage scorch marks on his flesh.

"It's nothing," Claw had reassured them. "They are just superficial. I will be fine to travel in a few hours. Most likely by tonight."

By midday, Bobby noticed that Claw began to move more. Not only was the vampire testing the strength of his arms and his legs but his burns were noticeably fading. Bobby ventured over to the horses and rummaged in the saddlebags for food. He dug out some cooked meat from their meal at the three-cornered tower, walked over to Katy, who was sat looking out across the marsh, and offered her some.

She just looked down at it and shook her head.

Well, that wasn't good.

"Katy?"

His sister said nothing and just resumed her vigil.

Bobby eased himself down onto the grass and sat cross-legged next to the eight-year-old. "There was nothing we could have done. There were too many constructs."

"Then there should have been more vampires." Her voice was small but resolute. Bobby could not miss the cold edge to it.

"There are no more. They were the last three."

"They should have made me one when I asked. I could have fought. With four of us, we would have had a better chance of success. Tigress and Scorpion…" Her words drifted off.

"Would still have died. You heard what Claw said. They knew how they were going to die."

Katy shook her head violently from side to side. "No. No. I can't believe that. We would have been able to change it. If I had been a vampire, I could have fought. I would have split those monsters open and drained them dry.

"And I would have enjoyed it!"

They were aware of a sound behind them. Claw had risen to his feet and was tentatively limping over to join them. "Katy, your brother is correct. There is nothing that we could have done. It was their time to die. No matter how many Children of Cain had been in that battle, the outcome would have been the same. No, all we can do is carry on with our quest. We must find Sam Spallucci. He is out there. I know it. I feel it."

Bobby frowned. "You mentioned him the other night, at the tower. Who is he?"

Claw's brown eyes looked off to somewhere that the children could not see. "An old friend. I knew him when I was first made a vampire. My transition was not exactly by the book and Sam helped me through, reuniting me with my mother. He has been a good friend to the Children of Cain.

"And we treated him awfully." He shook his head.

"What do you mean?"

The vampire grimaced, rolling a shoulder as he did, testing it for mobility as he considered his reply. "To use a phrase that Sam detested, *it's complicated*. Timelines were involved and it was believed crucial that he did not know certain matters from the future so as not to disrupt them. He was kept intentionally in the dark about crucial matters.

"This led to a certain amount of friction between him and the others."

"But not you two?"

Claw shook his head. "No. He was a good man and a good friend. And more."

"What do you mean?" Katy asked, finally tearing herself away from her vigil and joining the conversation.

Claw opened his mouth to speak but hesitated as his nostrils flared and he swivelled around, albeit unsteadily, drawing his knife as he did so. Bobby's and Katy's eyes were drawn to movement in the undergrowth as a familiar figure emerged from the dark shadows.

"The vampire means that he believes Spallucci is

the Man of Virtue," Cutter explained in his usual grizzled voice as he stamped his way out of the overgrown thicket and into the midst of the three companions. "What's more he would lead you on a fool's errand to try and find him."

"Cutter!" Katy squealed at the sight of the old-timer and she tried to run towards him, but Claw's free hand darted out and gripped her shoulder, dragging her back.

"It's okay," Bobby reassured the vampire. "He's our friend. We know this man."

Claw's lips drew back as he exposed his fangs. "Trust me, that *thing* you see there is neither your friend nor a man."

The children turned back to Cutter and their faces changed from ones of confusion to ones of shock as the old man's features began to ripple and moisten, transforming into something else. In a moment, the old man had disappeared. In his place stood something quite different. Clad in long, obsidian black robes, smooth-skinned and with slicked-back hair stood a Shadow Wraith.

But not just *any* member of the elite corps of constructs. The face of this particular one, its black eyes peering down at him, was one that Bobby knew well.

It was the one that had murdered his father.

# Bobby Normal
## and
# The Fallen

# Previously...

Bobby, a teenage boy from Irlingbury, and Katy, his fiery eight-year-old sister were entrusted to deliver the Eternal Talisman to a man called Jason, who was believed by his followers to be the Virtuous Man, the individual who could bring about the fall of Kanor and save humanity from the perils of the Divergent Lands.

With the help of a curious old man called Cutter, the two orphans did as they were asked. However, a plan that Jason had concocted to destroy a troop of constructs, the mindless clay golems of Kanor, failed disastrously and he blamed the children, ordering them to be burned at the stake as traitors.

Just in the nick of time, Bobby and Katy were snatched from their awful fate by Claw, Tigress and Scorpion, three vampires known as the Children of Cain. On returning to Irlingbury, the orphans discovered that their home village had been destroyed and its inhabitants slaughtered. They decided to travel with their new friends. As they did so, Claw told them how he was searching for the true Virtuous Man; someone he believed to be his old friend from before the Divergence, a person named Sam

Spallucci. Tragically, during a battle with the fallen angel Asmodeus and a cohort of his constructs, Tigress and Scorpion were killed and Claw was badly wounded. As the children waited for the vampire to recover, the old man Cutter appeared and revealed that he was, in fact, the Shadow Wraith that had murdered the orphans' father.

## Chapter One

Fire was a peculiar thing, Bobby thought to himself as the object of his musings spat and crackled in front of him. On one hand, it was a force of devastation, reducing buildings and their occupants to pitiful ash in just hours. He and his sister Katy, who sat aggressively poking this particular blaze with a long stick, had borne witness to this fact just three days ago when they had returned home to Irlingbury and found it burned to the ground, all human life eradicated. However, it could also be a source of safety, burning bright to keep any manner of fierce predators at bay, and a source of comfort, a reminder of the hearth at home for someone journeying through the barren wilds of the Divergent Lands.

The teenage boy stared across the burning wood at the creature that sat opposite. There was no way that it needed protection from hungry beasts and it certainly would not have any warm, fuzzy recollections of a home, a family. The creature that pretended to warm its hands by the campfire had no heartbeat, had no pulse; it did not require the heat from the flames. It certainly had nowhere to call home, having been fashioned from the very clay within the ground itself for one purpose alone: to kill without remorse all those who stood against Kanor, the Black Dragon, the devastator of humanity.

Just as it had Bobby's and Katy's father.

The youth swallowed and tossed a stray piece of wood onto the fire. He cast his eyes up towards the waning crescent of the moon above and blinked back salty tears.

When the Shadow Wraith that they knew as Cutter had arrived, pandemonium had briefly erupted. Claw transformed into a blur as he streaked across the small clearing only to come to a sickening halt with his neck in the firm grip of the construct. Katy screamed at the monster to let their new friend go as the vampire, still weak from its battle with Asmodeus, batted feebly at the creature's arm. Bobby saw red. He snatched up the Child of Cain's silver-tipped whip and the long weapon cracked out across the night air as it flicked around the construct's outstretched arm. The Shadow Wraith turned to the boy, a look of sadness on its face, and immediately transformed back into its old man form.

"Bobby," it said, "we need to talk." Then, gently, it lowered Claw to the floor and released its grip.

That had been a while ago now. Unable to muster up any kind words, Bobby had turned his mind to practicalities and had built the campfire around which all four parties were now seated. He lowered his eyes from the watchful moon and glared at the old man. "You wanted to talk, so talk."

The Shadow Wraith that looked like an elderly man tamped down a wad of smoking mixture into the bowl of his old pipe and ignited it with the end of a glowing stick that he took from the fire. "I'm guessing… that you know who I am," he said between puffs.

"You killed our father. In front of me."

The construct nodded. "That I did, and that action has haunted me ever since."

A sharp tutting noise came from Claw's lips. "A construct that feels remorse? You'll forgive me if I'm sceptical."

"There are more foolish things in which to put one's faith."

"Such as?"

The construct turned its head towards the vampire. "The belief that Sam Spallucci is your *Man of Virtue*." Bobby could not fail to recognise the disdain in the creature's words. "Spallucci is long dead and there is no virtue in this land."

"On the former, I beg to differ; on the second... Well, we have your kind to thank for that, don't we?"

Bobby frowned. "Claw's right. I've never met a construct that feels guilt. Why should you be any different?"

The monster in the form of an old man shrugged. "In short, I don't know. I have spent the last five hundred or so years doing what has been expected of me with no hesitation, no remorse. All of that came to a crashing halt when I killed your father. It was as if the hand of some unseen force had been thrust into my chest and had squeezed a beat out of my still, clay heart. My mind was transported back to my moment of creation. I was standing in All Saints looking upon Kanor and all I felt was revulsion and loathing, at both my creator and my centuries of actions."

Claw frowned. "You say that Kanor fashioned you?"

Cutter nodded.

"But the Shadow Wraiths are Asmodeus' *toys*."

"I was the very first. The Fallen may lay claim to our invention, but we, and the method of our creation, were gifts to him from the Black Dragon." He gave a darkly amused chuckle. "You really think that self-important narcissist would spend time studying how to improve the deadliest weapon on the face of the planet? Let's face it, he didn't even create the original model in the first place."

"You're talking about Asherah," Claw mused. "Back in Ancient Egypt."

Cutter gave another small laugh. "Indeed it was." He raised a questioning eyebrow. "Have you met the female Fallen?"

"Once, in passing. It was a very long time ago. *Eventful* would be the best description of how things turned out." The two long-lived beings sat silent for a while with their memories. Eventually, Claw asked, "So why are you here?"

The old man turned to the two children that he had made into orphans. "Bobby, Katy, you must not follow Claw on his quest for the Virtuous Man. It is folly."

"Why should we believe you?"

Three sets of eyes, one human, one vampire, one construct, turned toward the eight-year-old girl. It was the first time that she had spoken since Bobby had made the campfire and her small voice cut across the still night air. Bobby reached out and lay his hand on top of hers.

"I have committed possibly the worst crime to a child that a being can. I robbed you of your parent, causing you to have to fend for yourselves in this cruel world. Eventually, I found the courage required to try and atone for that sin and I followed you when you set out on your quest with the Eternal Talisman. I decided there and then that I must not let any more harm come to you. This is why I cannot hold my peace right here, right now. I say again that the man that he," Cutter pointed to the vampire with the mouthpiece of his pipe, "is looking for does not exist. Spallucci is dead. There is no Man of Virtue." He held up a gnarled hand as Claw opened his mouth to protest. "Your father was a good man. Not only that, he was influential. He was part of a growing movement that was rising up against Kanor. Removing him from the equation was supposed to squash that rebellion flat before it gathered momentum. However, your involvement with the disastrous shenanigans of Jason and your encounter with Asmodeus yesterday will ensure one thing and one thing alone, you will have been noticed.

"Kanor's forces will come for you."

"I will protect them," Claw protested.

Cutter drew deep on his pipe and blew out a long stream of smoke. Once again, he pointed the long implement at the vampire, swaying the mouthpiece from side to side: "And how did your last encounter with a Fallen work out for you? No, these children should come with me. I can protect them better than you." His voice softened. "It is the least that I can do."

"Katy," said Bobby, "what do you think?"

The light of the fire danced in the young girl's eyes. "I'm tired," she replied. "I want to go to sleep." And, with that, she curled up in front of the campfire, pulled a blanket over herself and closed her eyes.

Bobby ran his fingers through his sister's hair. "We need to think about this. Let us sleep on it. We'll decide in the morning."

Cutter nodded.

"In the meantime," the boy continued, "I think it

would be best if you left us for now. I think I speak for both of us that we find your presence somewhat unsettling."

For a moment, Bobby thought that the Shadow Wraith would protest, but instead, it rose to its feet, nodded and walked away from the clearing, leaving the tired children alone with their vampiric companion.

Bobby's sleep was far from restful. Sharp flashes of fleeting images caused him to toss and turn on the hard-packed ground.

To begin with, the dreams were warm and comforting. Images of his father drifted before his eyes: the kind man fashioning a leg for a chair, his strong hands gliding a plane along the smooth wooden surface; his father sat resting in his armchair, gazing into the crackling hearth; his father cradling an infant Katy in his arms and running his callused fingers through Bobby's unruly mop of hair.

But they soon took on a darker, more disturbing feel. The screams of his mother dying in childbirth; his father being led away by Teller's father; his father dying at the end of Cutter's arm.

As his father died in front of him, Bobby screamed out and all the onlookers of the barbaric execution turned to face him expectantly. They stood and stared at him as if waiting for him to act, looks of puzzlement on their faces.

All except one.

An old woman pushed her way through the crowd, leaning heavily on a stout, weathered walking stick, the hue of which was not too dissimilar to her old, wrinkled face, tanned by many years' labour under a harsh sun. As the rest of the crowd stood agape, motionless, she paused in front of Bobby, leaned on her stick and peered at him. As she did, Bobby could not help but gasp. Her eyes were unlike any that he had ever seen before. They contained no irises or pupils but were a mass of swirling water, small flashes of fire cascading within their azure depths. As he peered into those depths, he felt as if he were drowning and all around him the waters were singing in a three-fold melody. His head swam as he was lifted beyond the skies, far beyond the stars to which humanity had longed to travel so many centuries ago. He was carried up on the lilting tune that mingled with his blood, pumped his heart at such a rate that he thought the organ would explode, before being settled back down in a wide green field where a solitary oak tree stood sentinel. The old woman stood before him, but she was not alone. On her left stood a woman the age his mother had been when she had died; on her right a girl not much older than himself. Both of them looked at the confused boy with the same swirling watery eyes as the old crone.

As three, they nodded in agreement.

"This one," the old woman smiled, "will do."

Bobby awoke with a start, his hands flailing around his blanket, reassuring himself that none of what he had witnessed had been real. He was still in the small clearing. Claw was seemingly asleep on the other side of the fire, enveloped in his voluminous cloak which would protect him from the rays of the sun that were creeping over the horizon. Katy was…

Gone!

Bobby snatched back his sister's blanket and saw just flattened grass. He pressed his hand to the ground. It was still warm; she could not be far. The boy momentarily glanced over to the sleeping vampire but decided that his fiery sister had probably gone off in a huff. As such, she would need a gentler, more knowing hand to rein her back in. He rose to his feet and saw that she was not out in the open marshland where they had battled the constructs, so set off following the path in the other direction.

## Chapter Two

Bobby found that it wasn't exactly hard to follow the route that his sister had taken. It appeared that the irate eight-year-old had spent as much time hitting out at random bushes and patches of weeds as she had stormed off on her own to goodness knew where. Bobby couldn't help but smile as he saw first one plant thwacked in half, then another. He imagined Katy chuntering to herself as she whipped a make-believe wooden sword first one way then the next, striking down imaginary opponents that dared to get in her way.

There, was an annoying older brother: thwack!

There, was a mysterious vampire: chop!

There, was a deadly construct: hack!

Here, was a circle of adults who kept telling her she was *too young*: crunch!

As a result, it wasn't very long before he caught up with her.

The affronted sibling was stomping back down the route along which they had travelled to reach the Rishton wetlands. The current focus of her ire was a small sapling that definitely looked like it was now no longer going to grow into any form of a majestic tree.

The image of the large, elderly oak from his dream flashed into Bobby's mind and he shoved it away. He had more important things to deal with now rather than bizarre trees and surreal, watery-eyed women.

"Katy!" the teenager called out as he ran towards her. "Wait for me!"

The small girl stopped beating seven bells out of the offensive foliage and resumed her strident march away from the campsite. "Go away!" she called out without even looking back. "Leave me alone!"

Bobby paused briefly to roll his eyes then resumed his running. He quickly caught up with the irate girl. "Where are you going?"

"Home."

Bobby sighed. "Katy, it doesn't exist anymore."

"Then I'll start again."

"What with?"

"I'll improvise."

"They burned everything. It's just ash and cinders."

"I'll find a way."

Bobby changed tack. "Why didn't you wake me?"

Katy ignored the question and carried on stomping down the beaten-up road.

"Katy, I asked…"

"I heard you."

"Well?"

The small girl abruptly drew to a halt and Bobby had to prevent himself from colliding with her back. "Because you'd have stopped me."

"And why would that be a bad thing?"

Katy momentarily glanced back the way that she had come. When she turned to face Bobby, he saw that her eyes were wet. "I... I liked Cutter," she stammered, fighting back the tears.

"So did I."

"He killed Dad."

Bobby nodded.

"We trusted him. How can we trust *anyone*?"

Bobby sighed and knelt down on one knee, bringing himself to his sister's eye level. He reached up and thumbed a tear away from her cheek. "I don't know," he admitted. "Everything seems so... so... complicated." His final word was expelled with an air of frustration.

Katy shook her head, her dirt-encrusted hair swaying from side to side. "No, it's not. It's simple. We need to be strong. We need to stand on our own and survive. We don't need the others. We just need to learn how to be stronger than anyone or anything else."

Her brother frowned. "And how do you expect us to do that?"

The small girl shrugged, then stared wide-eyed over Bobby's shoulder. "I don't have an answer to that problem yet. However, what I do know is that, right now, we need to run!"

Bobby turned his head in the same direction and quickly rose to his feet as he saw a pack of hungry-looking dogs stalking their way out of the undergrowth further along the road.

*Is this to be my life now?* Bobby thought to himself as deceitful bracken lashed him across his protective arm. *Am I just going to spend my time running from one thing after another?* He leapt over a fallen tree and plunged further on into the dense undergrowth.

The dogs were in hard pursuit having emerged up

the path between the children and the campsite. The siblings had quickly deduced that to stay out in the open would have been suicide — the lithe dogs would have been upon them by their second or third footfall — so they had plunged into the scrubby woodland by the side of the road, hoping that it would prove more of an obstruction to the hounds than it did to them.

So far they seemed to have been correct.

But, only just.

When the children had been pursued a few days previous by the squad of constructs, they had had speed and agility on their side. The golems may have been relentless, but they had been big, bulky and relatively slow. So it had been possible for the siblings to put space between them and their pursuers, allowing them the opportunity to hide. The dogs, however, were far more fleet of foot and seemingly in desperate need of a quick, nourishing meal. So it was that they barked, yowled and yipped as they plunged through the dense woodland in pursuit of their quarry, seemingly snapping at the children's heels.

Bobby thought there were seven in total. He had managed a cursory headcount as they had set off at a cracking pace, desperate not to end up as a canine snack, but for all he knew there could be more, there could be less.

He prayed for the latter.

His ears were full of just three noises: the baying of the dogs, the crashing of his feet and the pounding of his heart, as Katy and he emerged into an opening surrounded by a copse of trees.

*Completely* surrounded by a copse of trees.

The children frantically scanned the densely

treacherous plants that seemed to corral them in for their pursuers. There was no way out save the way that they had entered.

And that way was now blocked.

One by one, the dogs slunk in through the same small gap in the trees through which the children had emerged. The wild canines' heads were low; their hackles were raised. An ominous, rumbling growl seemed to echo through the small clearing as the hunters ascertained just how much of a threat their prey would be. Not taking their eyes off the dogs, Bobby and Katy bent down and picked up the only weapons to hand, a pair of stout, arm-long branches. The children hefted them in their hands, testing the weight and simultaneously showing the dogs that they were not going to go down without a fight.

The dogs did not care.

They launched at the children.

Some years ago, his father had been commissioned to turn a particular piece of wood into a vase. One of the villagers of Irlingbury had found the piece of timber whilst out foraging for food in the nearby woods. It had been of quite a size, with a rich grain running through its middle. Rather than doing as many would and simply hacking it to pieces for fuel, they had brought it to Howard and asked him to make a vase in which to hold spring flowers. They had decided that they wanted something of beauty in their life.

Bobby had sat in his father's workshop as his father, in turn, had sat and stared thoughtfully for a long time at the piece of wood, occasionally turning it over in his hands, his eyes tracing the curves of the grain. Then, with a resolute nod, the woodworker had set about carving, shaving and hollowing out the timber until, some hours later, a beautiful vase sat on his workbench. It was a vibrant mix of varying shades of browns, tans and yellows. Swirling patterns spiralled around its body and whorls bloomed from their midst, drawing the onlooker's eye.

To put it simply, it was perfection.

When Bobby asked him how he had known how to produce such a gorgeous piece, his father replied, "Instinct. I studied what was in front of me before committing myself. Then, when I was sure I had all the details in my head, I acted purely on instinct. It is something you should apply to all walks of life. If you correctly link your eyes and your heart, your path will always be true."

These words echoed through his head as the wild dogs loped across the clearing. His eyes quickly scanned the situation in front of him. Four of the dogs were small and wiry. These were the ones who led the charge, their nimble bodies drawing speed quicker than their comrades. They would reach Bobby and Katy first. Behind them were two medium-sized canines. These looked older, more powerful. Their bulky muscles rippled on their shoulders as saliva dripped from their sharp teeth. Then, finally, the largest of the pack ran at the rear, but his size and powerful frame suggested that he would not stay there. As the smaller dogs snapped and harried their prey, he would stride through on his four sure paws before closing his powerful jaws around their future lunch's neck.

In short, Bobby surmised that they would have to fend off the smaller dogs first whilst preventing them from doing any damage before the heavier brutes came in to finish the job.

He had no idea how Katy and he would succeed.

The odds were totally overwhelming.

Mind you, they had survived a pitched battle with a battalion of constructs…

Bobby heard himself scream in rage as he swung his improvised weapon at the lead attacker. His stout branch connected with its brown muzzle and the dog yelped in surprise as it swerved off to the left, colliding with its similar-sized counterpart. Bobby continued to thrash and beat at the two smaller dogs, before swinging a roundhouse blow into one of the medium-sized dogs that had approached what it considered to be his unprotected flank. The dog snarled as the blow struck it alongside its tattered ear before lunging forward once more, this time accompanied by the two smaller hounds. Bobby found himself edging backwards to the wall of undergrowth as he swung increasingly more desperate blows at the snapping and snarling teeth that were drawing closer and closer. A quick glance to his right showed him that Katy was in a pretty much similar situation.

His heart finally sank when he felt sharp twigs and dry leaves brush up against his back.

It was then that the largest of the wild dogs launched straight towards him.

At first, Bobby screamed in abject terror at the sight of the deadly teeth plunging through the snarling pack towards his face. He then screamed in utter surprise as the dog flew across the clearing, where it remained pinned against a tree by a thundering horizontal torrent of water.

The other dogs judged quite rightly that their tasty meal was suddenly not worth the effort and, yelping in fright, they scattered as their pack leader squirmed against the forceful tsunami. As the dogs bolted, Bobby's eyes followed the pounding water back to its source and gaped in amazement. A woman with long dark hair was walking confidently into the clearing, her arm outstretched and the water miraculously flowing from her painted fingernails. She was dressed in what could only be described as a stylish manner: red leather trousers that fitted her form perfectly and a long flowing black travelling overcoat. Upon her face was a grin of intense enjoyment as she continued to bombard the helpless dog with her impossible water.

Eventually, the dog went completely limp and the woman ceased her bombardment, allowing it to fall lifelessly to the forest floor. She strode across the clearing, peered down at the deceased canine and poked it with her glossy boot. Seemingly satisfied with her work, she turned toward the two children.

Bobby reached out to Katy with a protective hand but his sister pushed it away, confidently walking over to the stranger, her face radiant with admiration. "Wow!" she breathed. "That was amazing!

"Can you teach *me* how to do it?"

The woman crossed her arms and smiled down at the girl who stood brazenly in front of her. "Well, aren't you the cutest little button?" Her voice was rich and her diction was unlike anything that Bobby had ever heard before. It oozed confidence. She stepped towards Katy and hunkered down. As she did, Bobby noticed that small flames flickered mischievously in her pupils. "Most people would run away from me, but not you." Reaching out one of her finely manicured hands, the woman ran her fingers through Katy's knotted hair. "But look at this," she tutted. "We really ought to do something about it." As she spoke, droplets of water eddied out from her fingers and wove in and out of the child's dirty hair, cleaning and unknotting the locks.

"You know," she seemed to muse to herself as water droplets ran along Katy's hair, washing out the accumulated grime, "I could take you to a grand palace where beautiful servants would pamper you and groom you. They would make you feel like true royalty. How about a bath in nice, hot water? Would you like that? You poor little thing, you look like you haven't had a decent soak in… well, forever."

"We had a bath in a pond the other day," Katy informed the stranger. "After some constructs chased us. We were seriously stinky."

The woman's red lips curled up in a genuine smile as she raised a slim eyebrow. "A quick dip with aquatic wildlife is no substitute for a nice warm soak, trust me."

When she seemed satisfied that Katy's hair was dirt-free, the curious woman snapped her fingers and the water evaporated, leaving Katy's hair the cleanest that it had been in a long time. "Much better," the woman mused. "Far more fitting."

"Fitting for what?" Katy asked.

"Why, fitting for a student of course," the stranger smiled. "You did say that you wanted to *learn*, didn't you?"

Katy's head rapidly bobbed up and down in excitement.

The woman held out her hand. "Well, come on, then. Let's go." She made to walk away and Katy made to follow, before pausing. She turned to Bobby. "Come on," she encouraged. "Let's go."

The boy just stood with his mouth agape. "What? Are you serious?"

Katy nodded. "Absolutely. Don't you see? Imagine what we can learn."

"Katy, we don't know this woman. Just because she rescued us from a pack of wild dogs doesn't mean that we can *trust* her. We don't even know her name."

There was a sense of movement from the edge of the clearing which resolved itself into the form of Claw, the vampire. Scowling out from under his dark hood, he growled, "Bobby's right. You *can't* trust her. And as for her name, it's Asherah. She's one of the Fallen, and she's trouble."

The Fallen peered at the vampire with what appeared to be a vague curiosity. "Have we met?" she asked, tapping a manicured nail against her chin. "Your face is vaguely familiar, but I don't recall all," she waved her hand dismissively at his cloaked attire, "...*this*."

Claw started to circle slowly towards Bobby, not once taking his eyes off the woman in front of him. The boy started to feel that he regarded her to be far more dangerous than the dogs she had just despatched. "Just the once. In Lancaster. You were leeching off a friend of mine before you tried to destroy his city."

Asherah clicked her fingers in recognition. "Oh yes, I remember now. You were the quiet one. Quite young, from what I recall. And I must say, that's really a harsh accusation you're throwing around there."

"You tried to get the entire city to commit suicide."

"I was in a bad place."

"From what I've heard, that seems to be a permanent state of residence for you."

"You listen to me, *little one*, when you've been around and done as much as I have, life tends to throw you an innumerate amount of curveballs. I can't help it if I'm just in the habit of picking them up and throwing them right back."

"Causing collateral damage in the process," Claw snapped.

"Then people should learn to duck." Asherah let out a deep sigh. "Anyway, enough of this. Come on, Katy," she held out her hand to the small girl, "let's go."

To Bobby's horror, his sister made to head off with Asherah, but before the eight-year-old could place her hand into that of the Fallen, Claw slipped between the two of them. "I can't let you do that," he growled.

The Fallen gave a disgruntled groan. "Oh, for goodness sake, will you just go away."

"I'm not letting you take the girl."

"But she wants to come with me. I can teach her so much."

"Of that, I have no doubt, but that doesn't mean that she should learn it."

Asherah looked around the vampire to Bobby's sister. "You see what he's doing, Katy? He's manipulating you, just like the Children of Cain have always manipulated humanity. They go off on their pointless little quests, dragging people along and eventually getting them killed. I heard what happened to the other two. Do you want to end up like them? Or do you want to be so powerful that no one can push you around anymore?"

"You're twisting things."

"Like hell I am!" Asherah erupted, her cool facade slipping. "I've watched your lot over the years, lurking in the shadows, thinking that you're so superior. Don't forget that while I was in Lancaster, I spent time with Samuel. He told me about how you and yours were constantly jerking his chain, getting him to do what you wanted whilst always keeping him in the dark. You used him like you use everyone else."

"Don't you dare talk about Sam! You betrayed him when you threw your lot in with Kanor."

"Well, it's not like he's going to complain now, is he? Samuel's dead."

Claw shook his head violently. "No. He's out there. I'll find him."

Asherah threw back her head and cruel laughter brayed from her mouth. "And there he is, the fanatical zealot dragging all those around him on a futile quest for his *Man of Virtue*. The prophecy is a lie! There is no Virtuous Man and, if there was, it definitely isn't Samuel. He's dead." She paused and the flames in her pupils flickered slightly as a melancholy filled her voice: "I was with him when he died."

Claw shook his head again. "You're lying. Just like you always do. You'd been sent Beyond before the day he was supposed to have died. It was the day that Lucifer and Abaddon fought at All Saints; the day the devices were detonated in Israel. I'd never forget that day. No one who witnessed it would — the utter devastation."

Asherah's lips curled up just a fraction. "Your little gang never really *got* him, did you? Like I said, jerking his lead this way and that, like a little puppy to play with one minute, then kick the next. Samuel was far more than any of you could ever have envisaged. You never truly saw just how resilient he was. Yes, I was sent Beyond, but who do you think came and saved me? Who do you think kept a promise he had made when he was holding me in his arms when everyone else had rejected me? Samuel kept his promise. He came for me. Then, no sooner had we set foot in this new creation…"

"So how *did* he die?" Claw butted in. "Who killed him?"

"Who do you think? Who wiped out almost everything that was beautiful about this insignificant piece of rock drifting through the blackness of space?"

The vampire stood silently as the enormity of what the Fallen had said sunk in.

Asherah nodded to herself. "So you see, your little quest is in vain. The prophecy was false. There is no Virtuous Man; there is only the Black Dragon. As a result, it's up to each and every one of us to stand on our own two feet and make the best of the cards we've been dealt. And," she smiled, "if that means you have to play with a marked deck to gain the upper hand, so be it." She held out her hand to Katy.

"You still can't take her."

The Fallen took a deep breath and a sly smile formed on her lips. "And you really think you can stop me?" It was then that Bobby heard a tune start to drift across the clearing. It took him a while to realise from where it was coming, but it began to dawn on the teenager that Asherah was humming the lilting melody. It grew in intensity, filling his head and making him feel weak at the knees. He slumped to the forest floor, as did Claw. His heart thumped in his chest and clouds parted as sunlight streamed in on the undeniable fact that the woman standing in front of him was the most wonderful person ever to have walked the face of the planet. How could he have doubted her? Of course she had his best interests at heart.

She shook her head and the song ceased.

Bobby felt empty and discarded.

"Cool," Katy whispered.

"It is rather. Come with me and I can teach you how to do that and so much more. You'll never be a victim again; never be a pawn in someone else's game."

Katy slipped her hand into Asherah's. The Fallen clicked her fingers and, with a loud snap, the two of them vanished.

# Chapter Three

For a while, Bobby and Claw walked in silence.

*Katy's gone: the teenage boy thought to himself.* She wasn't next to him, hitting at plants with a makeshift sword. She wasn't complaining that she was hungry, even though she had just eaten. She wasn't crying out that she wanted to be bigger and stronger, able to take down those that bullied and oppressed her.

Because she was gone.

Ever since his father had placed her gently in his arms, she had always been there. She had been his responsibility. When their father had been taken ill after their mother had died, Bobby had become the one to watch over his younger sibling. He had been the one to feed her, wash her, look after her.

To keep her safe.

He had failed.

What had happened? Why had she gone with Asherah, a complete stranger? Why had she turned her back on him?

*It was because she thought I was weak. She thought that I was going to go running after Claw on his quest for the Virtuous Man.* Bobby sighed. Did she really think that he thought more of that so-called quest than he did of her? Did she think that she would get more attention from the female Fallen?

As the two of them walked to where the horses were tied, the boy said, "I want to go after her. I need to rescue Katy."

Claw stood with his back to Bobby. His shoulders rose and fell under the heavy cloak. "Bobby, that's just not possible. You saw how strong Asherah is. That was just a mild taste of her power. I've seen her use it to do much worse."

"But there has to be a way. We can't just abandon my sister."

The vampire ran a gloved hand over his horse, which whinnied softly at his touch. "I'm sorry, Bobby. I need to resume my search for the Virtuous Man. Only when I find him can we end all this once and for all, with the death of Kanor."

Bobby felt his eyes begin to burn with hot tears. "Then she was right. You don't care about anybody else. You and your kind just use us and discard us when we're an inconvenience. You don't mind having us along for the ride, but when things get complicated, you just cut us loose."

"Bobby..." he began.

"No! There's no explanation. You claim to be looking for a Man of Virtue, yet what could be less virtuous than leaving a girl in the hands of a Fallen? Do you think Tigress and Scorpion would leave it like that? What about your friend, Sam? What about him?"

Claw's hood shifted from his horse to the two other riderless mounts then over to Bobby. "Scorp and Tigress would berate me and badger me until we rode off on any excuse to give Asherah a bloody nose. Sam…" He shook his head. "You really remind me of him, you know? A normal person that's been dragged into a very un-normal world. I hope you meet him someday. I think the two of you would really get on."

"Do you think he's dead?"

The vampire resolutely shook his head. "Not for an instant, and I know one other thing for sure."

"What's that?"

"He'd be telling me that we need to rescue Katy."


They travelled for three solid days. This time, Bobby rode solo and Claw rode with the spare steed tied to his saddle. The first day, for Bobby, was mainly spent overcoming his fear of the beast that carried him through the deserted countryside. As the centres of population became increasingly more sparse, until they were eventually cantering through what could only be described as wilderness, the teenager started to find his rhythm and was able to forget that he was atop an animal that could easily throw him to the ground then trample him under its powerful hooves.

He was helped in overcoming his fear by Claw's methods of distraction. These mainly involved talking. In fact, he talked far more than Bobby had ever considered him capable of. When there had been the three Children of Cain, it had normally been the garrulous Tigress who had filled the silences, with the mute Scorpion not saying a word and Claw seemingly comfortable to let the fiery redhead take centre stage. Now though, he talked almost incessantly, mainly about things which had happened in the dim, distant past. It was as if something inside of him had been uncorked and hundreds of years of memories had been released.

He described the world in which he had grown up as a mortal, the one where he had been reborn as a vampire. He talked about modes of transport that hadn't existed for over a thousand years. He waxed lyrical about famous people known as *celebrities,* of whom the whole world seemed to be in awe. He pooh-poohed politicians and world leaders who failed to stop a crisis in a far-off land that led to a whole country being destroyed by things that he described as *nuclear devices.*

"The Damascus Accord was a front for those in power pretending that they had smoothed things over," he explained. "They realised that their voters wanted the matter resolved so they made it appear that they had done just that. There was this famous shot of the American president standing on the steps of the conference centre waving a sheet of paper in his hand." He snorted in amusement.

"What is it?"

"Funny thing was, they found him dead in bed the morning that the devices went off in Israel. When they performed an autopsy on his body, it appeared that his heart had been burned to a crisp. No one ever claimed responsibility, but I have my suspicions."

He then neatly diverted the topic onto something called the *Infinity Gauntlet* and rambled on unintelligibly for three hours about a guy named *Thanos.*

Bobby glazed over at that bit. He felt a bit guilty at doing so as Claw was *really* enthusiastic about the whole thing, but to the teenager from a world without mass entertainment, it just sounded like words, words, words.

Eventually, when they reached a suitable place to

rest the horses, Bobby asked his travelling companion, "So, where are we actually going? Do you know where Asherah has taken Katy?"

Claw heaved the saddles off their steeds and settled the horses as he said, "I have a fair idea where she is. The Fallen has a palace, for want of a better word, over by a place called Sewell. Have you heard of it?" When Bobby shook his head, the vampire continued. "It used to be a small village next to a huge reservoir that was constructed in order to supply water to the local area, Irlingbury included. Asherah set up camp there as water is her elemental power."

"I remember you saying so before the battle at Rishton. She used it to drive off the dogs."

Claw nodded and began to lay a fire. "Remember, Asherah and Asmodeus are fallen angels. This makes them incredibly powerful. Far more so than Kanor's constructs. They used to exist in the Realm known as Heaven. There are two other realms: the Physical realm, which is this one, and Beyond."

"She mentioned that before, didn't she?"

Claw nodded. "It's a hell dimension. A terrible place, by all accounts. Asherah and Asmodeus both wound up there."

"How?"

"They were killed here in the Physical Realm. But I'm digressing somewhat. As I said, Asherah chose Sewell so she could be next to the water there because it's her element."

Bobby pondered this for a moment. "And Asmodeus' element is the lightning that shot from his hands when he attacked you."

Claw struck a flint, causing the tinder to spark into

life. He stretched his neck and Bobby could hear the tendons pop. "Correct. And it hurts like a bitch. Each angel has their own ability, their power. What we need is one to use theirs to defeat Asherah."

"And that's where we're going? To find another angel?"

The fire danced in the vampire's eyes as he sat silent for a moment. "He's someone I first met a long time ago." He pulled a face.

"What is it?"

"We didn't exactly hit it off." Claw poked the fire with a stick and embers rose into the night air. "But he's a good person and incredibly powerful. More so than Asherah, in fact. As long as he agrees to use his powers."

"What's this angel's name?"

"It's Michael. And he's not just *any* angel. He was the Archangel in charge of the army of Heaven."

On the evening of the third day of travel, Bobby found himself standing at the bottom of a craggy hill. Up above, the moon was but a thin sliver of silver, like a bow readying itself to fire an arrow into the dark.

"So, he's up there?"

Claw had removed his cowl and nodded. "As I said, Michael keeps himself to himself. He doesn't like visitors." The vampire paused as if recalling a previous visit. "He *really* doesn't like visitors."

Bobby nodded and, as they began the steep climb up the winding, overgrown path, Claw filled him in somewhat with regard to the former general of Heaven's army. On the day of the Divergence, there had been a huge battle between the angels and the constructs. It had been brutal and had not gone well. When Kanor had risen, Michael had refused to get involved and had walked away from his duties. The rest of the angels had retreated to the Heavenly Realm, leaving him here on Earth, an outcast.

"As you can see," Claw said, pointing out vague movement of large white blobs in the gathering gloom, "he turned his hand to other ventures."

"Are… are they sheep?"

"Immortal beings have to have a hobby," Claw grimaced. "Something to while away the long, tedious years of bitter regret."

As Bobby peered up at the not insignificant flock wandering aimlessly around past an old, gnarled tree, he became aware of a sudden change in the air around him. He shivered as the long grass upon which the sheep were munching began to sway back and forth. "Wind's getting up," he observed. "We'd better get a move on."

There was the smooth sound of Claw drawing his sword. "That's no ordinary wind."

As soon as the vampire had spoken, Bobby felt himself get slapped in the face by an unseen force. He cried out and staggered backwards. It was only the quick reflexes of Claw that prevented him from tumbling back down the hillside. The vampire's arm whipped out and his gloved hand caught the teenage boy by the arm. Bobby forced his head down and tried to resume his footing as an increasingly tempestuous gale circled around them. As the wind blew and howled, it seemed to gather up debris from the ground: sticks, grass, mud, stones. These snapped left and right, pummelling the two intruders, smacking into their shoulders, scratching at their faces. Claw stood firm footed and swiped around with his sword, his preternatural speed managing to bat away the worst of the debris. He began to doggedly advance up the path, pulling Bobby along in his wake, protecting the boy from the worst of the onslaught.

The wind began to shriek and, in its high-pitched wailing, the two of them could make out voices demanding that they leave, that they return to where they came from. Bobby blinked against the elemental force and, as he did so, he witnessed the most incredible of things. The debris that had been snatched up from the hillside was forming into the bodies of beings that stood in the maelstrom to block their way. Claw struck out with his sword at the beings made from leaves, grass, sticks and stones, trying to hack them apart, but every time his sword appeared to strike home, the matter from which the beings were fashioned would simply spread apart, ensuring that the sword just swept through without causing any damage. The matter would then resume its form, creating a hazard through which Bobby and Claw could not pass.

Bobby felt something hard pressed into his hand. It was the vampire's sword. Unable to speak across the howling wind, Claw pressed his hand firmly around Bobby's, the message clear: "Don't drop it." Then, he reached to his belt and unlatched his long whip. Flexing his arm, the weapon cracked out through the storm and lashed itself around a branch of the old tree under which the sheep stood, still quietly grazing as if nothing was happening, just a short distance away. Bobby felt a brief squeeze of warning, then the world was a blur and the two of them were through the maelstrom and standing under the tree, Claw's whip coiled around his wrist. As Bobby bent over to get his breath, he watched the wind finally drop, all the debris it had fashioned into guards falling lifelessly to the ground.

The two companions were about to resume their

journey up the hill when there was a clanking of heavy bells as the somewhat ramshackle flock of unkempt sheep wandered purposefully onto the track. Bobby tried to walk around them, but the flock shuffled as one in front of him, blocking his path. He looked over to Claw for help.

The vampire couldn't help but smile as he waded into the morass of damp-smelling fleece and grabbed one of the animals by its curled horns, intending to heave it out of the way. However, he swore loudly as another member of the ovine group butted him resoundingly on the rear. "Seriously? Attack sheep?"

The vampire and the boy were now completely surrounded by the flock and were unable to move forward or even retreat back down the hill. They appeared to be drifting helplessly in an ocean of wool and bleating.

"At least," came a deep voice from higher up the track, "they're not fatal. Well, not usually."

Bobby managed to force himself around so that he could see the source of the voice. Up above them stood a tall, broad-shouldered, dark-skinned man. He was dressed in simple homespun clothing and his tightly curled hair was wild and unkempt. "Not usually?" the boy called.

"Maurice there," the man pointed with a sturdy staff at the largest of the sheep, "does tend to have a foul temper, so you would be best not to provoke him. I'm going to call them off now and you're going to walk back down that hill. Don't come back."

"Michael! Wait!" Claw called out. "We need your help."

"I can't help anyone. You of all people should know that."

"You're our only hope."

Bobby noted that the Archangel raised an eyebrow. "You quoting one of your favourite films at me?"

"It's Asherah," the vampire continued, ignoring the comment. Instead, he gestured around the cohort of sheep to Bobby. "She's got his sister. We can't let her corrupt the girl, can we?"

"I can't help you."

"Please," Bobby called out, "at least let us up. We've travelled so far. We need somewhere to stay for the night."

Michael peered down through the gloom. "How old are you, boy?"

"About fourteen, I think. I'm not sure."

"The last time I helped a young lad, it did not go well."

"We can't live in the past, though."

"But it does have a habit of haunting us."

In his head, Bobby saw Cutter transform into the deadly Shadow Wraith. "That I certainly know, sir. However, we mustn't let those ghosts determine our future, must we?"

The Archangel leaned heavily on his staff. He nodded, opened his mouth and let out a deep braying noise. The sheep dissipated and wandered off, presumably to go back to their grazing. He turned and stalked back up the path.

Bobby and Claw exchanged glances and followed.

Atop the craggy hillside stood a small, precisely fashioned hut constructed from intricately hewn timber. In a little garden by the porch, rows of regimented vegetables stood to attention. "You can take the general out of Heaven..." Claw murmured.

"That life is far behind me now."

"Tell that to your carrots."

"If you're going to criticise my agricultural expertise, you can walk right back down that path."

Bobby stepped forward. "We're sorry, sir," he apologised. "It's just it's been a very long journey and we are somewhat drained. Both physically and emotionally."

The Archangel nodded. "The Lady of the Sea can do that to people. She sweeps in like a tsunami and devastates all around her." He glanced at the vampire, then back to the boy. "I was about to make a meal. Would you care to help?"

"You know I can't cook," Claw protested.

A smile formed on Michael's face. "That's okay then, as I wasn't asking you." He turned back to Bobby. "You know what to do with a carrot?"

"Since I was half my height."

The smile travelled up to the dark-skinned man's eyes and, for just an instant, Bobby was sure that he had seen the twinkling of flames in his black pupils before he motioned for the boy to follow him into the cabin. Inside, a table was already laid out with numerous precisely placed vegetables ready to be peeled, chopped and cooked. Propped up against a wooden beaker and standing guard over the ingredients was a small, tattered doll that had been fashioned from scraps of material. Bobby was about to ask about this curious anomaly when the Archangel enquired, "So, is Don Quixote still chasing windmills?"

Bobby frowned and picked up a short knife with which he started to prepare a bowl of the orange-coloured vegetables. "I don't..."

The Archangel chuckled warmly and peered out of

the window at the vampire sitting resolutely by himself on a stool on the porch. "It's okay. It's an old reference. Is he still on his quest?"

"For the Virtuous Man?" Bobby nodded and thoughtfully sliced up the carrots as Michael shredded some sort of leafy green. "He's looking for a man called Sam Spallucci. Tigress and Scorpion seemed to think he was dead though."

"I'm sure they do." Michael's knife paused mid-stroke. "Although, I believe you just used a past tense there…"

Bobby's head bobbed up and down in three short jerks. "A few days ago. We were ambushed by a squad of constructs led by Asmodeus. Scorpion was killed in battle and Tigress…" The image of the redheaded vampire's immolation filled Bobby's head. He fought back hot tears.

Michael nodded. "I understand." He slid the chopped leaves into a cooking pot and began to prepare an onion.

"I met Spallucci twice, you know?"

"When?"

"The first time was at his mother's funeral. The second was when he had been called in to investigate something that had happened in my church."

Bobby frowned. "Your church?"

The Archangel's knife hovered over the half-sliced onion. "His job was to work out why unusual things happened. I had been sent to watch over a boy a few years older than you. As a result, I was posing as a curate…" He paused when he spotted Bobby's confusion at the unfamiliar word. "That's an assistant priest at a church." When Bobby nodded at this, he continued. "Well, something *very* unusual happened and the senior priest at the church, the vicar, called Spallucci in." He looked down at the onion as if he could see the scene replaying on the allium's white flesh.

"What happened?"

"I'm not entirely sure. Something far more curious than what he had come to investigate." He finished his dicing of the onion and slid it into the pot. "How are those carrots?"

Bobby showed him the chopped root vegetables.

"Perfect. Let's put them in the pot and see how our friend is doing outside, shall we?" He adjusted the heat in the fireplace and headed out onto the porch, Bobby at his heel.

Claw was still sitting on the small stool, apparently peering out into the dark. "That's quite a drop there," he motioned to the edge of the hill, just past the hut. "You lost any of your sheep over it?"

"They have far more sense than most people do. They intuitively stay away from danger rather than apparently seek it out."

The vampire rose from his seat in one fluid motion and casually wandered over to the edge of the precipice. He peered over and gave a low whistle. "Yep, quite a drop."

"You want to be careful," Michael warned, his voice somewhat tense. "You don't want to fall over there."

Claw's shoulders gave a quick shrug. "Not too much of a biggie. Vampire, remember?" He gave the sheer drop one last look then asked, "What the hell are you doing here?"

Michael groaned and made to reply, but the vampire cut him short.

"No! Don't! No feeble excuses. You're the general

of Heaven's army. You dwelt in the Sanctuary of Yahweh. You looked upon the Presence of God! Why on earth are you sat on the top of a ruddy hillside, tending sheep? Why aren't you leading the world against Kanor?"

The Archangel swallowed. "Because I don't want to see any more pointless deaths. Every time I meddle, people die. *Good* people."

"You could defeat his construct army. You beat them at Megiddo."

"You weren't there." Michael's head bowed as if he were studying the ground in front of him, his voice low, barely audible. "The cost was too high. Gabriel… the thought of where he ended up when he used the Potency. That place is a hell." He drew in a deep breath and straightened himself up. "Besides," he waved a hand around him, at his hut, his garden and his sheep, "this is what I am now. I have no powers. They died many years ago."

Bobby saw one of Claw's eyebrows rise. "Really? And what was that down on the hillside? Just smoke and mirrors?"

The Archangel just shrugged.

"You can't hide up here. The world needs you. *We* need you."

"As I said, I have no powers anymore. Only the occasional parlour trick."

The vampire slowly shook his head, then gave a glance over the edge of the hillside. "I really don't believe that. Not one bit." He turned and his eyes fixed firmly on Bobby. The next thing the boy knew, he was sailing down over the side of the cliff.

Bobby had been told before, when he was small,

that when you faced death everything went slow and your whole life flashed in front of you. One day, a farmer had come to his father to trade for a new ladder. His old one had broken whilst he had been trying to repair the thatch above his front door. One minute, the farmer had said, he had been at the top of the ladder, reaching out to wedge some new straw into the gap in the roof, the next, he was standing on nothing and he was aware that he was falling, the top rung of the ladder clutched in his hand. "It was the most bizarre experience. As I fell backwards, down to the porch below, all that I had done passed in front of my eyes: every birth of my five children; the day of my marriage; the time I got caught snatching fish from old man Harper's backyard; the time I pissed my pants when my mother took me out into the roughs to collect berries. All those and many more casually wandered past my eyes and waved hello at me. It must have taken as much time as it would walking to Orchester, yet in reallty, I crashed to the floor in the blink of an eye." He shook his head and rubbed his dirty hand against his stubbled chin. "Everything moved so slow. So slow indeed."

Bobby, as he felt the wind scream past him whilst the ground below opened its deadly arms to catch his falling body, saw none of this. There were no reassuring images from his past to comfort a possible entrance through the doors to the afterlife. There were no feelings of regret for mistakes or mishaps from his previous years.

There was just terror. Complete, absolute, terror.

He was initially aware of just two things: the rushing air buffeting up past his flailing arms; his mouth open in a piercing scream.

And then there was a white blur shooting down towards him and he was snatched away from becoming a messy tangle of squished body parts on the valley floor below. His mouth gaped and flapped as he turned to see what held him, but no words came at the sight of the white-garbed, winged being with radiant skin and fiery eyes that held him tightly in its arms.

They rose up the face of the cliff and the being alighted gently on the grassy top of the hillside. It carefully lowered Bobby to the floor before bending down and asking in a familiar voice, "Are you okay?"

"Michael?" Bobby reached out with a shaking hand to touch the Archangel's transformed attire, but his fingers paused just before they met the fabric.

"Go on. It's okay."

The vestment felt unlike any sort of clothing he had ever touched. There was no trace of a weave or a stitch. The silken material slipped between his fingertips. He gazed up into his saviour's face. "Your eyes..." he breathed. "They're on fire."

Michael nodded. "This is my true form. Well, my true anthropomorphic form." He smiled as Bobby frowned. "A form that looks *human*. Technically, angels are beings of energy, which is why we can change appearance should we so desire. This is how I normally look when I interact with others."

"Like Asmodeus and Asherah do?"

Michael nodded again. "When they were in Heaven, they looked like me. But without this." He tapped at a burnished gold plate of armour that hung moulded to his chest.

"Because you're a soldier."

"*Was* a soldier."

Bobby ran a finger over the breastplate. It felt unusually warm to the touch, a slight vibration running through the metal. "Please. We could really use your help. You're the only person I've met who could be a match for Asherah. If Tigress and Scorpion were still alive, we may have stood a chance. But now…"

The Archangel sighed and looked from the boy to the silent vampire, to his crude cottage.

"Okay. But first, we eat and, as we eat, we talk tactics."

## Chapter Four

It was decided that Bobby, Claw and Michael would set off for Sewell early the next morning. It had been mutually agreed that, although the Archangel and the vampire could have travelled through the night, Bobby was in desperate need of a good night's sleep. Michael had made up his simple bed, bade Bobby a good night and retreated out of the small bedroom.

The exhausted teenager threw himself onto the bed and didn't even make it under the covers before sleep consumed him.

Not that it was very restful.

As he fell into a deep sleep, there was at first a peaceful dream waiting for him. Bobby found himself walking through a wide meadow. Small, red flowers that he did not recognise bloomed through the stems of wild grass. In front of him, skipping in the bright sunlight was Katy. She was singing to herself and, every now and then, she would stop and pick some of the flowers, bunching them together into a small posy. Bobby smiled to himself as he followed her through the lush grass.

"Who are they for?" he called out to his kid sister.

Katy bent to add more flowers to the growing bunch. "For Mother, of course, You know how she loves them."

Bobby nodded. Their mother was indeed fond of flowers. "She'll definitely love them," he agreed. "She'll put them in that vase father made for her."

Katy stopped and frowned. "Why would she do that?"

"What else would she do with them?"

The small girl looked down at the flowers. Their scarlet colour was running from the petals, pooling in a viscous puddle at her feet. "These flowers are not for the living," she whispered. "They are for the dead." When she looked back up at Bobby, the boy took a startled step backwards. She was no longer a small, eight-year-old girl, but a young woman. Her long brown hair cascaded down over her cloaked shoulders, framing her pale skin. "I killed her!" this older version of Katy cried as the bone-white moon rose over her shoulder. Then forming her mouth into a hard smile that revealed a pair of sharp fangs, she declared, "She was just the first!"

The vampire Katy leapt forward at Bobby. He turned and fled through the long grass that was stained crimson from the blood of the flowers. The horizon was empty except for one detail toward which he found himself being inexplicably drawn — a familiar, large oak tree. As he approached it, he saw the three females from his previous dream: the child, the woman and the old crone. They nodded as one as he pulled to a halt before them, then seemed to merge into one body before they said, "We are waiting."

Bobby snapped awake, gasping for breath and his

limbs tangled in bedclothes. The bedroom door flew open and Claw was by his side. "Are you okay? We heard shouting."

Bobby's eyes snapped to the open door and saw Michael standing there, concern in his fiery eyes. "It was just a bad dream. Nothing more." He felt the reassuring grip of Claw's cold hand on his shoulder, but the Archangel's eyes were far more cautious. "Is it time to go?"

Claw nodded. "The horses are ready."

Bobby swung his legs over the edge of the bed, then asked, "Why are we riding there? Isn't Michael able to…" He clicked his fingers.

"I'm afraid, that I am somewhat out of practice," the Archangel explained as they walked through the house and out to the waiting horses. "It would be best that I conserve my energy for our encounter with Asherah. Whereas she and Asmodeus have had continual usage of their angelic powers, I…" He held his hand out to his sheep.

Bobby frowned. "But you'll be able to beat Asherah?"

Michael climbed up onto his horse, his eyes dark. "Let's go and find out, shall we?"

The journey to Sewell took the best part of two days. There was a road that led straight there, but Michael and Claw both agreed that taking the direct route into the heartland of an area dominated by the female Fallen would have been exceedingly hazardous and foolhardy. As a result, they travelled cross-country, picking their way across bleak, abandoned fields, constantly watching the horizon for movement.

The Archangel's dark eyes were fixed firmly ahead as they travelled, his mind clearly elsewhere.

Bobby pulled up even with him as they passed a ruin of red bricks that had once been someone's home. "What was it like?"

Michael turned to face him and raised an eyebrow in question.

"Here," Bobby explained. "Before the Divergence."

The angel nodded and Bobby could see him forming an acceptable answer. "Different," he finally said. "Very different." He shifted in his saddle and the reins tapped against the side of his horse. "By the time of the Divergence, humans had spread all over the planet and had even started to go out into space. They achieved incredible things, bringing the planet back from the brink of ecological disaster; eliminating poverty and hunger. They had entered a golden era.

"At least for a while.

"Some said that it was due to the battle in Wellington between Abaddon and Lucifer, the revelation that they were not alone in the universe. Some said that it was the horror of the obliteration of Israel after the arrogance of the Damascus Accord imploded. Perhaps it was just a natural progression of events. I don't know. Perhaps it was a combination of all of these factors. But, when Kanor rose and the constructs activated, humanity never saw it coming. Half the population of the world was gone overnight, either turned into what they really were or slaughtered by their loved ones. The shockwave of the catastrophe left the rest paralysed in fear, making them easy pickings for the unstoppable army of constructs as they steadily worked their way through the population, carefully culling the herd, thinning them down to a manageable level for their master."

"Why didn't he wipe everyone out completely?"

"I don't know. Perhaps he needed a workforce? Perhaps he just wanted to watch them suffer? Who knows what that dark mind thinks?" The Archangel appeared to shudder and gave a deep sigh.

"Do you think it's possible to defeat Kanor?"

Michael was silent for a short while. "Our friend there," he inclined his head to the cloaked vampire behind them, "seems to think that a mere mortal, this *Man of Virtue*, is the one to overthrow the Black Dragon. Trust me, that's just a pipe-dream. No living being could beat Kanor. He is the most powerful creature who ever walked this planet."

Bobby frowned as he considered the Archangel's words. "You're talking as if you know who he is."

Michael's eyes held Bobby's and the fires burned fiercely in his pupils. "I have my suspicions. Something happened at the battle at Megiddo; after we beat back the constructs. To this day I'm not sure what it was or how it happened. One minute someone I knew was one person, then next he was someone else, someone I had watched him become before."

Bobby frowned. "You're not making any sense."

"You have to remember this, Bobby, before the Divergence hit, Time took a different path. Heaven and the Physical Realm combined to make an eternal paradise. Angels, being creatures of energy, can still recall that. We have two sets of memories that stand side by side. I remember my friend walking up to God Himself and being given his reward for saving us. He was given the highest rank of angels. The rank of Seraph.

"But, I also experienced a reality where that never

happened. *This* reality. In *this* timeline, Heaven and the Physical Realm never converged and when I joined my friend at the end of the battle of Megiddo, he became the very entity that he had just slain and, in his hand, that being held the thing that he had used to escape Beyond."

Bobby was about to ask who Michael's friend was when the Archangel's head snapped up and he peered at the far horizon. "Company," he murmured.

Claw's horse drew up next to them. "It's a small squad," he said, motioning to the line of figures in the distance. "Not surprising as we're only a mile or so away now. You think they've seen us?"

The Archangel shook his head. "They're heading away from us. If we keep moving, we'll be there for nightfall. We'll just have to keep our eyes open and," he glared at Bobby, "keep idle chatter to a minimum." Twitching his reins, he cantered his horse off in front of the other two.

"Don't mind him," Claw reassured the boy. "He's just been through a hell of a lot."

"So I noticed," Bobby replied.

Sewell was not what Bobby had expected. Not at all.

At Michael's suggestion, they had left the horses tethered in a small barn on what appeared to be a deserted farm a few minutes' walk outside of the settlement. "We will be more mobile in the town if we enter on foot," he explained. "Should we happen to get split up, we can rendezvous back here."

As they approached the large body of water, signs of civilisation started to become apparent. Cultivated fields filled the land with humans hunched over, hard at work. Not once did anyone stand up to watch the strangers passing by. The three companions rejoined the main road and proceeded with care through an increasingly urban settlement. Bobby gaped at the housing. It was palatial by the standards that he was used to. Along clean, polished streets, freshly painted wooden houses marshalled their approach to the palace that stood before the vast lake.

Bobby sniffed and his forehead wrinkled. "What's that smell?"

A brief smile crossed Michael's face. "Something you're not used to. Cleanliness. The Lady of the Sea is not a fan of filth and squalor. All these people may be her slaves, but she'll want them to… *look their best* in their servitude." He shook his head and let out an exasperated sigh.

At the intersection of every street stood a giant carved pole that was entwined with black and red ribbons. At the base of each were plates of food, tools and carved wooden figures.

"You can take the goddess out of Canaan…" Michael muttered to himself. "Kanor may rule the land," he said to the others, "but have no doubt that this is very much Asherah's own little kingdom. She's still living the glory days of old." He nodded to himself as half a dozen constructs rounded the corner and blocked their way, a Shadow Wraith at their head. "We can use this. Just follow my lead when the time comes."

"You will come with us," declared the Shadow Wraith as it flicked its arm out to one side, forming a cruel-looking curved blade.

"Now, why would we do that?" Michael asked, standing nonchalantly in the middle of the cobbled street as if he were out for a casual stroll. "It's a glorious day.

The sun is shining and the air is clear. My fellow travellers and I are just out enjoying the sights."

"Because the Lady of the Sea demands it."

The Archangel smiled and nodded knowingly. "Your mistress has demanded many things over the millennia. She's not always got what she wanted."

"Trust me," the Wraith threatened, "this time she will." He motioned with his blade and the constructs began to march toward the three companions.

Michael stood impassively, his arms by his side.

Bobby looked nervously from the angel to the vampire.

Claw had unclipped his whip.

A slight breeze began to tickle the hairs on the back of Bobby's neck.

When the cohort of golems was about fifty paces away, Michael thrust his hands out in front of him and a sudden blast of air rocketed down the street. Bobby braced himself in order to stand firm as the elemental force sent the constructs tumbling head-over-toe like wooden pins that had been knocked over by a small child. The pinwheeling golems reached out with their arms. Their elastic limbs stretched out to grab the nearest buildings to prevent themselves from being driven all the way down the street.

The Archangel kept up his unrelenting attack and, as he did so, began to walk steadily forwards. Bobby and Claw followed behind. As they did, Bobby became aware of a familiar sensation. A pounding one-two beat of feet was rising up from the ground through his feet and then his legs. He glanced over his shoulder and blanched as he saw a second cohort of constructs approaching behind them.

"We've got a problem!" he managed to yell over the roaring winds just as a clay arm wrapped itself around his middle and yanked him backwards. The road was hard and unforgiving as he collided with the ground. He cried out and tried to pull the smooth, clasping arm away from him, but it continued to coil up his body, wrapping itself around his arms, quickly immobilising him. Bobby tried to struggle as he felt himself being dragged along the floor, but it was no use. Instead, he looked on aghast as both Michael and Claw succumbed to the same sort of attack.

In a few moments, all three of them were coiled in the unforgiving embraces of constructs.

The Shadow Wraith stalked over to them, dusting itself down and stretching itself out. Bobby watched as tears in the fabric of its simulacra of clothing miraculously knitted themselves back together. "As I was saying," it glowered, "you will come with us."

Having no current apparent means of escape, boy, vampire and angel did as they were told.

If it hadn't been for the mortal dread of impending death, Bobby would have considered himself incredibly lucky to have entered Asherah's palace. As the three of them were frogmarched up the hill from the settlement and in through the wide wooden gates of the large stone building, his breath was taken away, and not just by the constricting coils around his chest.

The immediate inside of the building was a large courtyard that would have been open to the sky had the space above not been covered with brightly coloured fabrics that fluttered gently in a soft breeze, creating a kaleidoscope of hues as the sun above shone through the textile ceiling. More of the tall wooden poles stood sentinel around the courtyard, again entwined with black and red ribbons. The whole area smelt of something incredibly sweet and not unpleasant. Around the edge of the area, draped over piles of cushions or lying on long, plush ornate seats were numerous men and women. Bobby noted that they all had two things in common: they were all incredibly attractive and none of them was wearing much in the way of clothing. They all seemed to have a listlessness to their demeanour and a faraway look in their eyes.

There was movement at the opposite end of the courtyard and a set of rich, blue curtains swept apart at the touch of an unseen hand. Asherah slid into the room. She wore her long dark hair curled up atop her head, exposing her graceful neck. She was adorned in a sleeveless dress of flowing, pearlescent fabric that seemed to glitter in the colours from the awnings above. Her bare arms were stretched out to her sides and water was spiralling around her perfect skin. She smiled warmly as she reached out and let tendrils of water stroke and caress her lounging devotees who murmured contentedly at her touch. As the droplets of water passed from one to the other, each acolyte tried unsuccessfully to reach out and keep in contact with the flowing liquid.

Finally, the Fallen stood in the middle of the room and commanded the constructs, "Release them and leave us."

The Shadow Wraith did not hesitate to bow in submission and walked out of the courtyard, accompanied by his troops.

"Well, well, well," Asherah murmured in her rich voice as she sidled over to Michael. "This truly is a surprise. "I thought you had taken up a life of *shepherding.*" The word was brimming over with distaste.

"It passes the long, fruitless years," the Archangel shrugged. "At the end of the day, they're so much easier to control than people."

"But they're so much harder to bathe." The Fallen stood directly behind him, the fabric of her dress touching his clothes. "You know that I like to keep things fresh and fragrant."

"You seem to be doing a very good job of that. I must say that I'm very impressed at what you've carved out for yourself here."

Asherah placed her chin on Michael's shoulder and leaned the side of her head against his stubbled cheek. "Are you now?" she mused, fire twinkling in her dark eyes. Her manicured hand slid up his arm. "Is that why you so brazenly walked into Sewell? To admire my handiwork?"

"That," he replied, "and to bring the Lady of the Sea a gift." He looked at Bobby and Claw, his eyes pure flame. "Two, in fact."

Bobby felt as if the earth below him had vanished and he was falling without control. When he had been small, he had gone with his mother to play on the riverbank. She had told him not to go far, but he had been insistent that he wanted to watch the water flowing over the pebbles. She had agreed, but had told him to take care as the side of the river was slippy and treacherous. At first, he had stood back from the edge, peering into the rippling water, laughing as it tinkled over the small rocks. But the excitement and the beauty had lured him closer and it wasn't long before he was standing on a muddy outcrop overhanging the babbling brook. Something silver darted underneath him and he was just about to call to his mother that he had seen a fish, when the world around him disappeared and the outcrop gave way, causing him to plummet down into the cold water below. He scrabbled and screamed until he felt the hand of his mother on his arm, pulling him up to safety. For that brief instant, it had felt as if he was going to fall through to the other side of the planet.

His mother, however, was not with him when Michael betrayed him to Asherah.

Bobby felt his stomach lurch as he suddenly found himself trapped and powerless in the lair of one of the most powerful creatures on the planet. He stole a glance at Claw. The vampire was just standing impassive, motionless.

"And, pray tell," the soft voice of the Fallen purred into the ear of the Archangel as she wrapped a hand around his chest, "why would I want these two... filthy vagrants?"

"Claw is the last of his kind," Michael stated matter-of-factly, his eyes staring straight ahead, "and I believe that the boy could be special."

The manicured hand ceased in its caressing of the Archangel's chest, the Fallen's curiosity obviously piqued. "Special? How?"

"I believe you took his sister?"

Asherah walked around in front of Michael, her eyes studying the teenage boy. Bobby felt like a mouse being sized up by an adder. "She intrigued me. I saw potential in her."

"Well, he is from the same stock. Imagine if you had two of them. Your *own* powerful pair of children. Imagine how useful that could be..."

Bobby frowned as the treacherous angel let the implication hang. He felt like he was missing something here.

The Fallen crossed her slender arms and tapped her red lips with a coloured nail. "Bring the girl!" she snapped, and the devotee closest to the curtained doorway slipped out of the room. He returned shortly with a certain eight-year-old.

"Katy!" Bobby cried out. "Are you okay?"

His sister frowned at him and joined Asherah in the middle of the room. "Why are they here?"

"Apparently, they are a gift. Do you think I should accept them?"

"What if it's a trap?"

"Shall we find out?"

Katy nodded enthusiastically.

The Fallen affectionately ruffled the girl's hair and opened her mouth. At once, the room was filled with a harmonious song that caused the lounging acolytes to commence a deep groaning of longing and desire. Bobby felt his knees weaken and he was about to sink to the floor when another, louder noise cut across the song.

Michael had his right hand raised in the air and, above him, the coloured awnings of the ceiling were in the process of being torn to shreds as a swirling column of air descended from the sky. The air roared through the room, the tempest obliterating any other noise, including the song of the Fallen. Asherah screamed mutely in frustration and opened her mouth wider in an attempt to increase the volume of her song. At the same time, she raised her hands, balls of water forming at her fingertips.

Michael nodded to Claw and, in the blink of an eye, both the vampire and Katy were gone.

Michael sprung to Bobby's side and, as Asherah's elemental power surged across the room, he grabbed the

teenager's arm with one hand and clicked the fingers on
the other.

253

# Chapter Five

The first thing that Bobby was aware of when they arrived at the rendezvous point was the sound of Katy screaming blue murder. The second was that he was going to be sick. Turning away from the sight of an irate eight-year-old beating seven bells out of a bemused vampire, Bobby leaned against a rough lattice wall of the barn and emptied the contents of his stomach.

"I'm sorry," came the concerned voice of Michael, as he placed a reassuring hand on the boy's back. "The first time is always the worst for humans. Your physical makeup is not exactly designed for teleportation."

Bobby tried to nod but just ended up dry-heaving into the soiled straw. He braced his palms against the wall and forced himself to stand up, taking in long, slow breaths. As his stomach settled, he turned his attention to the commotion on the other side of the barn.

"How dare you kidnap me! Take me back! Right now!"

The teenage boy sighed. "Katy," he said. "Please, calm down. We came to rescue you."

The small girl diverted her anger away from the

vampire and towards her older brother. "Rescue me?" she snapped, her hands on her hips. "Why would you think I need *rescuing*? Am I a rabbit in a snare? A fish on a hook? I was exactly where I wanted to be! Did you not see that place? It was a palace, Bobby! A huge palace. I was clean. I was safe. I was respected. I wasn't being dragged off on some fool's errand by," she shot an evil glare at Claw, "people we hardly know."

Bobby tried to rationalise with his furious sister. "But Asherah is one of the Fallen. She is a servant of Kanor. She can't be trusted."

Katy shook her head. "You've got it wrong. All of it."

"How so?"

"She hates Kanor as much as we do. He did something unforgivable and she wants revenge on him. She only pretends to serve him. She says that one day she will turn on him and make him suffer for what he did."

Michael approached the girl. "What did he do?"

"He killed the only man who was ever kind to her, someone who she cared about greatly."

The Archangel shook his head. "Child, she's lied to you. I've known Asherah for an incredibly long time. The only person she's ever cared about in her long, power-hungry existence has been herself."

"No!" All three males in the barn took an involuntary step backwards as the small girl stamped her foot. "You don't know her like I do. She's kind, caring and genuinely interested in me." Her voice dropped to a near whisper and Bobby shuddered as she murmured, "I can be myself around her." She looked up, tears in her eyes. "Please... Please take me back.

"You'll regret it if you don't."

The Archangel and vampire looked to the teenage

boy for a lead.

Bobby frowned. This was not exactly going to plan. Had the Fallen brainwashed his sister? Had she sung her intoxicating song and made the girl believe that the beautiful woman had her best interest at heart?

Or was it something far more sinister?

Back in Orchester, Katy had killed Teller in cold blood, pushing him off a bridge. There had been no hesitation; she had acted on pure instinct. She constantly complained that she wanted to be stronger, more powerful. She was hungering to fight back against those who hurt them. Had she found someone that she believed could teach her the skills that she needed to stand on her own two feet?

Bobby looked at the vampire and the angel. The apprehension on their faces was clearly visible. There was no doubting that they saw the Fallen as trouble, just another soldier of Kanor.

But Katy wasn't them, was she? *Foulness!* Bobby thought to himself, *She's certainly not me, either.* What if she truly had found a path that was right for her?

Who was he to stand in her way?

How *could* he stand in her way?

He looked down into her dark brown eyes, saw a soul that was far stronger than his own and he nodded. Tears welling up in his eyes, he took his sister in his arms and hugged her tight.

"You're suffocating me," she protested.

"I know," he agreed. "And that's why I have to let you go."

Claw and Michael had protested. Lots.

They had claimed that a small girl could not possibly know her own mind, that she was being manipulated by Asherah and that, to take her back to Sewell, was signing her death warrant. However, Bobby had ignored all their words and simply climbed up onto his horse, pulling his sister up behind him.

"We all have to find our own paths," he said as he guided the black steed out of the barn. "Ours are no longer with you."

The two supernatural beings had stood in silence as the two children had ridden back towards the palace of the fallen angel.

As their horse cantered down the street lined with the poles decorated with ribbons and they approached the grand palace, Bobby didn't feel nervous. Instead, a curious calm came over him. Even when Asherah herself came out to greet them, residents of Sewell lowering themselves completely so that their faces touched the ground, the boy felt neither fear nor anxiety. Instead, he simply helped Katy to dismount and watched as the small girl ran into the arms of the awaiting woman who closed her eyes and held her tight.

After their reunion, Asherah stood and said, "Thank you, Bobby. That can't have been easy for you. I'm sure other influences advised you against such an act."

"Katy needs to make her own decisions." He looked lovingly down at his sister. "She is quite unique."

The Fallen tousled the girl's hair with finely manicured fingers. "That she is," she mused. "That she is." Then, turning back to Bobby, "But so are you."

The boy on the horse smiled wryly. "No. I'm just... *normal.* There's nothing special about me whatsoever."

Asherah shook her head. "No, far from it. Someone I once knew thought like that. He was wrong, too. Trust me on this, even if you can't on anything else; you are incredibly special.

"And that is why Kanor is obsessed with you."

Bobby frowned and clenched his reins tight, causing the horse below him to stamp its feet in irritation. "What do you mean?"

"He knows you exist, Bobby. He talks about you constantly. I'm not sure why."

The teenager just nodded. What else could he say after discovering that the person who devastated humanity had now set their sights on him?

"Where will you go?" Katy called up from her place at Asherah's side.

Bobby turned the horse around and began his lonely journey. "I'm not sure, he called over his shoulder. But I'll know when I get there."

It was about five days later when he finally crested a hill and saw the lonely silhouette on the horizon. A few hours later and he found himself dismounting in front of the old oak tree from his dream.

Underneath its wide canopy stood the most curious person he had ever lain eyes upon. She was female but seemed to constantly shift form from that of a small girl, to that of a middle-aged woman, to that of a crone so old and haggard, that Bobby was amazed she had the strength to stand.

After settling his horse, Bobby slowly approached the shape-shifting woman. "I'm here," he said. "Now what?"

"We need your services," said the girl.

"We have an important task for you," said the woman.

"We need you to save the one known as Sam Spallucci," said the crone.

# Bobby Normal
# and the
# Black Dragon

## Previously...

Bobby is an orphan from the Divergent Lands, a desolate world in the far future, where humanity has been reduced to a pitiful remnant. Along with his hot-headed eight-year-old sister, Katy, he was entrusted to deliver the Eternal Talisman to a man named Jason who was residing in the neighbouring village. A priest, Jason was believed by some to be the prophesied Virtuous Man who was destined to overthrow the ruler of this grim land, Kanor, known by those who survived the genocide as the Black Dragon. However, Jason sent his troops on a disastrous mission in which everyone apart from the siblings was slaughtered by Kanor's golem foot soldiers — constructs. To make matters worse, Jason blamed Bobby and Katy for the catastrophe, saying that they were secret servants of the Black Dragon himself.

The children were rescued by Claw, Tigress and Scorpion — three vampires that called themselves the Children of Cain. The supernatural creatures were searching for the man that Claw felt was the *true* Virtuous Man, his old friend Sam Spallucci. Tragically, Tigress and Scorpion died when the vampires and the orphans fought the fallen angel Asmodeus and his own band of construct soldiers. As the children tended to Claw's wounds, they were joined by an elderly man named Cutter. The old man had helped the two children numerous times on their adventures and they trusted him implicitly. However, the vampire Claw revealed that the siblings' ally was, in fact, a Shadow Wraith, an elite construct and a servant of Kanor.

Angry at the death of the two female vampires and the revelation regarding Cutter, Katy ran away. Bobby tracked her down before the female Fallen, Asherah, subsequently saved them both from a pack of wild dogs. Katy was impressed by the mysterious angel's powers so decided to leave Bobby and Claw in order to join her new saviour. Determined to rescue his sister, Bobby persuaded Claw to enlist the help of the reclusive Archangel Michael. Initially reluctant to get involved, Michael eventually accompanied the two friends to Sewell, Asherah's temple and stronghold. They successfully snatched the eight-year-old from the Fallen's insidious clutches.

However, Katy refused to remain with Bobby and Claw, demanding to be returned to Sewell, saying that it was somewhere that she felt she finally belonged. Bobby relented and returned his sister to Asherah before setting out on his own.

We join him as he arrives at a location that he has witnessed in his dreams. It is an old oak tree upon a barren hillside. Beneath it stands an individual who has visited him in his sleep — a being whose form continually shifts between that of a young girl, a middle-aged woman and an elderly crone. She informs Bobby that she wants him to save the one known as Sam Spallucci…

## Chapter One

Life, Bobby decided as he dismounted his horse and tethered it to a low-hanging branch from the voluminous oak tree, was indeed the most curious of things. Only a short while ago, his and Katy's entire existence had been centred around living on their wits, scavenging and stealing their next meal whilst avoiding the belligerent torments of the town bully, Teller.

The same Teller that Katy had pushed to his death from a bridge in Orchester.

Bobby sighed and rested his tired head against the warm neck of the chestnut brown steed. Taking a deep breath, he stood up straight, swallowed and, ignoring the curiously shapeshifting humanoid entity that was standing close by, wandered over to the vast tree. He allowed his fingers to trace the swirls and knots of the oak's rough bark. The patterned surface looked to him like a raging sea. Not that Bobby had ever *seen* a sea before. His father had just told him tales of people in the distant past venturing out on the vast watery expanses in search of new lands and undertaking great adventures. In the days before the rise of the Black Dragon, Kanor. In the days before the Divergence.

"My father would have loved this," the teenage boy murmured to himself.

"I am sure…" began the girl.

"…that he would have fashioned a great many items of furniture from its wood," finished the woman.

Bobby turned and faced the old crone. "You knew my father?"

"I know everything," stated the haggard old being.

Bobby leaned against the oak tree, crossed his arms across his chest and frowned as he studied the curious figure before him. Right now, he was not in the mood for mysterious riddles or insinuations. With Katy's departure and the revelation that Cutter was a Shadow Wraith, his world had been torn apart and thrown in front of a raging hog. Right now he could feel the heavy trotters pounding up and down upon his tired spine. His tongue was writhing behind his teeth, wanting desperately to spit words of anger at his latest tormentor.

However, the mention of his dead father brought back the memory of the brown-haired, gentle-faced man and a certain cantankerous customer. An elderly resident of Irlingbury had requested that Howard build him a fence to surround his small property. The old man had said that it was to stop children from strolling aimlessly across his vegetable patch, destroying his small crop of produce. Bobby's father had agreed to take on the job and produced a fence that had been fashioned from small branches and twigs from the scant supply of wood that he had scavenged outside the village. However, the customer had been less than impressed. He cried that if he had wanted a fence made from scraps then he would have simply scattered tatty bits of firewood around the boundary of his property. Howard politely explained that this was currently all the wood available for such a task as Kanor's troops had only recently levelled the woodlands nearby. There simply was not any wood of a larger nature. The old man had not backed down and had screamed that Howard was a charlatan and a fraud. He had marched off into his house and had slammed the door behind him.

Howard had simply nodded to himself, gathered up the fencing material, placed it on his handcart and trundled it back to his cottage.

Not once did he protest. Not once did he raise his own voice in anger.

Bobby had been amazed at his father's calm reaction and asked him why he had not demanded that the customer pay him for his work with the agreed goods.

"My son, we never really know what's going on in someone's life. We only ever see glimpses, fleeting images that are part of a complicated story. As a result, we should never, ever judge someone by their actions alone until we fully understand what has driven them to behave in what we might, ourselves, consider to be an unpleasant manner. Just a few weeks ago, that man's wife of many years succumbed to a fever. Their garden was her pride and joy. She would spend hour upon hour in it whilst she tended to her vegetables and flowers. She was a very common sight for all passersby. Now that she is dead, she is already fading from the memory of those who knew her. Indeed, the children of the village, who care not for the production of food and flora, just see the garden as a shortcut across the corner between two streets.

"Our friend there, mind, sees the actions of the children as an affront to the memory of his loved one. Naturally, he wants to preserve the garden as it was so that he can cling to that memory in his own final years. It is only natural that he should want to do so in what he would see as the most fitting manner possible. So, my guess is that when he came up with the idea of a fence, he imagined a much grander affair that was fashioned from nice smooth planks of timber rather than these pitiful remnants that I was able to acquire. I could have argued until I was blue in the face that there was currently no such timber available for his fence due to the actions of Kanor's troops, but it would have been to no avail. He would never have listened; never seen reason.

"Grief can do terrible things to folk. All we can do is nod, smile, wish them to walk well and stay safe whilst guarding our own tongue and prevent the matter at hand from becoming far worse than it already is."

Bobby continued to lean against the old tree and guarded his tongue.

The girl smiled. "Your father taught you well."

Bobby remained cautiously silent. Rather than replying, he studied the threefold being. Quite obviously not human, its eyes were pools of pure water. A deep blue, they swirled and flowed around their sockets making it quite impossible to figure out exactly what they were looking at. Her hair was grey and swept down over her shoulders as if it were a river in full flood. The creature was attired in what appeared to be a long dress fashioned from some sort of flowing liquid in which there were flashes of fire.

"That is why I feel you are suited to my task," continued the woman as her unsettling eyes regarded Bobby.

"But first," finished the crone, "you have questions. Two in fact."

The boy nodded. "Obvious one first, then. Who are you?"

"I," proclaimed the girl, "am the sea that flows between the three Realms of Heaven, Beyond and the Physical Realm. From the beginning of time, I have kept all three in check, ensuring that there is order in what would otherwise be chaos. The eternal song of creation sails upon my mighty currents, crying out to all who would lift their ears in order to listen. I am the Abyss."

Bobby nodded. "I've heard about the Realms before."

"From the Children of Cain," said the woman.

"I showed you to them," said the crone, "when they first met me."

This revelation pierced Bobby's armour of calm. He pulled away from the large tree. "They didn't mention that."

"It is of no concern," shrugged the girl. "It was a long time ago and much has happened since then."

"They were younger," explained the woman, "and were somewhat... preoccupied."

Bobby shuddered. He closed and reopened his eyes. "Show me," he demanded. "Show me what you really are."

The crone nodded and all around them changed. Bobby was no longer standing upon a hillside in the Divergent Lands. Instead, he found himself suspended in complete darkness. For a moment, blind panic overtook him and he screamed helplessly into a void that swallowed all sound.

All sound except for one.

Out of the darkness came a voice that was impossible to describe.

"... ... ..."

It reached his ears as a threefold rhythm and it beat an enticing melody against his tympani that sang of beauty, of hope, of creation. Then, in the darkness there was Light.

An explosion burst from a distant point and the void was filled with song. The song coalesced and flowed as a mighty ocean. As its waters boiled with fire, it split the darkness in two. On one side was a place infused with light; on the other was a place of blackness. Then the song rose in volume and intensity and a third place formed, split from the other two. This was a place of vibrancy, of life. All three Realms coexisted in harmony with the mighty Abyss surging between them, keeping them apart and separate.

And, all the time, the threefold rhythm crashed upon the shores of the three Realms. As it did so, Bobby could now hear words attached to the rhythm:

*We are one...*

*We are one...*

*We are one...*

But there was more. Even through the immensity of the universe's might and grandeur, Bobby could sense more.

*Would you see it?* came a soft voice in his head.

"Show me," the boy replied.

Beyond the three Realms, a fire erupted into the surrounding darkness. Bobby watched as it expanded in size and illumination. A six-winged figure rose above all that existed. In its hands, it held a chalice and a sword. Its lips moved in time to the threefold song as it swung the sword and all creation cascaded down into the bowl of the chalice until there was nothing apart from a small, solitary ember.

Bobby gasped and crashed to the dew-soaked floor under the great oak tree. He looked up at the shifting form of the ocean that kept the universe in check.

"The Eternals," explained the girl. "When they sing their song as one, all will be destroyed."

"When?" Bobby managed.

"It has happened," said the woman.

"It will come to pass," explained the crone.

"Everything?"

The Abyss nodded: girl, woman, crone.

"How can I stop it?"

"That is the wrong question."

Bobby nodded. "Who is Sam Spallucci?"

A small fire cracked and popped as the day grew late. Embers floated up into the air, accompanied by frenetic sparks from the burning bracken and scavenged fragments of wood. Bobby held his hands out to the flames, warming them against the growing chill.

The soothing heat reached his skin but not his insides.

What the Abyss had shown him had chilled him to the core.

Everything swept away.

Absolutely everything.

No Earth, no Divergent Lands, no constructs, no Kanor.

Some might say that was a good thing. They would say that it was an end to this brutal cycle of destruction brought about by the Black Dragon. They would point out that the world, as it stood, was a rabid dog in agony as poisonous insanity consumed its brain; that it would finally be at peace as its owner cracked its skull open with a heavy rock. Let the being rise that would destroy everything! Let it bring an end to the carnage and chaos! There would be peace once more. Humanity had been given a chance and had failed. It had birthed Kanor from its loins, allowing the Black Dragon to spread his obsidian wings and decimate its hapless parent to a pitiful remnant.

But not Bobby.

As the teenage boy watched the fire dancing in the growing twilight, he knew that there had to be a way to prevent the devastation. Not just in his gut; not just some instinct. The Abyss had told him so.

What's more, there was a bonus.

"Sam Spallucci is a pivotal character in the history of humanity," the girl had said.

"If you save him…" continued the woman.

"…then Kanor will not rise," finished the crone.

A piece of wood collapsed in on itself and a plume of embers spiralled into the air as the fire changed shape. One small action had altered the structure of the hearth.

One small change in history could prevent the rise of Kanor. Prevent the Divergence from ever happening.

Bobby let that possibility hang suspended in his mind. What would that actually mean? If he went back and prevented the rise of the Black Dragon, what would that actually do? Everything would be different. Absolutely everything. No constructs, no poverty, no pain.

But what else would not exist?

He himself was a child of the Divergent Lands. If they did not come to pass, then how could he go back to prevent them?

The Abyss had added a new word to his vocabulary: paradox.

"You will be a thing out of time," explained the girl.

"A thing that should not exist yet does," said the woman.

"You would not be the first of these things as they have happened before," continued the crone.

Bobby sighed. Yes, life truly was far more complex than it used to be.

"What about Katy?" he had asked the shifting persona of the ocean that encompassed reality. "What about all the other people that have existed since the Divergence? Surely, if I prevent the rise of Kanor, then they will cease to exist."

"Do you think they enjoy their existence?" asked the girl. She waved a hand across the air in front of her and an apparition appeared. It showed a cohort of constructs marching through a small village putting to the lance all those who stood in their way.

"If you prevent the Divergence, you will prevent all this pain," stated the woman, her watery eyes holding fast onto the boy.

Bobby shook his head. "But life is far more than that. There is love here in this world as well as pain. Mothers give birth to babies who are cradled in the arms of their fathers. There is still beauty. You just have to look for it."

"But there is suffering too," said the crone. "You need look no further than the end of your nose in order to see the pain that this world endures."

"Why me? Why should I be the one to bring about change?"

"Because I know you will. I have already seen it."

So, as surely as the sun rose in the sky each morning, Bobby's destiny was already laid out in front of him. According to the Abyss, he had no choice.

According to the Abyss…

"No," he had said. "I can't do it. I won't. This may be a terrible place, but it can change. Humanity is resilient. It has existed this long, even under the crushing yoke of Kanor, so it can continue to survive and then, someday, it will rise up once more and overthrow him. He is called the Black Dragon, but he is just a man and men die. Kanor will perish one day. It may be in my lifetime; it may be in the future. But he will die, just as all men do. Then, on that day, humanity will be reborn.

"It doesn't need me to go back and erase all that has happened since the day of the Divergence. That would make me no better than that being you showed me eradicating all the universe. I do not have the right to alter what has gone before."

Then the Abyss had done something truly unsettling. The girl, the woman and the crone had all smiled. "You say that now," they said, "but you will change your mind. When you do, you will travel to the church in Wellington, to the lair of Kanor himself. There you will lay your hand upon the font, the stone basin at the back of the church and I will transport you back to a time before all of this. I will take you back to a world before the Black Dragon rose and scorched the land and I will deposit you in a city called Lancaster.

"There you *will* find Sam Spallucci."

Then, without saying another word, the manifestation of the Abyss had simply vanished, leaving Bobby standing on the barren hillside under the old oak tree. Cursing under his breath, he had climbed up onto his horse and ridden as far away from that spot as he could before the night had begun to creep upon him.

So here he was sitting in front of a small fire with sleep tugging at his eyes as the soothing warmth reached out to him. Here he was, adamant that he would defy an entity that had mastery over time and claimed to know his fate.

Here he was, drawing a line in the dirt and saying that he would not cross over. Contrary to what the Abyss claimed, he was the master of his own destiny.

And, with that, Bobby allowed his eyes to shut and he drifted off to sleep.

## Chapter Two

Bobby did not sleep well. As he lay on the ground in front of the dwindling fire, his mind was not filled with images of a being wiping a universal slate clean or of the Black Dragon rising into the air, scorching the ground below with his infernal breath. There weren't even any constructs marching into a grubby, defenceless settlement, subjecting all the villagers to brutal deaths.

There was none of this.

There was just Katy.

He was chasing his sister as she ran through a similar meadow of scarlet flowers to the one which he had seen in his previous dream. Bobby kept reaching out to grab her, to pull her back, but she was always just that bit too far ahead of his grasping fingers.

Not that she wanted to be caught.

His sister was laughing happily to herself as she ran her fingers through the small red blooms. As she did so, her hands came away stained with their colour. Rather than disturbing her, this caused Katy to laugh even more. "Look, Bobby! Look!" she cried with glee over her shoulder, lifting her hands above her head for him to see.

As Bobby watched, the red pigment on his sibling's fingers began to drip down onto her head. The two children stopped and Katy lifted her face to her hands. Opening her mouth she let a drop of the liquid fall upon her tongue. "Yes!" she cried. "Yes!" and she thrust her hands into her mouth, devouring all that she could of the viscous substance.

Bobby reached out again, but still he could not grab his sister, even though they were both standing still. She seemed to be drawing even further away. The boy frowned at the impossibility of the situation then gasped as his sister aged. Now she stood in front of him in what looked to be her early twenties. Her now pallid skin contrasted against the black cloak that she wore over her shoulders. "See what I am become..." she hissed.

Bobby's nose twitched as the familiar smell of burning reached him and, behind the older Katy, the horizon erupted into flame. A wicked grin formed on her mouth and a pair of sharp fangs were all too clear to see at the edges of her red lips.

"See what I am become..." she repeated as she turned and sprinted towards the flames, drawing a sword as she did so.

Bobby screamed silently after her and tried to follow, but he kept stumbling. Looking down, he saw that his path was strewn with corpses, all bearing agonised death masks. Again he cried out and again his voice was silent.

Katy turned to face her impotent brother. This time she had a boy of Bobby's age clasped in her arms. The teenager was terrified and was screaming for his life.

"See what you let me become..." Katy growled as she thrust her face into the unfortunate lad's neck and ripped at his skin with her sharp fangs. Moaning joyfully, Katy drank deeply from the ravaged skin as the boy finally fell limp and she threw him, discarded and empty, with the other corpses. "You could have stopped this, but you didn't," she declared. "You let me become this." And in a motion that was faster than Bobby could comprehend, Katy was nose to nose with him, the blood of the dead boy covering her face and assaulting her brother's senses.

Bobby awoke with a shout and with an overwhelming sense of confusion.

The nightmare was not the only cause of this abrupt awakening.

The pricking sensation of a clay lance at his throat was also a contributing factor.

Bobby silently cursed his idiocy as his horse jolted underneath him. His hands were bound in front of him, the cords digging into his wrists as a reminder that one must never let down one's guard in the Divergent Lands. His encounter with the Abyss had caused him to be distracted and it had cost him his freedom.

He considered himself fortunate that it had not cost him his life.

His mount was tethered to that of a Shadow Wraith that rode in front of him. Another rode behind and the three horses were flanked with numerous constructs that marched in their ubiquitous precision.

*Thud... thud...*
*Thud... thud...*
*Thud... thud...*

As soon as he had awoken, Bobby had realised that trying to run would have been pointless. Not only had one construct been holding a lance to his throat but he had been surrounded, as he was now, by a full cohort.

"You will come with us," one of the Wraiths had instructed and that had been all. Nothing else. No threats, no explanations. They had simply motioned that he should mount his horse, to the saddle of which he had then been bound, and they had set off away from where he had spent his dream-filled night.

Something was going on and Bobby had no idea as to what. On the plus side, he was still breathing, so he took that as a win and decided to wait and see what would happen next.

He didn't have to wait too long. After half a day's ride, they arrived at an enormous building that rose out of a flat plain. Human guards stood at the gateway and stamped to attention as the party rode through into a large courtyard. The lead Shadow Wraith leapt gracefully from its steed and pointed to Bobby. A construct turned and whipped out an extended arm like a lasso. It snaked its limb around the boy and lifted him effortlessly from his saddle before depositing him on the cobbled floor.

"Thank you," Bobby smiled politely.

The construct, needless to say, did not reply. Instead, it turned, fell into step with the rest of its cohort and marched off into the complex.

Bobby shrugged, faced the two Wraiths and raised a questioning eyebrow.

"Come with us," one of them replied before shoving Bobby towards a large pair of wooden doors at the edge of the courtyard.

As he approached the doors, Bobby paused and gazed up in wonder. Never had he seen doors of such a size. The amount of timber required to manufacture them would have been immense. No mean feat in a land where

Kanor's forces systematically slashed and burned the woodland. Whoever owned this fortress was certainly a person of great power and obscene wealth.

He had only ever seen one such building before. The temple of Asherah. Which probably meant…

As the massive doors swung solidly shut behind him, Bobby's suspicions were confirmed. He found himself standing in a long room with a golden throne at the opposite end of a long, red carpet. Dotted along the edge of the carpet, and leading up to the majestic seat of power, were numerous statues. They all showed the same man in what Bobby took to be heroic poses of some sort. There he was fighting a man with a head resembling that of a bull. There he was decapitating a crazy figure of a woman with snakes in her hair. There he was standing proudly on a boat with other men in unrecognisable clothing. There he was… Bobby frowned. The statue of the man seemed to have some sort of contraption over its head and its clothing was large and bulky. It seemed to be stepping down a small ladder from a weird little house on legs onto a very bumpy surface.

*Each to their own*: he thought as he walked past the statuary and up to the throne upon which was seated an individual whom he had last encountered on a battlefield.

"Kneel before Lord Asmodeus," growled the Wraith. Bobby felt a rough shove between his shoulder blades and he collapsed onto his knees.

The male Fallen waved a hand of dismissal at the two Shadow Wraiths and they departed in silence. He was lounging nonchalantly with one leg over an arm of the golden throne and was attired in long blue robes that curled around his arms and legs. "So, *Bobby Normal* (I believe that's your name), what do you make of my grand palace? I bet you've never seen something so fine before, have you?"

Bobby was tempted for just a brief moment to say that he had preferred the temple of Asherah but, before his mouth snapped the words out, he caught sight of the two thunderbolts on the top of the throne and decided better of it. "It's truly unique," he said, "and completely beyond my comprehension."

Asmodeus seemed to consider the reply as electricity flickered absentmindedly across his knuckles. He nodded and flicked a finger. Bobby flinched involuntarily as a shower of sparks flew across the air towards him. However, they landed on the bonds between his hands, burning them apart and setting his wrists free. "Thank you," he said, rubbing at his wrists.

"You see, Bobby, I can be quite magnanimous when I want to be," drawled the fallen angel, idly watching more electricity dancing across his fingertips. "I find it can be quite useful." He paused and lifted the index finger on his right hand. A spark of electricity grew in size just above his fingertip.

Bobby swallowed.

Asmodeus ignored the boy's growing discomfort and just appeared to study the dancing electricity as it continued to grow in size. "So, let's get straight to the point, shall we? My *employer*," Bobby could not help but notice the disdain in the word, "appears to be somewhat fascinated with you. Back at Rishton, I could have fried you to a crisp, but there would have been dire consequences." He finally shot a glance at the kneeling prisoner. "And not just for you." Repositioning himself so that Bobby became his entire field of vision, Asmodeus leaned forward, the spark of electricity on his finger directly between him and the human. "Tell me, why is Kanor obsessed with a street urchin?"

This was not good. Bobby stared at the dancing spark of energy and wracked his brain for an answer. The wrong one could lead to agonising repercussions.

"I don't know," he answered honestly then shot his hands out in front of him as Asmodeus made to flick his wrist. "Wait! I truly don't know. I am a nobody! Normal, like you said. Yet I seem to have been dragged into this incredible world of yours. I don't know why. It perplexes me, confounds me and baffles me. Why should the decimator of humanity be obsessed with a teenage boy from a small village in the middle of nowhere?" He paused, considered his next words very carefully and then continued: "I am sure that an esteemed Lord like yourself has far more insight into the matter than a lowly individual such as me."

Bobby closed his eyes and awaited the agonising surge of electricity.

It never came.

Opening his eyes, he watched Asmodeus palm the spark and then frown momentarily before allowing a smile to spread across his face. "That does make sense," he nodded. "If I cannot comprehend the mind of my *master*," there was the animosity once again, "then how can I expect you, a mere human, to do so?"

Bobby decided that now would be a good time to perform a bit of prying, whilst the Fallen was enjoying having his ego stroked. "If I may, my Lord? It appears to me that you do not enjoy having your angelic self pushed around by the Black Dragon."

Asmodeus slouched back on his throne, a sullen look on his face. "You may be just a human, Normal, but you seem to be quite perceptive. My relationship with the Black Dragon is… *complicated.*"

"How so?"

The Fallen opened his mouth to speak but there was a commotion and the doors were thrown open as a Shadow Wraith entered. "Apologies, my Lord," it called across the room, "but it is urgent."

Asmodeus beckoned for him to approach the throne.

"We have located them."

The angel raised an eyebrow. "Really? Well, that *is* good news. Where?"

"Those who defied you are a day's march north of here. We can muster a cohort and be upon them before sunset tomorrow."

Asmodeus clapped his hands with glee and a shower of sparking electricity plumed from between his palms. "Excellent. We shall hunt them down, pounce when they're not expecting it and ram their heads upon poles in the torched remains of their village. No others would dare to defy me when they see the consequences of their futile actions." He rose from the throne. "Normal, our little chat will have to be put on hold." To the Wraith: "Have him taken to the dungeon. I'll ready my troops for the hunt." With that, he strode gleefully out of the throne room.

The Shadow Wraith turned to Bobby and grabbed him roughly by the shoulder.

As Bobby was not-so-gently escorted through the twisting corridors of Asmodeus' fortress, he knew that he should have felt sick to the pit of his stomach with worry and terror. The weird thing was that, instead of a blind panic coursing through his body, he was experiencing a peculiar sort of calm. As he passed numerous constructs marching through the passageways, he considered just how many times he had run into them out in the wide world. He couldn't quite put a number on it, but the encounters were certainly starting to rack up.

And he had survived every one.

Was it luck? Was it skill? Was it the ability to run crazily fast when being pursued by a murderous lump of clay on two legs? Perhaps it was a combination of all of the above?

Would it be the same this time?

Well, Bobby surmised, he wasn't dead yet. He had been captured and brought alive to the Fallen. Then, when in Asmodeus' presence, the angel hadn't even lain an electrically charged finger upon him. Bobby had the feeling that Asmodeus valued him more with a pulse than as a charred piece of meat.

What actually worried him though, as he was pushed into a small cell at the end of a dark passageway, was that this was the second time he had been told that the Black Dragon knew of him and was *obsessed* with him. Asherah had said exactly the same thing. This really did not sound good.

The bars clanged shut and Bobby turned to watch the Shadow Wraith stalk away, leaving two constructs standing motionless in front of the cell. The imprisoned teenager blew out a long breath, stretched and took in his new environment.

After no more than a few seconds, he decided that there wasn't really much to see. Stone walls, bucket, straw: that was all. With nothing else to occupy his interest, he turned his attention to his guards.

"So, do you do this a lot? Guarding, I mean. Must make a change to the stompy-stompy, stabby-stabby. Get a chance to rest and have some peace and quiet? Or, perhaps this is punishment duty? Did you do something wrong? Let someone go who you should have skewered? I can imagine your great leader has a bit of a temper when things don't go according to plan. We used to have someone like that back in Irlingbury. We had this crazy person who from time to time would just lose it. No one ever knew why. He just stormed around the streets every now and then, screaming and shouting at people. One time, he took his toilet bucket and threw it at a passerby. The look on her face! You really should have seen it." Bobby paused. "But, of course, you wouldn't have been able to, would you? Not having eyes. I guess you'd just have slipped your long tongue out and wriggled it around like you do, scenting the air." He shook his head. "The stench would have made even one of *you* cringe."

Bobby paused. The constructs hadn't moved at all. Were they even listening?

He rested his head against one of the bars. "I don't normally talk to myself. I guess I'm just not used to being on my own. I have a sister, you see. She was always there with me. Normally eating or complaining, but always there. More often than not, she was the one who'd be filling the silences. She's younger than me, you see? So, she has a lot more unanswered questions bubbling around inside of her. That and..." In his head, Bobby watched Katy pushing Teller to his death. "That and something else..." He closed his eyes and just stood there with his head leaning on the bars to his cell.

The sound of footsteps broke his reverie and he straightened up, opening his eyes to see who was coming.

It was a Shadow Wraith.

Correction, it was a very familiar Shadow Wraith.

Bobby watched as Cutter marched down the corridor with absolute authority and presented himself before the two guards. "Our Lord demands that I take the prisoner to him right now."

The two constructs stepped aside, allowing Cutter access to the cell. The Wraith placed his hand over the locking mechanism and Bobby heard the wet sound of transformation as his "flesh" slipped into the metal workings. Cutter twisted his wrist and the door swung open. He withdrew his key-shaped hand, shook it, and his fingers slid back into position. "Come," he said to Bobby, gesticulating with the newly formed digits.

Cautiously, Bobby emerged from the cell, passing between the two guards. Cutter gestured for him to walk in front, which he did. When they had turned a couple of corners, the Shadow Wraith bent forward and whispered in his ear, "Stay close and do as I say."

"Why? So you can get me safely to your master?"

"No, Bobby. So I can get you out of here alive."

Bobby's heart leapt, but he kept his emotions in check and carried on walking. As they retraced his earlier journey, the boy and the Shadow Wraith passed numerous constructs, all of which stood to one side to let their superior pass. Not once were they challenged.

That was until they emerged into the courtyard of the fortress.

As soon as they stepped foot into the yard, Bobby's heart sank. It was far busier than it had been when he'd arrived. Now there were dozens of constructs swarming out of arches and doorways around the perimeter of the courtyard. They were all making their way to the central area where they were falling into line, forming an army.

In their midst was the same Shadow Wraith that had taken Bobby to Asmodeus. His head rose from his task at hand and his attention was diverted from organising the troops to the arrival of the two newcomers in the courtyard. Frowning, he marched over to Bobby and Cutter. "What's going on here? Where are you taking the prisoner?"

Bobby watched as six constructs peeled off from their formation and stamped over to behind their commander. This was not looking good.

"Well," Cutter began, "I could tell you that Asmodeus has requested the presence of the boy, but then again, for what good that'll do me, I might as well tell you that the moon is made of cheese."

The commander frowned and made to speak, but his words were cut short as Cutter's left hand transformed into a lance and impaled the Wraith's face.

"Run for the gate!"

Bobby didn't need telling twice and he darted towards the main gate of the fortress. All around him, hell was breaking loose. He could hear Shadow Wraiths screaming commands, constructs stamping to action and human vassals presenting arms. One of the human guards jumped in front of him. Bobby kicked him squarely in the shins, causing the traitor to drop his pike and squeal in agony. Another grabbed Bobby by the arm but the boy dropped down into a roll, taking his would-be captor to the floor. As the teenager came back up to his feet, he stamped down angrily onto the man's face. Blood and cartilage erupted from the guard's nose.

The ground beside Bobby shook as a giant construct marched up towards him. He jinked left and right, making himself harder to target. However, his plan failed as he felt his feet swept out from beneath him. Cursing as he fell to the cobbled floor, he struggled onto his back and saw the construct's extended arm wrapped around his ankle. Bobby kicked with his free foot at the clay coil but the golem ignored the futile effort and relentlessly reeled him in.

There was a deafening roar from the melee in the courtyard and Bobby's attention was diverted from his impending fate. A knot of constructs was sent flying like twigs before a storm as a mass of fur and teeth burst from their midst. The simulacrum of a gigantic wolf bounded across the battlefield, throwing to one side any being that dared to block its path. In one final leap, it descended upon the extended arm of the construct and clamped down with its ferocious jaws. Bobby felt the coil around his leg slacken.

Cutter presented his back to the teenage boy. "Get on!" his gruff voice growled.

Bobby climbed aboard, clung on tight to the wiry hair and kept his head low, close to the powerful shoulders, as Cutter propelled the two of them out of the fortress and off to freedom.

# Chapter Three

Cutter made sure that they were a safe distance from the fortress of Asmodeus before he allowed himself to slow down. His wolf form drew to a halt and he let Bobby dismount. When his passenger was securely on the ground, the wolf transformed into his usual shape of an old man dressed in ragged clothes.

"Are you okay?"

Bobby nodded, his eyes studying the grassy floor at his feet.

His rescuer sighed and walked over to a thicket of thorny bushes. Grumbling as he parted the treacherous branches, Cutter pulled out a long staff and a tatty-looking travelling bag. After slinging the bag over his shoulder, he rummaged in its depths until he found some dried fruit.

"Here. Eat this."

The teenager just stared at the offering.

"Bobby…"

"You think this makes everything okay?"

The old man's face filled with sorrow and regret. "Please. You need to eat."

"Why would I eat anything you offer me?"

"Because you look like you haven't had a square meal in days. What have you been doing?"

"It's none of your concern." With that, Bobby turned and began to walk away.

Cutter shoved the fruit back into his bag and trailed after the angry teenager. "You're just going to walk around while Asmodeus sends his goons out looking for you? That doesn't sound like a good idea."

"You have a better one?"

"Yes. Let me take you far away. Somewhere safe."

Bobby shook his head. "Well, what do you know? A cowardly construct. Who would have thought?"

"Right, that's enough of this swill." Cutter marched in front of the boy and thrust his staff defiantly onto the ground. "Out with it! Come on. Let's hear it!"

Bobby glared up at the old man. "What's there to say? You killed my father. You single-handedly tore my life apart! How in all the Divergent Lands can you possibly think I could ever forgive you for that? So, you burst in back there and sprung me from my cell. Thank you, kindly. Much appreciated. Now, go! Get out of my life! I don't need you anymore."

Bobby made to push past the old man, but Cutter's hand snapped out and grabbed him by the wrist.

"Let go!"

"No. Not until I've said my piece."

"What? That you had no choice? That you were made that way? Only following orders?"

"I could. But it would be pointless. Words mean nothing, Bobby. They are just fawning vanities that the guilty use to smooth rushing waters. Actions speak far louder. Judge me by my deeds. Weigh them as a baker weighs their grain. Look at what I've done and see if they balance out. I've been following you now since you left Irlingbury with Katy and Persephone. That was the first time that I intervened, when Teller was chasing you on the outskirts of the village."

Bobby frowned as he remembered the event, just before he, Katy and the girl entrusted with the Eternal Talisman had escaped down into the tunnels. "They thought they saw me down the street. That was you?"

Cutter nodded and there before Bobby was standing a simulacrum of himself.

"Well, that's weird."

His reflection nodded and shifted back into its previous form. "Constructs can look however they want. They can blend into a crowd and pass for humans. You could be walking along and have no knowledge that they are right next to you until the lance thrusts out of your dead heart. If you wander off on your own, Asmodeus *will* track you down. He will drag you back to his stronghold and he will do whatever he desires to you.

"It won't be pretty."

"So, you think I should just run away and hide?"

"It is the sensible thing to do."

"But it's not the *right* thing."

Cutter crossed his arms. "What else do you have in mind then?"

"Something that might help you win back my trust."

They found the villagers who had defied Asmodeus shortly before the sun reached its zenith. Cutter had transformed into a sleek black stallion and they had galloped northwards, just as the Shadow Wraith had described, locating the rag-tag bunch of people encamped by a stream.

The boy and the horse looked down on them from a nearby hill.

"I think," Bobby said to his currently equine partner, that you ought to transform before we introduce ourselves. Don't want to terrify the people we're here to save."

The black horse nodded and shifted form. "About that. Just how do you intend to save a weary bunch of fugitives from an organised and vicious army of constructs."

Bobby gazed down into the valley below, mentally totting up the number of humans. There seemed to be about five dozen. "There's a good amount of them."

"But, even from here, you can see they are broken," Cutter protested, leaning heavily on his staff after he took it from Bobby. "You don't know what they've already been through, but knowing the forces of the Fallen, it will have been brutal and harrowing. They will have suffered and will have already seen loved ones fall to the lance."

"Then it's a good job I've got something that they've never possessed before."

"Please don't say *hope*," Cutter grumbled.

A smile touched Bobby's lips as he prodded Cutter's chest with a finger. "Oh no. Something far more useful than that. Someone who knows exactly how constructs think and how they can be outsmarted." With that, he headed down the hill to the refugees.

It quickly became all too apparent to Bobby that Cutter had been right about the fleeing villagers. They were disheartened, tired and scared to death.

As a result, the news that an army of constructs

would be upon them by nightfall was not received very well.

"We must flee this place at once!" cried a stout man in a tunic that matched the redness in his jowly face. "Let's pack up and head north."

"We can't outrun them," protested another villager. "They will slaughter us." He slammed his face into his hands and began to weep.

Similar notions circulated around the crowd. About half began to pack up their meagre belongings whilst the rest simply sat down and awaited their fate.

"No! Wait!" Bobby cried. "Listen to me. There is another way."

Eyes brimming with fear turned towards the teenage boy.

"We can fight."

A woman pushed her way through the stunned group. "Are you insane? Have you not seen what fighting has already brought us?" She waved a hand at her companions. "Look at us. We have little enough energy left to walk let alone take on an army of mud buckets. Boy, you don't know what we've been through. You've not seen what they did to our loved ones. Who are you to tell us to fight?"

Bobby swallowed. He felt the unbearable weight of so many people staring at him. What he said now would affect their fate for good or ill. He knew he had to get it right.

"No, you're right. I don't know what you've already been through. You look to me like a bed sheet that has been wrung out after it has been washed; you hang heavy where you stand and are not what you used to be. You are defeated and broken. You are a shell of what I imagine you used to be. But, let me tell you this, neither running nor lying down to die will solve your problems.

"Because they're not just your own.

"They are the shared problems of all of us living in the hell forged by the Black Dragon. Look at yourselves. Your tiredness and your fear are not your greatest problems. The fact that you are divided in what you should do is what is preventing you from striking back. And that is what Kanor and his forces use as their greatest weapon: division.

"Think about it. How often did you socialise with people from other settlements? How often, when a trader came to your town did you eye him with suspicion? More often than not you were probably afraid that he was a quisling for one of the Fallen or, even worse, a construct in human form."

Some heads started to nod.

Bobby pressed on. "My home village was divided in the same way. A man named Teller was placed in charge of running things. He, his son and his cronies spied upon the rest of us and reported any misdeeds to higher powers. It was because of them that my father was put to the lance.

"And no one did anything about it.

"Instead, people went on with their lives as if nothing had happened."

"They murdered my daughter," snarled the woman.

"What was her name?"

The woman's eyes turned towards Cutter, who had asked the question.

"It was Anna. She was named after my younger sister, who died when I was but a teenager."

The old man nodded. "I'm sorry to hear that...?" He

paused and allowed the woman to fill in the unasked question.

"Martha. My name is Martha." It was obvious to all that she was fighting back tears.

"Martha," continued Cutter, "what was the charge?"

"They accused her of plotting against Kanor. She was a child. Just a child! They dragged her screaming into the village square where a damned Wraith sliced her head off with a scythe he'd fashioned from his arm. We took them by surprise. It was only a small group, a Wraith and two of the mud buckets, and we were able to over-power them."

"What did you do?"

"Fire. We rained fire down upon them. With long poles, we harried them into an old barn and we torched them. We baked them solid then dragged their corpses out into the square where we ground them up and danced on their dust.

"But, someone must have betrayed us. An army came the next day. So many were killed. We had no choice but to run."

Cutter nodded. "You did what you had to do at that time."

"But now," Bobby said, "you can do something else. You can turn and fight. You can beat them back and, in doing so, send a message to the rest of the Divergent Lands that we can stand up for what we love, that we can beat them.

"We will be divided no more.

"We will stand together against our common foe.

"The Black Dragon."

A few hours later the preparations for battle were

well under way. To Bobby's utter amazement, none of the villagers had packed up their things and fled into the surrounding countryside. All had decided to remain where they were and fight.

"It appears that you truly inspired them," observed the gruff voice of Cutter as he came and stood next to the teenage boy.

Bobby looked up from the dry, brittle bracken that he was packing down into the ground. "I just hope it was the right thing to do."

The creature in the form of an old man grunted to himself and nodded. "Only time will tell."

Time. Bobby shuddered at that word. The Abyss claimed to have mastery and knowledge of time. She had stated that he would go back in time to save this Sam Spallucci character, yet here he was preparing for battle.

A battle which would inevitably cause the death of numerous people.

All around him, those same people were busying themselves with their allotted tasks.

Which ones would live?

Which ones would fall to the lance?

It was impossible to tell.

Bobby shook his head. "I shouldn't be doing this," he muttered. "*Why* am I doing this?"

A steadying hand gripped his shoulder. "Because someone has to." Cutter paused before continuing. "You were right, Kanor's greatest weapon is humanity's own divisions. That's how he was able to rise so quickly and eradicate them. Sure, a sleeper army of murderous constructs lying in wait certainly helped, but if humans had been more cohesive then they could have worked together better to fight the new enemy." He gestured to the digging and labouring fugitives. "Look at them now. They are united. They at least stand a modicum of a chance. Far more than when they were arguing amongst themselves. They even have a leader."

Bobby and Cutter watched silently as Martha went from worker to worker, making sure that everyone was well and understood their allotted tasks.

After a while, Bobby turned to face his companion. "Were you there? On the day that Kanor rose?"

Cutter shook his head. "No. I and the Shadow Wraiths that followed me came much later: when the Black Dragon realised that he needed generals to martial his foot soldiers. I've been told what it was like, though, by the Black Dragon himself."

"You've actually seen Kanor?"

"Of course I have. He created me. Remember, I was the first Shadow Wraith. The rest may have been constructed by Asmodeus, but Kanor used me as a blueprint.

Bobby frowned. "Is that why you're different?"

"You mean, is that why I have a conscience?" Cutter shrugged. "I don't know. I just know that there are so many things I have done that I cannot bear the guilt of anymore. I have to do what is right. I have to help you overthrow Kanor."

Bobby studied the Wraith's old, haggard features. He allowed his eyes to travel over the creases and furrows that covered the face of the monster that had murdered his father. He took in the grey hair that was knotted and unkempt and the lips that were dry and chapped. They settled upon the grey eyes that, in return, were studying him. For a moment, construct and boy stood there in silence, simply staring intently at each other.

"Excuse me…" the voice of Martha broke the awkward moment. "Could one of you possibly check on something for us?"

Cutter nodded and, in doing so, broke eye contact with the boy that he had orphaned. "Certainly," he said. "Are you following my instructions precisely?"

The woman nodded in reply.

"I don't need to remind you that constructs are relentless. The firetrap we're setting here needs to be very wide. Even when it catches fire, they'll keep on coming."

Martha nodded once again.

"Good. I'll give it a look over." With that, he hobbled over to a ditch that the woman and her companions had been digging.

Then, as the Shadow Wraith and the female human peered down into the freshly dug earth, they froze.

Bobby frowned and cast his eyes around him. Everyone was motionless, captured in what they were doing. Some were pushing down on spades, others were lifting dry bracken into ditches. Whatever they had been doing at that precise moment had become a fresco illustrating their preparations for battle.

"Why are you wasting your time doing this?"

Bobby sighed and turned to face the girl as she became a woman.

"You will fail," said the woman.

"This is pointless," said the crone.

"You said that I was a paradox," snapped Bobby, jabbing an angry finger at the Abyss, "something that shouldn't exist in time yet does. Well, I choose to make an event that is the same as me. You say that I will fail, yet I believe that I can triumph."

The girl cocked her head thoughtfully. "No you don't."

"You believe you will fail," said the woman.

"You know that many will die," stated the crone.

Bobby tore his eyes away from the transforming entity and looked around the field of preparations. So many people. So many were depending upon him.

"You could walk away right now," suggested the girl.

"Go and do what needs to be done," said the woman.

"Save Spallucci," urged the crone.

The teenage orphan rubbed the heel of his hand against a wet tear duct. "Why is he so important to you?" he forced out. "What does he do?"

"If you save Spallucci," began the girl.

"There will be no Divergence," continued the woman.

"And Kanor will not rise," finished the crone.

"But none of these people will have ever existod!" shouted the boy, his frustration finally exploding from him. "These people are a product of the Divergent Lands. If the Divergence never happens, then I will have ripped them out of existence. At least going into battle they stand a chance of surviving."

"Do you really believe that?"

And, once more, the field was full of the sounds of activity, of humans preparing to battle against overwhelming odds in order to survive.

Bobby hung his head and refused to cry.

# Chapter Four

The plan, as it stood, was quite simple. They were to lure the constructs in to engage them, then set fire to the buried bracken in the firetrap. For most of the day, the group of villagers had been following the precise instructions of Cutter concerning the digging of wide trenches in a narrow valley between two rises. He had then sent them to scavenge from the local environs all manner of dry material that they could find. This had then been packed into the earthworks. When they were finished, the trenches were full of dry bracken and scrappy pieces of wood: fuel that would ignite quickly and produce intense heat in an attempt to bake the constructs solid.

The hardest part of the excavation had been digging up the inclines of the low hillsides, ensuring that, when the material was ignited, it would form an effective enclosure, trapping the constructs in a kill zone.

As Bobby stared down from one of the hills at the deathtrap, he felt his stomach knotting inside of him. Below, as the light began to fade, villagers were lighting homemade torches, readying themselves to set fire to the dry material as soon as they needed to.

"It's impressive," Cutter slowly stroked his stubbled chin as he stood next to the teenage commander. "You've certainly united them."

"It's your tactical advice that has guided them."

"But...?"

"But, is it enough?"

"You doubt my plan?"

Bobby ran his fingers through his sweat-soaked hair. "Of course I do! We're taking on a whole cohort of constructs with a pile of kindling! What could possibly go wrong?"

Cutter shrugged. "A lot of things, naturally. But the alternative is for these good people to keep on running until exhaustion overcomes them and they simply lay down to die. At least, this way, they have a fighting chance."

Bobby opened his mouth to reply, but his response was cut short as an excited shout rose from below.

"They're coming! They're coming!"

Bobby and Cutter turned their heads and, from their vantage point, watched as a lone male villager ran frantically from the south. He darted across the deathtrap, his arms waving above his head.

"Where are the others?" Cutter growled. "Three went out to lure the constructs in this direction."

Bobby frowned but was immediately distracted by an all-too-familiar beat that pursued the lone villager.

*Thud, thud...*

*Thud, thud...*

*Thud, thud...*

The cohort of constructs rounded the base of the opposite hill. They marched as one: relentless, driven, unstoppable. Their feet rose and fell in perfect unison, each step solid and precise. They only paused when they reached the mouth of the valley. As they faced the villagers who stood before them, the constructs changed formation. They moved from their usual two-abreast phalanx and spread out to fill the entire width of the valley, creating an impassable row of three deep. As one, their arms transformed into deadly lances then together they marched on into the valley.

Slowly, carefully, the villager acting as bait edged backwards. It had been emphasised to him that his role in the charade was crucial. If he ran back too fast then the constructs might pick up speed and overshoot the killing zone. Too slow and he would be trapped with the golems when all hell broke loose.

As it was, the man played his role perfectly.

As he emerged from the firetrap, the wide band of constructs was situated perfectly in its middle.

"Now!" Bobby screamed from his spot on the hillside.

As the constructs marched as one, so the villagers responded in unison. Dipping prepared arrowheads into the flaming torches, they lifted up their hunting bows and let the fiery projectiles fly into the midst of the oncoming army. The arrows struck home and the bracken and dry wood caught the first time. Flames roared up from the ground, enveloping the constructs.

"More!" Bobby yelled. "More!"

The villagers were only happy to oblige. Bows which were more accustomed to firing on rabbits caused arrow after arrow to rain down upon new targets. More and more of the valley erupted into fire. It became a Hell on Earth, a veritable infernal pit with the creatures of clay standing in its midst. Bobby could feel the heat from the fire searing the hair on his arms as he peered down into the inferno. What he saw made his heartbeat quicken.

The constructs were standing there, baked solid. They were now immobile, a long wall of clay from one side of the valley to the other.

He gaped through a beaming grin. It had worked! Not only that, but it had worked so quickly and without the loss of one single life.

"We did it!" Bobby gasped. "We beat them!" he turned to Cutter and paused in his jubilation. The old man was thoughtfully stroking his stubbly chin as he peered down at his hard-baked kindred. "What? What's the matter?"

The Shadow Wraith's eyes were now following the procession of villagers as they swarmed down the hillside towards their brave friend who had acted as bait. Backs were being slapped and cheers were going up as celebrations were had.

"They just stopped in the middle of the valley. Why didn't they keep marching forward?" Horror spread across the old man's face. "Get them out of there," he growled. "Now!"

But it was too late.

*Thud, thud…*

*Thud, thud…*

*Thud, thud…*

The celebrations petered out as the villagers turned to face the northern end of the valley. Through the rising smoke, they could make out a large, wide force of constructs advancing towards them. At their head rode not just one or two, but six Shadow Wraiths.

Panic overcame the humans and they searched for a means of escape from the oncoming assault. Their way back was blocked by the impenetrable wall of clay lances and fire. This meant that the only way out was up. Screaming, they began to clamber up the hillside opposite from Bobby and Cutter, only to be faced with a descending row of lances.

It was then that the sound of death began to fill the valley.

The first to fall were those who were highest up the hill. As was their wont, the constructs struck methodically and without mercy. Limp bodies were thrown down onto those below, causing the panicked villagers further down the slope to stumble and fall. These were then easily picked off by the advancing troops who marched solidly over their fresh corpses. The row of constructs advancing down into the valley now came into play. They surrounded the remaining villagers and, with the Shadow Wraiths harrying them from atop their mounts, they pushed them to their ultimate goal: the flaming wall of fire and lances.

Bobby could stand to watch helplessly no more. Ignoring Cutter's protests, he leapt and bounded down the hillside, reaching the fiery deathtrap before he even took a breath. Ignoring the screams of death, he grabbed a relatively larger piece of old timber from the flames and charged into the battle, furiously swinging the fiery end at anything that got in his way. In front of him, he saw Martha slump to her knees as a construct rammed its lance through her chest. Bobby charged the golem and struck it with the fiery wood. The construct simply rose from its grisly task and turned towards Bobby before advancing. The teenager watched the lance rise up level with his face and transform into a club.

Bobby was vaguely aware of the sound of running behind him before the club swung down upon his head and everything turned black.

# Chapter Five

"Hello, Son."

Bobby opened his eyes. The world was at the wrong angle. The small part of it that he could see, anyway. Pushing himself up to a sitting position, the world righted itself.

Sort of.

It was level now but it was still very, very wrong.

From his seat on a wooden sofa that was covered in homemade cushions and blankets, Bobby gazed around the small, homely living room where he had awoken. The hearth roared, producing a soothing heat. Apples lay in a smoothly polished wooden bowl upon a small, finely crafted table. A woven rug, the patterns of which he remembered tracing with his infant finger, lay on the otherwise bare wooden floor.

His father sat in a chair opposite, smiling gently at him.

Bobby frowned. The last thing that he remembered…

He ran his hand tentatively across his scalp. No blood, no bone, no damage.

"Am I dead?"

His father smiled in amusement and shook his head.

"Then what is this?"

Howard's brown eyes held his son. "I can't say that I'm entirely sure, Bobby."

"Are you real?"

"As real as you need me to be, I guess." The long-dead woodworker rose from the chair he had fashioned shortly after Bobby had been born and crossed the small living room to sit on the sofa next to his son. He slipped his arm around the teenager, drew him in close and waited.

He didn't have to wait long.

Bobby began to cry. "It's so hard without you, Dad. So hard."

"I know. I know."

"Every day's a struggle. No matter what I do, life just seems to get harder and harder. So many people have died. Innocent people. I can't stop it."

"You're just a boy," came the soft voice of the adult. "How can you *expect* to stop it?"

"But someone has to! This can't go on forever. It's not right!"

"And why does it have to be you?"

Bobby sat cradled in his father's arms, tears tracking down his cheeks. "Whichever way I turn, it's always there, confronting me. I can't escape it. If I turn my back on it, it just walks around and stands before me once again.

"I'm so tired."

"I know, Son. I know."

"And Katy…"

Bobby felt the spirit of his father sigh beside his cheek.

"I failed."

Howard drew back and, placing his workman's hands on his son's shoulders, looked the lad straight in the eye. "Now, that is far from the truth."

"But, she left me. She ran away to be with Asherah."

"And why should the actions of your sister be your fault?"

"I drove her away! She left because she was cross with me."

"No. Katy did what she did because of something far darker."

The image of the older and vampiric version of his sister rose up in Bobby's mind. "What's wrong with her?"

"I don't know, Bobby. I truly don't. But, whatever demons Katy is fighting, they are not of your doing." Howard ran his callused fingers through his son's dark mop of hair. "She has always been strong-willed, defiant. So opposite to your kindly nature. She needs to find her own path. She needs someone to teach her how to control the raging tempest inside of her."

"But, Asherah…?"

Howard's head rocked from side to side. "Do not dismiss the Fallen offhand. She is a somewhat complex being."

Bobby frowned. "If you say so, I guess." He looked up at his father's kind face, one he hadn't seen for so many years. "It's good to see you."

"And you," his father smiled, before a more serious demeanour swept across him. "So, what are you going to do now?"

"What do you mean?"

"Well, in a moment, you're going to wake up, with an awful headache, I might add, and you're going to be faced with a choice. What will your answer be?"

Bobby nodded. "Should I go to Wellington? Should I travel back in time and save Sam Spallucci?"

Howard returned the nod.

Bobby ran his fingers through his hair. "I don't trust the Abyss," he said. "There's something… *slippery* about her. She feels like a prize fish you might see basking in the summer sun at the bottom of a clear brook. You creep up on it, carefully keeping out of the sunlight so as to not scare it with your shadow. Then, slowly, so slowly, you slip your hands, fingers outspread, under its belly and you grasp it, only to feel it slide effortlessly out of your grip. Yes, she's just like that fish. She is what she is. She's not pretending to be anything that she isn't, but she knows so much more than I do, just as the fish knows that it is safe from my grasping fingers. I could kneel by that small brook all day and never manage to get a hold of the fish; I could spend my entire life trying to fathom what the Abyss is up to, what she really wants, and never form a coherent answer."

"You could walk away."

Bobby's head sank down to his chest. "I know. Like you said, I'm just a boy."

"And how would that make you feel?"

"As rotten as the last apple in the barrel."

Howard smiled. "Humanity is a very precious thing, Son. It is like a fine cloth that has been woven and then embroidered with an intricate pattern. However, someone is teasing at a loose thread, unravelling all the time and effort that its creator has spent on it. If they continue to pull then, one day, there will be nothing left."

"But how can I be the one to put things right?"

"Perhaps it's not your job to do so? Perhaps this Spallucci chap is a dab hand with a darning needle?"

"And in saving him, I save humanity?" Bobby pondered this for a moment. "But if he prevents the Divergence, what about everyone who has lived since Kanor rose?"

"Do you really think they've had lives worth living? Perhaps they will be born into new lives. Better lives?"

"I hadn't thought of that." Bobby rested his head against his father's chest once again. "I miss you."

"And I miss you too. But I'll always be with you."

Bobby nodded. "In my thoughts and my dreams."

"Exactly. Walk well and stay safe, Bobby."

"Walk well and stay safe, Dad."

With that, the teenage boy allowed his eyes to slide shut.

Bobby opened his eyes for the second time and winced. His father had been correct. He had a hell of a headache.

Rather than lying on a long chair in his childhood home, he found himself lying on a soft patch of ground, the grass moulded to his face. Carefully, he pushed himself up and, after the world had stopped swaying, took in his immediate surroundings. In front of him was a roaring campfire. Its heat was welcome as the night had drawn in and the stars looked down from a clear sky. Without the dancing flames, Bobby would have been chilled to the core.

He was not alone by the fire. There were two others, both familiar.

On his left, bound tightly across his chest by what appeared to be a piece of rope, knelt the sole surviving member of the group of villagers that had gone out to lure in the construct cohort. The man's clothing was ragged and torn and his face was a patchwork of bruises.

But that was not all.

As Bobby studied the purple marks on the wretch's face, he saw blood trickling down from the man's closed eyelids. Bobby moved closer to study him and the man flinched. His head snapped back and forth with his eyelids still shut. "Who's there?" he called out. "Please! Please!"

"Quiet down," came a rough voice from the other side of the fire, "or I'll take your tongue as well as your eyes."

The villager slumped nervously back into his former position and Bobby turned his attention to Cutter.

The old man was tending to something on the fire. "How are you doing?" he asked.

"Better than," Bobby motioned towards the blind villager, "hlm, apparently. What did you do?"

Without taking his eyes off what he was tending to on the campfire, Cutter replied, "Well, first I rescued you from the construct that had just bludgeoned you unconscious. Then I grabbed our guest over there and brought us to this place which is quite safe... for now. As you slept, I had a chat with our friend about loyalty and what would make a man throw it away as if it were a warm pot of piss. Then..." He pulled a stick out of the fire and the aroma of cooked rabbit caused Bobby's stomach to growl. "I cooked you some food." He offered the meat across to the teenage boy.

Bobby nodded and took the meal. "Thank you," he said before devouring the tasty morsels. "How long was I unconscious?"

"Most of the night." Cutter rummaged in his pocket and drew out a pouch from which he emptied some smoking material into his pipe. Taking another stick from the fire, he lit the bowl and inhaled deeply. The aromatic fragrance of the mixture mingled pleasantly with that of the cooked rabbit. "How are you feeling?"

Bobby finished the meat and glanced across at the prisoner. "Cautious," he replied. "Why? Why did you do that to him?"

The old man drew heavily on his pipe and regarded the prisoner on the other side of the campfire. "I needed answers."

"But, blinding him?"

"Bobby, that wretch sold out his entire village. It was he who was the original informant and then told the force of constructs that were pursuing us about our am-bush. He watched as the rest of his team were put to the lance. He did nothing. He then led the constructs back to us and stood by as everyone else was massacred.

"And do you know why he did all this?"

Bobby shook his head.

"Tell the boy your grand reason," Cutter called across the fire. "Tell him why you sold out your friends."

The man's shoulders rose and fell. His head jerked from side to side.

"Do you want me to come over there and resume our little chat?"

The man's head shook more violently.

"Then spill your story."

"They… they said I was useless. They said that I was no good at my job."

"Which was…?"

The man mumbled something unintelligible.

"We didn't hear you. Why don't I come and get your tongue and it can whisper in our ears after I've cut it from your mouth?"

"I emptied their cesspits. They said I didn't do a thorough enough job."

"So, you betrayed them all and let the constructs slaughter everyone."

"No! No! Please. It wasn't like that. I didn't betray them."

Cutter rolled his eyes, dragged himself up from his spot by the fire and stamped over to the prisoner. "Here we go again. Really? You're still claiming this was all a big misunderstanding? Tell me then, just how did you escape when the others died?"

"I ran. I just ran. The mud buckets let me go."

"They let you go?"

"Yeah. I got a head start and they followed me as per the plan."

"Really?"

"That's right."

"The thing is, if a construct has you at the end of its lance, it won't hesitate to kill you. They let you go because you told them about the trap. You betrayed your friends and family."

"That's crazy! Why would I do that and, anyway, how would you know what a construct would do?"

Bobby's hands flew to his mouth as Cutter's arm shot out far longer than humanly possible, a sharp point at its end, and thrust through the chest of the blind prisoner.

"You'd be surprised…" Cutter murmured as the dying man twitched and spasmed on the lance.

When he was sure that the man was dead, Cutter withdrew his arm and took a deep draw from his pipe before blowing a long stream of smoke through his pursed lips. "So there you have it. The guy who shovels shit had a chip on his shoulder after a bit of criticism and decided that the correct response would be to have the rest of his village slaughtered." He turned to Bobby. "And people call *me* a monster."

Bobby sat silently, his eyes fixed on the slumped, bleeding corpse.

"I've been on this rock a good number of years now, Bobby. It's the same all over. People... *humans*... are selfish. They look out for number one. They do whatever they can to better themselves. They will trample over the fresh corpses of children should it mean they have a better life."

Bobby shook his head. "No. That's not true. It's not humans. It's this world. It's the Divergent Lands. It's what Kanor did to them that makes them do awful things like..." he pointed to the corpse, "he did."

Cutter raised an eyebrow. "Really? So it was all pansies and puppies before the Black Dragon rose, then? There was no war, no poverty, no jealousy, no hatred?"

"Well, yes, there was, but that was due to..."

"To what? People treating other people like the muck this vermin was supposed to shovel?" Cutter chuckled darkly and refilled his pipe. "Yes Bobby, Kanor has done terrible things. I should know. I've done them for him. But it was no different before his rise. Humanity is a perverse, corrupt monster that rose from the ground and devoured all that stood before it, before turning on itself. Did you know that they had weapons that could have obliterated the entire planet? The entire planet, Bobby!

Kanor may have decimated them, but humanity could have wiped its own entire species from the face of the Earth. They even tried a few times. Once, they desolated nearly a whole country. Millions dead in the blink of an eye!"

"Just like your kind did on the day of the Divergence?"

"But, we had no choice. We were created that way. We were the weapons, not the one wielding them. Humanity…" The Shadow Wraith shook his head. "They were innocent at some point, I guess. But, somewhere along the way, someone gave them a nice, long pointy stick and showed them which end was safer to hold whilst jabbing it into their neighbour."

Bobby pondered this. "But, if that's the case, then surely, it's still not their fault. Someone corrupted them."

"Maybe," Cutter shrugged. "Maybe they just decided that the sound of screaming was a beautiful melody to which they could rock their dying babies to sleep at night. What can you do about it? Go back and find the exact point in time that a human first picked up a rock and caved in the brains of his brother?"

"No, but I can stop all," he waved his hands around him, "*this* from happening. I can give humanity a second chance to get things right."

Cutter's eyes narrowed and his dark pupils twinkled in the firelight.

"And just how do you think you could achieve such a momentous task?"

## Chapter Six

"This is a terrible plan."

As Bobby stood at the edge of the wide lake that surrounded the towering edifice of All Saints church, there was a distinctly large part of him that agreed with Cutter's succinct appraisal of their current situation.

It had taken a few days to travel from their previous location, even with the Shadow Wraith transformed into the shape of a strong black stallion. This had given the equine simulacrum plenty of opportunity to voice his opinion on the task at hand.

His first bone of contention had been the trustworthiness of the Abyss. "How can you believe anything that she tells you?" the horse had demanded. "She is a timeless ocean that encircles reality. What would it serve her to dabble in human affairs?"

"But, you could ask the opposite, couldn't you?" Bobby had replied. "She has no personal need to interfere. Like you said, she is a being outside of our…" He sought in vain for the correct word, eventually just waving his hand around them at the barren land across which they travelled. "…all this. So, perhaps she's just being benevolent? Perhaps she is looking with pity on the mere mortals that she sees suffering through time?"

"Perhaps," Cutter had grumbled. "Perhaps she is just using you?"

"To what end? As you said, she is an ocean that surrounds our Realm. Whatever could she want?"

The second point that Cutter raised was regarding the man that Bobby was supposed to save. "Why Spallucci? You know nothing of the guy."

"Claw held him in high esteem."

This had provoked a harsh snort from the horse's nostrils and an annoyed stamping of its hooves. "Seriously? You buy into this *Man of Virtue* garbage? No. It's a fallacy. There is no such person."

"Not if he's already dead. What if I went back and saved Spallucci and he turned out to be the Virtuous Man? What if he's destined to stop the rise of Kanor? What If that's the Man of Virtue's role in all of this?"

"I don't like that many *what ifs*..."

"But it could be a chance for us to stop all this horror from ever occurring."

"And how do you expect to find him? The world is a very large place."

"She said that she would transport me directly to Lancaster, the city where he lives. It shouldn't be too hard to find him there, I would imagine."

"Towns were much bigger back then, Bobby. I'm not sure you really know what it is that you're letting yourself in for."

"But I have to try," the boy had said. "If I don't, who will?"

So, in due time, they had arrived at Wellington. Bobby had dismounted at the edge of the town and Cutter had resumed his old man form. "I am guessing that I do not have to say that we need to exercise the utmost caution here," he had warned.

It had been like walking through a town that had died. The crumbling buildings were decaying bones; broken glass was rotten flesh. Not a sound resonated through the place, not even the breath of the slightest breeze. Everything was still, inert. Bobby had thought that the place would be swarming with constructs, but this was not the case. The two of them made their way through the ghost town unimpeded until, finally, they found themselves on the side of a vast lake that surrounded the old church.

Bobby looked up at his companion. "What now? How do we cross?"

"On that." Cutter raised a gnarled finger and gestured to a figure looming out of a misty gloom that hung over the glasslike surface of the lake. The sound of water lapping against wood and the creaking of rusted metal reached the teenager's ears as he witnessed a ghastly figure emerge into view. Slowly, with no apparent need to hurry his task at hand, a man used a long pole to push a thin boat towards them. Dressed in tattered rags, the ferryman was tall and gaunt. A dark cowl covered most of his head, but Bobby could just about make out a face of long, drawn features that possessed a pair of milky eyes.

The boat eventually bumped up against the stony shoreline and Cutter climbed aboard as Bobby tentatively followed.

The ferryman held out a pale withered hand, making a grasping motion with his bony fingers.

"There's no need for that." Cutter's voice was low and menacing.

The ferryman struck his hand out once more.

"What does he want?" Bobby asked.

"Payment."

"Surely we have goods that we can give him?" Bobby took his pack from his back and made to open it in order to look inside for something suitable.

Cutter placed a hand on the boy's shoulder. "Trust me. You are no longer in possession of the payment that this being requires. You handed it to someone else quite a while back."

Bobby frowned as he tried to work out what the old man meant before realisation dawned on his face. "The Eternal Talisman! Its purpose was to see the Virtuous Man across the lake? But how can we cross?"

"Simple," Cutter smiled as his skin began to ripple. "I pull rank." He pulled himself up straight and there, in the boat, stood his true form. That of a Shadow Wraith.

The ferryman leaned forward and peered closely at the construct with his milky eyes. Then, nodding in acceptance, he thrust the long pole into the water and pushed them away from the shoreline. Cutter grunted in apparent satisfaction and transformed back into his usual shape.

The journey across the lake was a short one and it was in no time at all that the barge thumped to a halt. The silent ferryman stood passively as his passengers disembarked. Then, when his services were no longer required, he pushed the boat back out into the mist.

"No going back now," Cutter mused, rubbing an arthritic hand against his stubbled chin. He turned and gazed up at the old church. "I haven't been here for a very long time. It hasn't changed." He took a deep breath and made for what appeared to be the entrance. Bobby followed him up into a  stone porchway. Before them stood the remains of an old wooden door. The material of the door looked like it was black but it was rotten and its scant remains were covered in mildew.

Bobby wrinkled his nose. "The rot makes it smell sour."

Cutter grunted. "That's not just the stench of decay. It's an odour of something far more unpleasant. Magic." He approached the remains of the rotten door. "Shall we?"

In the pit of his stomach, Bobby felt the swelling waves of a sea of nausea but, in his head, there was nothing but clarity. This was where he was meant to be. Everything over the last few weeks had led him to this place. Every single step, every action, had brought him to stand here upon the threshold of the lair of the Black Dragon.

He had a job to do and do it he would.

Bobby nodded and stepped past Cutter into the old church.

The inside of the ancient building was everything that Bobby had expected. The first thing that struck him was the rise tenfold of the foetid stench. He found himself retching and holding a fist to his mouth as he controlled his body's reflexive reaction to the foul odour. When he had brought his gagging under control, he looked around and decided that, before Kanor had chosen it as his dwelling place, the church would have been a place of beauty. Large windows reached to the roof. Long ago, they would have allowed sunlight to stream through on the worshippers, bathing them in a rainbow of colours from what looked like stained glass. Now, though, the glass was mostly shattered and the roof itself was ripped apart above where Bobby and Cutter were standing.

Bobby cast his eyes around into the gloom of the dead building. On his right, a long screen seemed to traverse the main body of the church, passing under gigantic stone arches. Atop it was a decayed figure of a man on what appeared to be a cross, his arms spread out wide and nailed to the wood. At first, Bobby winced, thinking it was some sort of victim of the Black Dragon, but then he realised that it was a wooden carving. Breathing out in relief, he looked down the other end of the building, to his extreme left.

And there he saw the font.

Tapping Cutter on the arm, he made to step towards the stone bowl, but the old man's hand shot out and grabbed him by the wrist. Bobby turned and frowned at his companion, but then followed his eyes into the darkness on the opposite side of the church.

There was movement.

To begin with, it was just the hint of a shadow but then the movement took form and stalked out of the darkness, taking the shape of not just one construct but many. Bobby felt his guts lurch as he heard the sound of transformation next to him. Glancing quickly at Cutter, he saw that the man's arms were now a pair of deadly lances.

"Run!" Cutter barked. "Go for the font!" and he sprung into the middle of the church to confront his kindred.

Bobby needed no repetition of the command and his feet pounded beneath him as he darted to his left. His ears were aware of the sound of fighting but his eyes were focused on his goal, the stone bowl at the back of the church. He leapt over old wooden seats and ducked under fallen beams as he homed in on his target. A loud cry came from his right but he ignored it. He knew that there was nothing he could do to help his friend. He had one task and one task alone.

He had to reach the font.

And he almost did.

He was just crossing a clear patch of flooring when a loose flagstone rocked under his foot and his ankle twisted. Screaming out in pain, Bobby fell to the floor, the stone flags cracking against his knee. He rolled to his feet, making to lunge for the font, but there was a terrifyingly familiar wet sound behind him and he cried out as an extended clay limb wrapped around the wrist of his outstretched hand. He felt himself pulled sharply around and was face to eyeless face with a gigantic construct that towered above him.

Bobby was transported back many years to that day when he had first encountered one of these mud buckets, back in the village square of Irlingbury. He remembered how the rest of the villagers had been terrified, how they had held their breath as the monster had loomed over the small boy.

As the construct in front of him raised its lance, Bobby now found himself doing as those villagers did all those years ago. The eyeless beast opened its wide gash of a mouth and its dark tongue slipped out from between its clay lips. The tongue snaked to and fro as it scented the air between itself and its captive. The raised lance paused mid-air.

A demonic roar exploded behind the construct and its lance fell, dismembered, to the floor.

The golem staggered around to face its attacker and was presented with a sharp scythe that cleft it straight down the middle. Both halves of the monster slipped silently to the ground to reveal a battered and frantic Cutter.

As Bobby crawled to his feet, pushing the lifeless arm from his wrist, he winced at the sight of a wide hole gaping through the old man's shoulder. Cutter's eyes followed those of the boy and he shuddered as the wound miraculously closed shut.

"Now," the Shadow Wraith that had saved his life said, "while there is still time."

Bobby nodded and turned towards the font.

As his hand reached out, the sound of someone clapping reached his ears.

He paused and turned around. There, walking down the middle of the church was a robed figure. It wore a dark cloak, the cowl of which obscured its face. Carefully, it sidestepped the pools of clay that Cutter had left in his wake.

"Marvellous!" came the dry male voice. "Absolutely marvellous! Such a fine show. I haven't seen the like in many, many years."

Cutter stepped in front of Bobby, shielding the boy. "Leave him be."

The robed figure stopped, slid his hands into his sleeves and appeared to cock his head in thought. "Now why would I ever harm the boy?"

"You just set your constructs on him!"

"Did I?" The cowl appeared to study the wet pools of clay that were disturbingly edging themselves away into the shadows of the church. "Did any of them actually harm him? I think not." He walked up to Cutter and said, "You really are so suspicious, you know. Mind you, that was to be expected, I guess."

Bobby could just make out a touch of a smile in the

shadows of the cowl as it turned to face him.

"Hello, Bobby," came the voice. "Please allow me to introduce myself. I'm Kanor. But then, I'm guessing you've already worked that out. You are such a bright lad, after all."

Bobby swallowed his nerves and forced his tongue and lips to move. "What… what do you want?"

"Why, peace of course. Just like everyone else. It's just that, you know, I achieved it. So, there you go. Good for me!"

Bobby pushed past his protector. "Peace! Peace? You call all this peace? Seriously?"

"How else should I describe it, Bobby," Kanor shrugged. "Tell me, when was the last time you saw a war? When was the last time you heard of humans taking up arms against each other? Never! That's when. And you have me to thank for it.

"I united humanity. I thinned the herd. There were so many of them. Far too many, in fact. All with their different beliefs and cultures. All with their own differing opinions on how to move forward. You know, many years ago, someone once said to me that humanity, as a species, doesn't do different. So, I made it all the same.

"In doing so, I brought peace."

"But… you slaughtered billions!"

Kanor gave another shrug. "What can I say, a difficult nut needs a large hammer with which to crack open its shell."

Bobby shook his head and felt his feet turn beneath him. He felt himself spin around, leaving the crazed ruler of a dead world behind him. One foot slapped down on the stone floor in front of another as they propelled him towards the font. He watched his arm, reaching out under the command of sheer rational thought and emotion, touch the rim of the font…

And suddenly he was somewhere else entirely.

325

# Epilogue

The Shadow Wraith stood before his maker. The question that went through the created being's mind was, "What now?"

The hooded figure turned his back on his creation.

Cutter lifted his arm. It was still in the shape of a scythe, the deadly weapon with which the monster in front of him had blessed him. He could use it now. One swift strike would dispatch the being who had caused the deaths and suffering of billions.

He lifted his arm and took a purposeful step forward.

Then stopped, immobile in his tracks.

He pushed with all his might against his arm, willing it to sweep down and cleave his creator in two. But the limb remained motionless.

Kanor paused. His cowl moved slightly before he nodded and turned towards the font. "Well?"

A column of water rose from the depths of the stone bowl. The Black Dragon stood patiently before it as the swirling liquid took the form of a girl, then a woman, then a crone before gracefully stepping down onto the stone floor. As its foot touched the ground, the same flag-stone that had only recently caused a teenage boy to stumble rocked under the weight of the fluid entity.

A small smile touched the lips of the ever-changing face of the Abyss.

"It is done," said Kanor.

"I know," said the girl.

"Of course you do. You know everything. Even how you were supposed to die."

"…and there will be no more Sea…" mused the woman.

Deep within his hood, the Black Dragon grunted.

"You seem… *conflicted*," observed the crone as she walked slowly around humanity's decimator.

"Will this work?"

The girl paused in front of the cowled figure. "What an odd question, you ask."

"You know it will," stated the woman.

Kanor approached the font that bore the acrostic of his name. "That's not what I mean. I mean…"

"The end of everything," the girl finished.

"I've sacrificed so much because of it."

The woman: "You have done what had to be done."

The crone: "And there is more still to be done."

Kanor nodded and traced a finger along the words that were engraved along the edge of the font. "My army is ready. It is time to start sending them back through time; time to sow the seeds of my rising. You can definitely do this?"

"The blood spell was broken when the battle was fought in this place," explained the girl.

Kanor nodded. "The day of the event in Israel. I remember it well."

"As you should," said the woman.

"It was the day that Sam Spallucci died at your hands," finished the crone.

A dry chuckle emanated from the dark cowl. "Indeed it was. Indeed it was." Kanor turned to face the figure of Cutter who still stood with his scythe arm outstretched above his head. "So, we had better begin. This one first, I think. I have a very special job for him."

"I'll never serve you again," Cutter growled, tugging defiantly at his immobile limb. "I broke your hold over me."

Raucous laughter filled the church. "Oh, God. That's so funny. It really is." Wiping tears of laughter away from his shadowed eyes, Kanor came nose to nose with his creation. "I really did do a good job on you, didn't I?"

Confusion swept across the Wraith's face.

"Don't worry. In a few seconds, all will become clear." Then, leaning forward and whispering in the construct's ear, a solitary word left Kanor's lips, "Chimera," before he took a calm step backwards.

Cutter's mouth formed a round O shape and he stared up at his outstretched limb. Shaking his head, he transformed it back into an arm and, flexing his fingers, he sank down in reverence onto one knee.

"What is my master's bidding?"

329

Bobby Normal will return in
Sam Spallucci: Lux Æterna

A.S.Chambers

## Author's Notes

Many moons ago, I was working on *Sam Spallucci: Dark Justice,* the fourth book in my Sam Spallucci series. During the course of the story, my paranormal investigator gets dragged into the shadowy world of the Children of Cain, the vampires in my ever-expanding Spallucci-verse. In one of the final scenes, Sam finally comes face to face with a construct, a clay-based golem created by the devastator of humanity, Kanor. It is a truly terrifying experience for Sam as the faceless behemoth towers over him. This is a creature which has been created with one sole purpose: to eradicate all those who would oppose its master.

When I finished the scene, I read it over and a curious thought edged its way into my head: *What would this creature look like to a child?* So I took the basic elements but reworked them from a child's perspective. The resulting scene became Bobby's first encounter with a construct in Irlingbury market in *Bobby Normal and the Eternal Talisman.* Needless to say, I was pleased with the result and decided to let it evolve into a full story.

I was immediately drawn to setting the adventures

of Bobby not in the present, but in the land post-Divergence. The Divergent Lands. By the time of writing *Dark Justice*, the Divergence had been mentioned a lot in Sam's cases, most prominently in *Ghosts From The Past*, so I felt it would be a good time to explore what was actually going to happen. Plus, they sounded like a fun place to explore! A few months later and I had the first draft of *Eternal Talisman*.

However, there was a problem.

I didn't like it.

I wasn't sure what was wrong, but I felt that the story lacked something. It all felt rather vanilla. In my Sam stories, Sam got into trouble plus there were convoluted shenanigans. On top of this, people died. A *lot* of people died. I mean, when you tot up the body count of *Ghosts From The Past* it's a right royal bloodbath! The Bobby Normal story I had written, lacked this and I felt it was bland because of it.

Now, at this time, I hadn't read any young adult fiction since I was a teenager back in the days of Noah. Back then, it had all been picnics and ginger beer with cheerful resolutions. So this was still the image I had in my head of this genre. As a result, I shelved my Bobby Normal project for a while, determining that I needed to go away and read some more up-to-date material. My inspiration came in the form of the *Jedi Apprentice* books by Jude Watson. They followed the early relationship between Qui-Gon Jinn and Obi-Wan Kenobi in the Star Wars universe and, for me, they were a revelation. Watson crafted stories where it was okay to show youngsters having angst and seeing people die. After devouring the lot, I returned to my project and wrote the scene where Bobby witnesses the execution of his father. In that action, the floodgates were breached and the book, then the series, that we have now rapidly took shape.

As I was re-working the first book, something became apparent to me. I didn't want these books to be random monster-of-the-week adventures, single stories that the reader could just dip in and out of. My Sam Spallucci books weren't like that, being part of this expanding universe, so I wanted these new creations to be the same. I set my sights on five books that would stand alone but be connected in a serialised form, drawing Bobby to his *ultima thule*: a confrontation with the Black Dragon himself before being catapulted into the modern-day adventures of Sam. Along the way, I had Bobby interact with characters with which my readers would already be familiar, along with some new ones. The vampires, the Children of Cain, had to play a major role as I already knew that some of them would crop up in the Divergent Lands and I loved weaving Asherah into the life of Katy Normal as I was working on *Sam Spallucci: Fury of the Fallen* at the same time. As a result, I was able to develop the Fallen's character across two books simultaneously. If you read both of them carefully, you can see her say certain phrases in both books. It also meant that I was able to not-too-subtly set Katy up as a major player in my future *Divergent Lands* trilogy, which is due to be written after I've finished my Sam Spallucci series.

My favourite new character had to be Cutter. I was watching *Breaking Bad* and *Better Call Saul* when I started the series. My favourite character in both series has to be Mike Ehrmantraut, played by the outstanding Jonathan Banks. Cutter is unashamedly based upon Banks' portrayal of this ex-cop who is dragged ever deeper into the murky world of drug cartels as he becomes an enforcer for Gus Fring. His battered appearance and world-weary demeanour fitted Cutter perfectly. We root for Mike just as we root for Cutter. Even when we start to see things that make us doubt his intentions, we still like him as a character. All I will say here is that you haven't seen the last of the Shadow Wraith yet.

So, what does the future hold for Bobby? Well, as the little *Bond-esque* comment says, he will be seen next in *Sam Spallucci: Lux Æterna*, where he arrives in Sam's world before becoming a major figure in the penultimate Sam Spallucci book, *Dare The Dragon*. As for that, well that way spoilers lie, so I think I'll just leave it there.

If you enjoyed the books, please let me know over on social media. There are links for all the socials plus links for my other books over on my website: www.aschambers.co.uk.

In the meantime, walk well and stay safe!

ASC, January 2024.

## About The Author

A.S.Chambers resides in Lancaster, England. He lives a fairly simple life of walking in the countryside, gazing at mountains and rescuing his cat from the dastardly machinations of net curtains.

He is quite happy for, and in fact would encourage, you to follow him on Facebook, Instagram and Twitter.

There is also a nice, shiny website:
www.aschambers.co.uk

www.ingramcontent.com/pod-product-compliance
Lightning Source LLC
Chambersburg PA
CBHW051237210726
48287CB00002B/285